VEGAS
CRUSH

georg kolochev

Defense

2

dedication

For those who are,
and always will be...
VEGAS STRONG.

1
vegas baby!

Pam

Mm-mmm. There's that tall, long-haired Russian. "Curious Georg," as he's known on Instagram. Or was known, before his account went stagnant. Kind of a bummer. His account was pretty fun to follow. Georg in big sunglasses and a silly hat. Georg pouring a bottle of Russian vodka over some half-naked woman's stomach. Georg half undressed, asleep on a purple couch, a mustache drawn on his face in black marker.

What can I say? I'm a sucker for trouble.

We went on a date once. Kind of twice. The first time doesn't really count because we were just the plus-ones to our friends Evan and Holly. The second time, we sucked face up until that big dummy Viktor started a fight and shut down the evening. Fight notwithstanding, I still think the sucking face elevates it to a date.

Anyway, I saw him at Evan and Holly's wedding a few months ago but he mostly just stared at me with a brooding look on his face. Which was hot, I guess. I mean, who doesn't like being stared at intensely by a guy who can rock a suit with no tie while he nurses a vodka on the rocks?

No one likes that?

Oh.

Never mind then.

Not gonna lie, I totally flip through the gossip sites looking for pictures of him. I'm a sad little groupie. Not a puck bunny though. More like a Georg-specific bunny. Though I'll lie if anyone ever calls me out on it.

My mother would say that I shouldn't waste my time on a guy who's probably drunk eighty percent of the time he's off the ice. And I know I shouldn't. So, I won't. I mean, the prohibition on fraternizing with team members sort of stops me anyway, since I'm on the staff now.

Woo, boy. I'm the newest physical therapist for the Crush. Grad school is done and my best friend and social media guru, Holly, put in a good word with Max Terry, the team's owner, and got me an interview. Which I nailed.

Because I am awesome.

"You excited?" the guy next to me asks. We're both in athletic polo shirts emblazoned with the Crush logo on the front.

"About the job? Or the hockey?" I turn my head to look him over.

He gives me a funny little half-grin. The guy is pretty cute, actually. Blond, blue-eyed, muscular, and fit. He's wearing black chinos and trainers. "Um...both?" he says with a laugh. He holds out a hand. "Dale Moncrief."

We shake hands. "Pam Jenson. And yes, I'm excited about both. The Crush had an amazing season last year, so I'm thrilled to now be part of the team."

"What will you be doing for the team?" he asks, running a hand through his hair. It's short on the sides and in the back, but a little longer on top. Boyish. Rakish.

"Physical therapy. Just finished grad school at UCLA. I worked really closely with the soccer teams there."

"Awesome," he says. "I'm an athletic trainer."

"They really seem to be beefing up the training staff this year."

"Well, when you have a championship-level team, you tend to want to make sure they stay in winning form," Dale says. "Did you follow the Crush before you started here?"

"I did. My best friend is the social media manager here. She just married one of the players."

"Oooohhhh, a breaker of policies." Dale grins conspiratorially. "Bad girl."

I laugh. "More like good girl. Holly's about the most rule-followingest person you could meet. If you knew her—"

"What about you?" Dale asks, leaning over and nudging my shoulder with his. "You follow *all* the rules?"

I bite my lip and lower my eyelids flirtatiously. "Wouldn't you like to know."

A crash on the glass turns my attention back to the ice, where Georg and last year's star rookie, Mikhail, have had a run-in during scrimmage. Mikhail, the hothead, throws off his helmet and starts yelling about penalties, while Georg grins and wiggles his rear end at his teammate, telling him to lighten up. Then he looks over at me and winks. This makes me crack up for some reason.

Dale notices. "You know him?"

"Kind of. Not real well, though."

"Well, he is known to be a bit of a womanizer. Be careful of that one."

"I can handle myself, but thanks."

"I'll bet you can," he says with a wide grin. "No doubt about that." I *think* he believes he's appealing.

The head of our team of therapists, trainers, and nutritionists gives us what I suspect is the annual start-of-season pep talk. He talks about keeping our players in top form, and the importance of communicating with each other about concerns that might cross the borders of what we do. He reminds us that we're always to be professional—with each other and with the players.

As the scrimmage goes on, he points out different plays and tosses out stories about specific injuries that he's seen from each type of play. He focuses on concussion protocol and stresses that we are not a team that puts players back on the ice before they're cleared by a doctor. Dale makes snide comments under his breath every so often. Some of them are funny, but others miss the mark. I think he's trying to paint himself as a rebel, or maybe he wants to keep my attention off my Russian friend who keeps looking in my direction, much to my surprise. Either way, I wish Dale would just stop while he's ahead. The guy might think he's all that, but he's slowly massacring any attraction I *might* have felt.

My mind wanders to Evan and Holly's wedding. It was so beautiful, set in the mountains, on a vast deck with an incredible view. I've never imagined myself settling down with someone like that. My eyes start to wander and my interest eventually wanes. I'm not like Holly, who has always been cautious about relationships. I'm in and out, and always on the lookout for the next shiny boy toy.

I'm not a slut, though. Seriously. Just want to put that out there.

FIRST DAY on the job is in the books as I head out to my new condo, which is really Holly's old condo in a cute little suburb of Las Vegas. It worked out perfectly for me to take over her place after she moved in with her hubby. I looked at Evan's apartment complex, too, but decided I liked the quieter pace of the suburbs. After living in student housing for the past six years, I was ready for something private and quiet. Evan's building was full of young professionals, athletes, and performers, all with a penchant for partying in common. I like to party—don't get me wrong—but I want to be able to get away from it sometimes, too.

I didn't have a lot of furniture that I wanted to lug here from Los Angeles, so my first order of business was to pick out some new stuff. I've been sleeping on an air mattress for the past week, so when the delivery truck pulls up with my new bed, I feel like celebrating. I know I'm going to fall in love with that bed.

Bonus. The two movers are buff and tan. I flirt shamelessly while they unload my new bedroom, living room, and dining room furniture. I probably splurged too much, honestly, but it was time. Six years of communal living, of ramen noodles, of whatever-I-could-scrounge furniture. Now that I was adulting, and creating my own space with my own stuff, it was all part of the evolution. And not items found at the Goodwill, which is stop *numero uno* for any poor graduate student.

One of the movers wears a wedding ring but the other, a ginger with bright blue eyes, flirts shamelessly right back at me.

"New to town, then?" he asks with a teasing smirk.

"Yep, just moved here. I work for the Crush," I answer, leaning against the doorframe while he and his partner put together my bed frame.

"Good gig," he says appreciatively. "You a cheerleader?"

"Ha! Hockey teams don't have cheerleaders."

When he smiles, a super adorable dimple appears in his cheek. "I know. You're just too cute to be, like, their accountant or something."

"Awww... Flattery *could* get you everywhere, my man. I'm actually a physical therapist. So I get to work on muscly dudes all day for a living. Not a bad gig at all."

"Well, I'm a muscly dude," he answers with a grin. "I've got this pain in my shoulder..."

The other guy snorts. "Stop flirting and help me out

here. We've got two more deliveries before we can be done for the day."

I slink away downstairs to start dinner, and the guys head out shortly after. Of course, I find the guy's name and number on my new nightstand later that night when I go to bed.

Oh yeah, Vegas is going to be a whole lotta fun.

2
"that" pam

Georg

"Who are you, and what have you done with Georg Kolochev?" Evan asks as I slip off my soaked workout tank and pull on my undershirt and shoulder pads.

"*Trakhat'sya*," I hiss, giving him the middle finger.

He laughs. "There he is."

"Did you see they hired that Pam in the therapy room?" I stupidly change the subject to the one thing that's been on my mind ever since I heard about it.

"*That* Pam?" He shakes his head at me in disgust. "Seriously, dude, as in Holly's best friend?" He's more than a little sarcastic as he continues, "Yes, I know she works here now. We put in a good word with the bosses to get her hired." He leaves off the, *you ignorant fuck*, but I hear it regardless.

Loud and clear.

"Shouldn't they hire skilled therapists though? I mean, a nice rack is great, but it doesn't help with a sprained ankle." The second the words are out I regret them. I don't even know why I said anything, let alone a dick comment like that.

"Don't be a pig," Evan snaps. "You know she's not some dummy. And seriously, why are you so sweaty? Or is that booze sweat?"

"It's not booze sweat," I answer, glad the conversation has turned in a new direction. "There's a new trainer, too. He's a hard-ass."

"You were in the gym? Doing a workout?"

"You're being a cunt." I toss a shoe at him.

He laughs again, putting his hands up. "Okay, okay. Sorry, friend. I'm just messing with you. You look good. Fit. Been working the weights while I've been on holiday, yeah?"

"I thought we were all working the weights on the off-season. Some of us got fatter, though, I see."

Evan narrows his eyes and lifts his shirt. "Abs of steel. Can't be talking about me."

"Sympathy weight since your lady is seven months pregnant?" I jibe.

He scoffs out a curse and pulls on his jersey. "Come on, Mr. Universe, let's go see what your new buff body can do on the ice today."

He tromps out of the locker room while I finish pulling on my gear. I have to admit that winning the cup, being in the All-Stars...it really put things into perspective for me. I want to win. I want to play well. And I can't get past where I am now if I don't focus on keeping my body in shape.

Of course, seeing Pamela Jenson at work is a motivator, too. We had a few hot moments last spring...

But I think she thinks I'm an alcoholic loser. It was awkward as hell seeing her at the wedding this summer. I couldn't stop myself from staring at her like some B-class creeper. See? Awkward. Probably more for her than me, as I enjoyed the view.

Once I'm laced up, I head to the rink. Everyone's doing warm-up laps, stretching out. I take a few laps before heading to one end of the arena, where the defensive coaching staff and our GM, Bud Bellikowski, are gathered.

"Nice of you to join us, Kolochev," my teammate Kellen says under his breath. "Did a hockey honey make you late?"

"*Mudak*," I spit at him.

He smacks me in the calf with his hockey stick. "I don't speak Russian, but I'll bet that wasn't a compliment."

I give him a fake smile. "I called you an asshole."

He grins. "I've been called worse."

"And I was only one minute late. I was in the gym."

"With a honey?"

"Athletic trainer, fuckface."

"Guys," yells Bellikowski. His combover is wonky. He must sense it because he awkwardly runs his hand through it, putting it mostly back in place. "Stop the side chatter and pay attention."

"Sorry, sir," Kellen and I both answer in unison.

"I was explaining that this is an important season for us," Bud says. "Teams will be out to prove that our championship year was a fluke, that we can't make it to the playoffs again. We've got seats to fill and we fill them by winning. So I need my defensemen to be vigilant. I need you blocking shots on goal, controlling the neutral zone, and keeping the puck in front of our wingers." This is not new strategy or information. It's how we're to play our game. What's new is the additional pressure to prove we're worthy of the cup we won. *And that we can win it again.*

Everyone mumbles assent and he tells us to have a good practice before bumbling off, his soft-soled, cheap dress shoes sliding against the ice as he toddles the few feet toward the gate.

We start drills, Kellen and I next to each other as we work on pass accuracy.

"Did you see Kazmeirowicz's old lady?" Kellen asks. "Looks like she's gonna pop."

"Couple more months," I say. "She looks like she's supposed to look for being seven months pregnant."

"I can't believe he settled down, let alone has a baby on the way."

"Meh." I give a shrug. "He's in love. Leave him be. Holly's great."

"She's hot, that's for sure," Kellen says. "Speaking of hot. I've been having shin splints so I went to the therapy rooms. There's a smoking-hot blonde working there now. Have you seen her?"

"Yes, I have," I answer nonchalantly, despite the urge to go crazy ape-man on his ass. I don't like him talking about her.

"So hot. Rack I'd like to smother myself in," he says wistfully.

"Aren't you dating someone?"

"Yeah, but a man can always look."

I roll my eyes and skate over to Evan so we can drill several new plays. The relaxed first few days of practice have suddenly become a lot more intense as we work through several complicated plays and speed and agility drills. By the end, I wish I hadn't worked out at the gym this morning. I also wish I hadn't had that fourth drink at the club last night, but who was counting? Unfortunately not my dumb ass when I should've been.

After showering off, I head out and decide I should go to the therapy rooms to at least welcome Pam to the team. I mean, we had a…moment. Or whatever. It doesn't mean we can't be professional. I'm all about professionalism. All day long. Yep, when it comes to my job, I keep things straight.

She's working with our second-string goalie, who pulled a muscle in his shoulder during our defense intensive today. She's got him facedown, his arms pulled up and contorted in a way that looks like it must hurt.

"Don't break the players," I say as I walk in.

"It's what they pay me for," Pam shoots back.

"Yeah, Kolochev," my teammate jumps in. "Don't you have a bottle of vodka to drain or something?"

"That's real nice," I say lightly, even though the words smart a bit. "Thought we were on the same team."

"Did you need something, Georg?" Pam asks, still pulling on the guy's arm.

"I just came down to welcome you to the team. It's good to see you here. And…I know you will do great."

Well, that was painful…and lame…and fucking stupid.

"Thanks," she says softly. She won't even look at me,

so I stand, awkwardly shifting from one foot to the other, until I realize I'm making things weirder.

"You're welcome." My response just cranks up the weirdness another notch until it feels unbearable and I'm compelled to make it stop. "Then…okay. See you around, Pam."

I leave, feeling like a major asshat. What was I thinking? She'd just throw herself on me? That we'd just fuck on the therapy table like two horny teenagers? No, I mean, we haven't fucked, so that wasn't likely anyway. But maybe she might flirt with me a little—that didn't seem so far-fetched. Obviously, that's incorrect. Professional Pam is exactly that. Professional.

And me?

My team thinks I'm a drunkard, so maybe I really do have a bottle of vodka to drain.

3
heartburn much?

Pam

I finish with the goalie and give strict instructions for Ibuprofen with alternating heat and ice as he gets off my table. Wincing as he hobbles out, he mutters something about not being sure whether to propose marriage or curse my name. Seems about right.

Georg was so weird though. It's sweet that he came down to greet me or whatever, but he was so frigging awkward. It was kind of cute, I guess. I don't know.

I head upstairs to meet Holly, who's big belly looks so out of place on her skinny little body. Crazy lady still ran miles until recently. She's fitter than most non-pregnant ladies. Show-off. She pushes herself up from her chair, her extremely *efficient* cubicle filled to the brim with photos of her and Evan now. They've made a happy life together in a very short period of time. It's sickening, really. Especially to women like me, who have no serious interest in settling down or finding "the one" or whatever.

"How's it going?" she asks, grabbing her purse.

"Good," I answer. "I really like the work a lot. Georg came down to say hello."

Holly's eyes go wide and smirk plays on her lips. "You ever going to tell me what happened between you two in LA?"

"My lips are sealed," I say, as a gorgeous redhead wanders up.

"Hey, Holly? Before you go, could you approve this plan for preseason on Snapchat?"

"I took a look at it earlier," Holly answers. "I've got some thoughts, but can I share them with you tomorrow? It's nothing major, but I want to brainstorm for a second."

"Oh." The redhead looks slightly defeated. "Okay, that's fine. I was just hoping we could give it to Fiona tomorrow."

"Shouldn't be a problem," Holly tells her. "By the way, Scarlett, this is my very best friend in the whole world, Pamela Jenson. Pam, this is Scarlett Woods."

We shake hands. "Hey. What do you do here?"

"I'm an interim communication team member," she says. "I'll be filling in for Holly while she's on maternity leave."

"Ah." I nod. "Cool."

"And you?"

I take in her curvy figure, sky-high heels, and perfect makeup. She's pretty, I'll give her that. But she seems unsure of herself, or her work or something. I guess being an interim anything would probably take a person down a peg professionally.

"I'm a physical therapist."

"Oooh," she says with a smile. "Get to be hands-on with the players?"

I laugh. "Indeed I do. It's not a bad gig. I get to fix them and inflict pain. It's like a non-sexual S&M shop."

"Jesus, Pam," Holly says with an eye-roll.

Scarlett just laughs. "I like her. I mean, you married the hottest guy on the team so don't pretend you didn't notice the abundance of muscles around here."

"Okay, time to go," Holly says. "See you tomorrow, Scarlett. We'll work on that plan first thing."

We head out and down to the pub outside the arena. Holly orders a Sprite and complains of heartburn, then orders like three fried appetizers.

"Counterintuitive much?" I ask after the waitress walks away with our order.

"Can't help it. Baby wants fried cheese sticks," she explains. "And jalapeno peppers."

"Yikes. This is crap you wouldn't have eaten if someone had paid you before you got pregnant."

"I know." Her face wrinkles into an adorable cringe. "I don't know, I just want it all the time now. Evan says I should let myself indulge every once in a while, so…"

"So you're loading up tonight, got it," I say with a shrug. "I won't judge. As long as you don't judge the giant margarita I'm going to drink."

"Of course, I wouldn't. So you said Georg came down today?"

"He did. Didn't seem to have a purpose. I've never seen such a hulk of a man so…uncomfortable. It shouldn't be cute, because he's a giant, but it was. Very odd."

"He likes you, Pammy."

"He didn't seem to like me at your wedding. And I haven't heard a thing from him since LA, really."

"Well, that doesn't mean anything. I mean, I saw the way he looked at you in Colorado."

"Like he wanted to chop me to bits and bury me in the back yard?" I ask.

"No, it was less stalker and more smolder. I saw it." Holly lifts her chin as if to dare me to argue with her. She's feisty now that she's preggo.

"He smolders, no doubt," I agree. "But if he wanted me, he'd have come and got me. Besides, he's not long-term material anyway. He parties way too much. He probably needs rehab."

"That's not a lie," Holly says. "But what do you care about him being long-term material anyway? You kick dudes to the curb the minute they start to get serious."

"My mother raised me well." I try not to sound bitter.

"Your mother just rid herself of her fifth husband."

"Your point?"

Scarlett wanders in as we're talking. She walks over and says hello, and Holly scoots over, inviting her to sit for a minute. She looks relieved at the invitation, but says, "I don't want to impose."

"The more the merrier." I gesture to the seat next to me. "Please sit."

"I was just going to pick something up to take home," she says.

Holly shrugs. "We just ordered. Feel free to join us. I was just grilling my friend here on her visit from Georg Kolochev."

"Oh, he's super sexy," Scarlett says. "That long hair. The scruff. He's such a bad boy."

"Oh, he's bad all right." With the sarcasm dripping off my words like the mozzarella in Holly's cheese sticks, I give her a smirk.

"Are you...dating?" Scarlett asks.

"No, definitely not. We hung out a time or two in the spring. Besides, the non-fraternization policy and the nature of my job means I couldn't date him even if I wanted to."

Scarlett's face falls. "Yes, you're right. Of course. I mean...I wouldn't step over a line. You know. I get it. Just looking. No touching."

I don't say it, but I want to get in Scarlett's pretty face and tell her I don't give a flying crap if she screws players —she just better stay away from Georg. I know he's not mine, but the thought of him with someone else just— well, it really upsets me.

"You okay there, champ?" Holly asks, breaking me from my thoughts. "You look like you're the one with heartburn."

"Speaking of heartburn," I state as the waitress comes back and unloads a tray worth of appetizers. I look at Scarlett and say, "She's having grease for dinner tonight."

"It's just an appetizer," Holly retorts as she stuffs a cheese stick into her mouth. Mouth full, she says, "I'm haffin' dinner wif Eban later."

I feel both of my eyebrows go high on my forehead as I witness this madness. Holly does not shove cheese sticks in her face. She does not talk with her mouth full.

And she does not stuff herself with junk before going to actual dinner. Pregnant women are bizarre.

"So Fiona seems kind of severe?" Scarlett asks tentatively.

Holly lets out a little huff. "She can be, but she's a pro at media management. She just takes a while to warm up. Just do a good job and you'll be fine."

"That's good advice." Scarlett nods earnestly. "I'm sure I won't ever do as good a job as you have. I mean, I followed the Crush accounts all last season. You killed it. I applied for the communication specialist job mainly so I could learn from you."

"That's sweet," Holly says. "It's not brain surgery. Just be creative. The guys are mostly up for anything."

"So we don't manage their personal social media use."

"Obviously not," Holly answers with an eye-roll. "Otherwise we'd have too many pictures of players drinking shots from between silicone breasts, right?"

Scarlett laughs. "I thought that during the interview for the role when I was asked if I believed integrating their personal social media with their professional pages was wise."

"I'm glad you obviously said no. They have the right to have their own online presence. The only time we get involved is if there's something illegal or borderline—and usually the guys will take whatever it is right down."

"Georg Kolochev's account..." Scarlett starts.

"Tell me about it," Holly responds with a sigh. "He hasn't posted in a while but most of his stuff is party, party, party."

"Is it true he's an alcoholic?" Scarlett asks.

"That's probably none of your business." It comes out far harsher than it should have.

Both women stare at me from across the table, looks of shock on their faces.

"I don't mean...I mean, I'm sorry if I..." Scarlett stammers.

"I'm just saying that we shouldn't make assumptions about people. And we shouldn't judge them just because they have pictures of themselves partying on Instagram." I try to tone down the aggression as best I can.

Scarlett nods, looks at her phone, and comments, "Oh, well, I'd better be going. Thanks for letting me hang."

Scarlett leaves in a hurry and Holly stares at me, a look of mild amusement on her face.

"Jealous much?" my friend asks. "You bit her head off."

"She *was* annoying."

"Man, you are a crab today," Holly says. "Have another drink. Chill out."

"I mean, there's a policy. We can't date the players," I comment, as if this is even remotely connected to why I was so mean to Scarlett.

Holly opens her mouth but then shuts it again. She reaches out and grabs some fried nonsense and pops it in her mouth.

The benefit of being here in Vegas is having my bestie around. I missed seeing her and being able to throw all my chaos her way when needed. And I think that Georg Kolochev falls under the category of chaos. Yes, I'm attracted to him, because as Scarlett said, he's super sexy.

But there have been moments where I've seen more in his expression. More than the party boy manwhore. More than the man who drinks vodka for dinner. More than the embarrassed confusion on his face earlier. Just...*more*.

"I like him, Holly," I finally admit. But I just don't think it could work. I'm, well...me. For one. And for two, he's Georg. We're on two different ships, sailing in different directions."

"Two ships, sailing in different directions?" she repeats. "What kind of horse manure is that?"

I shrug, grinning. "Change of subject. I need to know if you and Evan still do it while you're preggers, and if so, how is it possible?"

"That's a very personal question, Pamela." She eats another cheese stick. "But since you're my very best friend, I will simply share that we do indeed make love and that it requires some strategical ingenuity."

"Aren't you worried he'll, like, poke the baby?" I tease.

"Do you even know a single thing about human biology?" Holly responds by throwing a piece of fried cheese at me.

Truth be told, I know a lot about biology. There are many other things I don't know about, though. Relationships. Sex. Long-term commitment.

Sex.

And did I mention sex?

4

naked conversations

Georg

Practice has been good all week. We have a couple of rookies on the team who've been fun to mess with. This one kid, Mikhail, is a total hothead. I love fucking with him on the ice just to get him riled up. I swear, these rookies come in with such chips on their shoulders. It brings me great pleasure to take them down a peg...or five.

As I'm pulling off my gear, ready for the weekend, I hear two guys in the shower talking about trades. And then I hear my name. So, naturally, I stroll back and turn on a shower, interrupting their conversation.

"Heard my name," I interrupt. "Know something I don't?"

Nothing like having a conversation like this while everyone's naked. It just sort of removes all the pretense and deceptiveness.

"Nah," they answer at the same time.

"I thought I heard my name and the word trade in the same sentence, though," I say as I soap up. I wash my cock and balls as I ask the question, just to make it more awkward.

"Just heard they might be making some high-level trades to cut budget. Send high earners off, bring younger guys with lower salaries in," the one guy says. He shuts off his shower and wanders off, clearly done with this conversation.

"I don't think it's true," the other guy adds. "Why cut people who helped lead you to a championship?"

And then he's gone, too, and I'm left soaping myself alone, with only my own thoughts to keep me company.

Of course, the first thing I do once I'm clothed is call my agent.

The next morning, we're in Max Terry's office.

"Good to see you, Ned." Max holds out a hand, a gold watch on his wrist, his shirt cuffs monogrammed.

Ned Saunders, overweight and sweaty, holds out a hand and shakes. I can see the distaste on Max's face. Ned has sweaty hands. I don't shake his hand because it's just disgusting.

"Good to see you, too," Ned says. "What's this rumor we're hearing about trades?"

"On Georg?" Max asks. He looks genuinely surprised.

"On high-cost players," I answer.

"Not sure what you're hearing or where you're hearing it," Max says, "but I've got no intention of messing up a good thing. We took a hit when Chalamet retired and replaced him with a couple of rookies. I didn't go big because I didn't feel like we needed a superstar. We've got you and Evan—the dream team."

"So I'm not on the chopping block?"

"Not so long as your play stays good and your off-ice adventures are kept to a minimum. I can't have bar fights and middle-of-the-night calls for bail this year," Max says.

Ned is picking his way through a bowl of mixed nuts on Max's office coffee table. He's literally touching nuts with his bare, sweaty hands, and then putting them back in the bowl. It really is disgusting. And I *really* need a new agent.

He seems to sense me staring at him so he straightens up and takes a handkerchief out of his jacket, then wipes his sweating forehead. "Georg was part of a winning combination out there last year. Having him on the trade list would be bad for the team."

Both Max and I stare at him like he's grown two heads. Did he hear any of the last five minutes of conversation, or was he so completely engrossed in finding the perfect cashew to actually listen and do his job?

"Yes, well," Max says. "We've established that Georg is not on the trade list, Ned."

"Oh, well, that's great," Ned replies unenthusiastically.

Is this asshole for real?

"Max, I appreciate your time," I say, cutting off this painful bleed session before I turn the floor red. "I assure you I'll work harder than ever this season. I've been working closely with the athletic trainers and am already seeing good progress on my personal health goals."

"I'm glad to hear it, Georg," Max says. "We pulled in new staff throughout that area to assure you all access to the best support possible. Nutrition, exercise, therapy… whatever you need, it's available to you now. We want to double up on the cup, so to speak. So keep up the good work."

I shake his hand and wait for Ned to pipe in with some sort of bonus conversation, something about making more money if I have another strong year on the ice. But, no. He's back to the nuts. He basically grabs a handful and shoves them in his suit jacket pocket before waddling out, not even bothering to say goodbye to the guy who has my professional fate in his hands. All I can do is cringe, thankfully receiving a sympathetic look from Max Terry, who shakes his head along with my hand.

"You need a new agent, son," he comments under his breath.

Ain't that the truth.

As I walk back down the hallway, ready to call Evan's agent and beg him to take me on as a client, I literally bump into someone. When I look up from my phone, I realize it's Pam.

"Oh, sorry," she says. "I was totally texting and walking. Dangerous business."

I laugh. "Same. Sorry."

She gives me a little smile and her cheeks darken a bit. Is she blushing? Ugh. She's so beautiful. Voluptuous with pretty, dark brown eyes. Long blonde hair. Even in that drab uniform they have her in, a stupid polo shirt and sensible shoes, she's a knockout.

But that ship has sailed, I think. There was chemistry between us, for certain, but she held back. And then at

Evan and Holly's wedding, I couldn't even get the courage to walk over and talk to her. Like some teenage boy with a crush.

"Are you enjoying your work here?" Lame start to a conversation I know, but I need to say something that doesn't involve staring and drooling.

She nods. "Very much. It's exciting to put all that schooling to use finally."

"The guys are nice to you, yes?"

"They've been great. Really sweet."

"Probably trying to butter you up," I tease.

"For what? I mean, I'm kind of mean when they're going through their therapy exercises. They probably curse my name."

"No. No way. They know those exercises will keep them on the ice. They probably fake injuries just to come and flirt with you."

Pam pushes her pretty pink lips to one side and bats her eyes at me. "Well, I guess they can fake injuries all they want. It's job security for me."

"I might have to intervene, though...in the flirting. Don't want you getting in trouble with these *khuligany*."

Pam makes an adorable face while she tries to figure out what I just said.

"Well, it's good to see you," I say with a wink. "Hopefully I'll see you around again soon."

"Yep," she says, seemingly unaffected by my pathetic attempt at flirtation. I need to step up my game, I think. "See you, Georg."

She walks off without a backward glance, which

shows me clearly where I stand. As much as I'm enjoying the view from behind *very* much, her eyes are *very* much fixed forward.

And that's the way it will stay.

5

thank you, georg

Pam

"He's got a torn rectus abdominus," the team doctor explains. "And his ribs are subluxated and malaligned. There's also a contusion from the tear, which will complicate therapy simply from a pain management perspective."

"So this looks like at least six weeks to me." I look over the notes on this injured player. "Maybe eight."

"In an ideal world, he'd have eight weeks, but we really need to speed him up if we can," Coach Brown adds. "I can put him on IR for preseason but I need him on second string once the season starts."

"I'll do my best, Coach. No promises."

"I need you to do more than your best," Coach replies. "On any player you treat. I don't want them out there on fresh injuries but they need to fight through the last of it sometimes. You know what I mean? The longer they're off the ice, the longer it takes to get them back up to fighting weight."

I nod. "I do understand. I'll start him on electronic

stimulation right away. We'll alternate heat and cold, and work in a strong anti-inflammatory. Once he's comfortable enough to handle it, we'll do some manipulation on the ribs. I suspect the malalignment may have played into the severity of the tear, so getting the ribs back in place will probably promote faster healing."

"Great. Keep me posted on his progress," Coach says dismissively.

My eyes follow him as he heads out, off to put out the next fire for an organization as big as the Crush. It's nothing I haven't heard before.

"Welcome to pro sports," the doc says.

"College sports are just like this," I say with a shrug. "Lots of pressure to perform, even when the athlete is not ready. It's not a great situation."

"Yes, and they make a lot of money within a limited pro timeframe. They pressure themselves as much as anyone else pressures them. It's a really thin line to walk. Let me know if I can be helpful as you get started," he says before setting out after Coach Brown.

"Thanks."

From there, I head to find Dale, the personal trainer I saw on the first day of work. His office is down closer to the team gym. And, of course, he'd have to be training with Georg. I think about walking back out but just as I'm about to sneak out the way I came in, Dale turns and addresses me. "Hey there, I was hoping I'd see you today."

I raise a hand in a kind of lame little wave. "I can come back when you're not busy."

Georg is craning his neck to get a look at me from his

position on one of the machines. Dale tells him to go jump on the treadmill and do a five-minute walk. He does as he's told, but not before staring at me for a good fifteen seconds. The look is intense. I might even call it smoldering. Yes. Okay. I would definitely call it smoldering, since I can feel it right between my legs. Woo, boy, I'm in trouble.

"So, what's up, pretty lady?" Dale asks a little too jovially.

"I came in to talk about the plan for this player with the torn rectus abdominus," I answer. "I don't want him getting soft in the six to ten weeks he'll be on the IR list."

"He's not going to make it ten weeks," Dale says, shaking his head. "You know that, right? He'll be lucky to get six before he's back on the ice, and I'm betting more like three."

"Three?" I ask, incredulous. "He would in no way be ready."

"I'm not saying he'll be ready. I'm saying he'll want to get back on the ice."

"Well, my goal is to hold him off as long as possible," I answer. "But in the time we do have, can you work up a plan that will allow him to work arms and legs with minimal core engagement?"

"I sure can." He gives me a leering grin. "Anything else I can do for you? Take you to lunch? Drinks? Dinner?"

"Well, it's nine in the morning, so don't get ahead of yourself there, Dale."

"Pfft. Fine then. I'll ask again later."

Georg nearly falls off the treadmill, he's trying so hard

to listen to our conversation. The scene grabs both Dale's and my attention, and Dale jogs over and asks, "Are you okay, buddy?"

"*Kusok der'ma*," Georg spits in Russian.

"No speakie Russkie," Dale says. "English please, big guy."

"*Trakhat' tebya*."

I let out a little giggle and both turn to look at me. "What did he say?" Dale asks.

I shrug. "I don't know, but he usually saves his Russian for swears and insults, so…"

Georg laughs but doesn't offer a translation. It reminds me of our date night last season when he tried to teach me a few Russian cuss words. I don't remember any of the words, but I do remember how funny he was that night. Georg has a great sense of humor.

"All right, well, I guess I'd better get back to kicking this guy's ass, then," Dale says. "Burpees for you, funny guy."

"Okay, well, don't kick it too hard. I don't need to see him on my PT table later." I turn to leave knowing both sets of eyes are on me as I walk out. I hear Georg say something in Russian, followed by "fucking burpees," and it makes me laugh again.

LATER THAT EVENING and most importantly, after the blazing Vegas sun slips below the horizon, I decide a walk around my neighborhood will have to do for my daily exercise. It's incredibly hot outside, so a tank top and shorts with flip-flops is the best I can manage. I'm not an exercise fiend...not like Holly anyway. I mean, I do Zumba and yoga semi-regularly, and I'll hit the gym periodically, usually just to scout guys.

Now I'm a curvy girl. Always have been. Big on top, small at the waist, some definite ass on the bottom. This is a figure that can be hard to dress. Fitted clothes make me look like a porn star and attract the wrong kind of attention. Baggier clothes make me look overweight. But I wore mostly baggy clothes through high school. Especially after my mom's husband-number-three decided to come into my room every time my mom was out. The first time, I woke up to his hand rooting around in my pants. He made all kinds of bribes to keep me quiet about it, and I thought it was done. A couple months later, he was back in my bed, naked and hard. He grabbed at my breasts and told me how gorgeous my body was before humping my leg, spraying his gross orgasm all over my bare leg.

I was fifteen. Very developed compared to other girls my age. I thought it was my fault, so I started wearing sweat pants and baggy T-shirts to school nearly every day. It didn't stop him. He still came in to sweat on me, grab at me, and come on me about once a month for nearly two years.

My ex-stepfather is due for parole pretty soon, but I try not to dwell on that too much.

I need a distraction. I've been through all kinds of therapy and usually I'm pretty good about managing my feelings about what happened, but sometimes it rears its head and I end up feeling the dread of anxiety in the pit of my stomach.

Flirting helps. Feeling in control of my sexuality helps.

There's a hot guy washing his car about two streets away from my condo. He looks up as I pass, his eyes moving along my curves as I give him a subtle smile. He gives a lopsided grin back before our flirtation is interrupted by not one but two small children, who run out yelling, "Daddy." He turns a smile on his kids, running a hand through his hair. And yep, there's the glint of sun on metal against the wedding ring on his finger.

I keep walking, ashamed of myself. Annoyed with him.

When I get back home, I'm sweaty and anxiety-stricken. Thinking about the past always gets me worked up. It makes me want to control my sexual situation to the nth degree. And what really gets me worked up is thinking about how poorly I've managed my sexual life these past years. I am twenty-four years old with a master's degree and a great job. I usually feel pretty good about myself.

And I'm still a virgin.

Yep. Inquiring minds want to know: How is a sexy, flirty lady like Pamela Jenson a virgin? Well, she panics every single time she tries to have sex, that's how. She has a literal panic attack whenever it comes time to "do the deed," and so she sucks the guys off and sends them packing, her embarrassment too intense to ever see them again.

Yes, I just spoke about myself in the third person. Sue me.

The fact is that even after multiple years of therapy, I'm still a hot mess when it comes to sex. And while I've certainly gotten close, I've never actually had intercourse. When they lean in close and I feel their breath or hear them panting...

Stop. Don't go there. You're safe. You're an adult and are in control.

I place my dinner order online—thank you, Papa John's—and jump in the shower, so ready for an evening of Jack Ryan in my pajamas and a pizza. I'm too hyped up. I need to relax.

The water is hot, not scalding but close, and it feels good to wash the day away, wash the thoughts away. I force myself to breathe, force myself to think about good things, fun things. How I love my new job. What a great steppingstone it is. How happy I am for Holly and Evan, who will be parents soon.

And Georg. Silly, messed-up, wildling Georg. Beautiful Russian bad boy, Georg.

Under the water, I find my hands traveling to the sensitive places between my legs. I wash, but my fingers linger there. Georg's face comes to mind. A nose slightly crooked from a break or two. Green eyes, vibrant like spring grass. Long hair, usually messy. Wide shoulders. Sharp cheekbones. The small scar above his right eyebrow. Very much my flavor.

Memories of dancing with him, kissing him, come at me like a flood and I'm swept away. I switch the shower control to the massage setting, letting the hard spray of water hit my clit. It feels too good to stop. I need the sweet burn of an orgasm to clear my head. I push my hips forward as I work the water sprayer over my clit, flexing my muscles, pushing myself toward the peak as I think about Georg Kolochev.

His hands on my waist. The way his lips felt, hot on my neck. His tongue when he sucked on my lobe, something I'd never enjoyed before. The strength of his leg muscles as they virtually held me up as I melted from his touch. And then his words…whispers of erotic want murmured in Russian that felt like honey as I absorbed them…

An orgasm pounds through me, leaving me sagging against the shower wall. I have to catch my breath before I turn that stream of water on my hard nipples, the pressure of the water causing pain, feeling like little bites. I imagine it's Georg's teeth there and I come again, less intense but no less delicious.

I breathe a quiet "thank you" to Georg for helping me get off, for helping me get past the icky memories of the past. For helping me conquer the anxiety that had filled my belly with dread, replacing it with the endorphin rush that comes from a good orgasm.

Did I mention I'm the only person who's ever made me come?

I get back to my plan, the one where I'm wearing my soft, blue silk PJ's and snuggled on the couch with my cheese pizza and a beer. I didn't even have to answer the door to the delivery guy. I tipped online and told them to leave it on the mat and just ring the doorbell. Modern technology is too easy sometimes.

I wish navigating my love life was as simple as ordering a pizza delivery from behind a screen.

I know that Georg Kolochev is off limits. Our work policies alone prevent me from dating him. I know Evan and Holly got around the fraternization policies, but I don't think I could. I think, just by virtue of having my hands on these guys during PT, I need to stay professional. And I know how it would end. We'd have a good time. I'd think I was ready. I'd freak out and end it. And then what? I'd have put my career in jeopardy for nothing. For a fling.

No, it's not worth it.

No matter how much I want it.

6
a froot loop intervention

Georg

I'm trying to figure out if it is possible to like and hate someone at the same time. I like that this new trainer, Dale, is taking the time to help me get in better shape. I hate that he's a Mr. Universe lookalike and clearly has his eye on Pam. *Fucker.*

We're working on core, so he's demonstrating the ridiculous shit he wants me to do—hanging with my elbows in some kind of strap setup that'll use my core strength to hold me up. He looks like a professional gymnast as he does it, the bastard, with his eight-pack abs, his perfectly unmarred skin, his bulging pectoral muscles. Puke. I want to puke just looking at this Ken doll.

And, because I *only* have bad luck, Pam wanders into the gym just in time to see this ridiculous display of testosterone.

Dale jumps down and flashes Pam a grin. "Hey there."

"What a thing to walk in on, Dale." The fact she

smiles at him grates on me more than I'd like. "Preparing for Olympic trials, are we?"

"Just hanging out," Dale answers, "waiting for you."

"Hanging out," I repeat, along with a fake laugh. "You're so *pun*-ny."

"Attitude will get you nowhere," Dale snaps cheerfully. "Your turn, Georg. Hop up there."

I strip my shirt and climb up, positioning my arms in the stirrups. At first, it's not too hard to hold myself up. Dale watches for a few seconds, then turns his attention to Pam. She shows him some sort of file, but her attention flits to me every so often, slyly. I'm determined to stay here until she leaves. I do not want to fail in front of her.

I count in my head and it's about sixty seconds in that I start to feel the burn. I'm trying to focus on staying up here, to not notice the way Dale's posture is, the way he leans casually toward Pam, not so close as to be unprofessional, not so far away as to give an impression of disinterest.

I want to MMA this guy, to drop down off this thing, onto his shoulders, my legs squeezing his head, taking him down. I *need* to pummel him.

Suddenly, I'm feeling kind of nauseated. Not kind of. A lot nauseated, actually. I give up, having lost track of time, and hop down, running for the locker room. I barely make it in there before my vision blurs and my skin goes cold and clammy. I put my head between my knees, trying to will my body back to normal.

Dale follows me in. "Hey," he calls out. He finds me bent over like a lightweight, unfortunately. "What's going on?"

"Just felt dizzy and nauseated for a moment." I wave him off. "No big deal."

He reaches out to grab my wrist, checking my heart rate before looking at my pupils. "Stick out your tongue and say 'ahh.'"

"Ahh."

"I think maybe you're a little dehydrated or maybe low blood sugar. What did you eat today?"

"Cereal," I say reluctantly.

"What kind?"

"Froot Loops."

He raises an eyebrow. "Are you fourteen?"

"No."

"There is zero nutritional value in Froot Loops," he says. "Especially for a grown-ass man. Especially for an athlete. You need to get something with fiber, whole grains, and so on. And frankly, more protein, more fruits and veggies. I'll bet you eat like a bachelor, which for an elite athlete confuses me. You need speed and strength, Kolochev. Surely you know this."

I just shrug in response, refusing to look at him. *Smug bastard.*

"Go see Devon in nutrition. Have her give you a daily schedule. Get on track with your diet or you're going to start eating into muscle. You're doing great with these workouts, but your body can't sustain them or build muscle if you don't give it the right fuel, both before and post workouts."

"Got it." I am so done with this conversation.

"You made it two minutes, by the way," he says.

"Longer than I anticipated. Good job. Showing off for a certain blonde therapist?"

"Nope." If he doesn't shut up soon, I might do something I *know* I'll regret later.

He winks. "Liar. I was showing off, too. It's okay. She's hot."

I can't even speak a response. I just get up and stalk out, and head down the hall to see Devon Pearson.

The Crush organization has a habit of hiring very attractive women. Most of the women who work here—from the top brass to the housekeeping staff—are attractive. Some are thin and some are thick. Some are tall and some are short. Some are white and some are brown. But none of them are ugly. I think that's on purpose, though even our dumb-dumb of a GM isn't dumb enough to admit it.

All of that has led up to me saying for the record that Devon Pearson is in a whole other sphere of beautiful. She's the kind of beautiful that belongs in magazines. She's the kind of beautiful that makes men forget how to form coherent speech. I am not joking. Why she's a nutritionist and not a model is beyond me. She's nearly six-feet tall, perfectly proportioned, totally symmetrical, with slightly up-slanted eyes, lush, dark hair that falls in waves down her back, and a gorgeous set of perma-red lips.

I'm not stupid enough to think she would ever, in a million years, be attracted to me, so I'm not intimidated by her like some of the guys are. That said, I don't mind being sent to her office from time to time. Eye candy and all.

"Georg Kolochev," she comments as I wander in and flop down in one of her office chairs. "What brings you here today?"

"Dale's worried I'm not eating right."

"Are you eating right?" she asks, challenge in her voice.

I shrug. "I had Froot Loops for breakfast."

Devon looks at her watch. "And lunch?"

"Does water count?"

"No, it does not. Seriously, Georg?"

Another shrug. "I'm not always hungry."

Her lips form a flat line. "What else is going on in your life right now? Why the big push for fitness? I mean, you've always been fit as an athlete, but not totally committed above and beyond the necessary minimum to play the game."

"I am flatline on increases."

"And..." Devon asks with her eyebrows raised.

Isn't that enough information? I shrug. "I need to be better...stronger." I want the big paychecks like Evan gets. He is a scorer, but I am with him on each assist almost. Yet I don't get the big bonuses, the big multi-year, seven-figure contracts. I make good money, yes, but I am not where I want to be. But I don't share all that with Devon because she's asking the right questions. She's a nutritionist, not a psychologist.

"And that means what with regard to this spur in fitness training?"

Clearly, I was wrong. I sigh and shove back in my chair. "I need to prove last year was no fluke. I need to attract a new agent who can represent me better. Or at all, really. Ned is not cutting it for me anymore."

"Ned drinks a lot, yes?" she asks.

"He does. And he eats a lot. And he sweats a lot. It is hard for anyone to take him seriously."

"Do you think maybe he needs to head to rehabilitation for his drinking?" she asks.

"Who knows." I lift a shoulder. "His drinking is not my problem. His lack of ability to do his job *is* my problem, though. In the meantime, I need to train so that I can attract a new agent."

"Well, I think you could consider asking him to kick his drinking habit. You can ask him to focus on himself like you're focusing on yourself. I assume you're cutting the drinking as well?"

"I wouldn't go that far, Devon." I put two hands up to halt this conversation.

"Well, you should go that far," she snaps. "You'll never get past the plateau you've hit if you don't cut the booze, my friend."

I don't answer. Silence is the only answer I give anyone who tells me I need to stop drinking. Devon proceeds to ask me a plethora of questions about carbs, proteins, fats, and what combinations do what. After she checks for allergies and what foods I love and hate, she prints off some weekly meal recommendations and hands them to me.

"Please think about what I said, Georg. And stick to these meal plans for the next couple of weeks. See how it feels. It should be enough calories to sustain your increased workouts. And I'm guessing you'll have more energy and stamina."

"More stamina is never a bad thing." I give her a wicked grin.

"Get out now." She shoos me away with her hands. "That stuff doesn't work on me."

With a chuckle, I thank her and head back out into the hallway, reading the meal plans as I walk. Lots of fish and chicken. Lots of vegetables. Lots of fruit and whole grains. Definitely more work than I'm used to...

"Hey, Georg?" Devon calls from her cubicle.

"Yeah," I answer, turning to look.

She jogs the few feet and hands me a Post-it Note. "I realize this is a big change. There are services that pre-prep all of this and deliver it for you each week. I've written them down here."

"Bless you for reading my mind." I rub my eyes, suddenly tired. "Thanks, Devon, I appreciate this."

"Anytime, Georg."

I HEAD off to grab what I've decided I'll call my "Last Meal"—a burger and fries—and feel immediately better.

I also drink two beers before calling Ned.

I start in with the demands the second he picks up and I know it's not voicemail. "Ned, I need you to draft a preseason memo for management. Ask them to reward me based on performance."

"Oh, I don't think they'd—"

"I was one half of the top-scoring duo on the ice last year," I say. "Evan got bonuses like crazy. It can be negotiated. And I'm motivated to hit whatever goals they want to see."

"Well, I just don't—"

"*You just don't* what, Ned? Do your job? *Pridurok!* You get paid to represent me. So why don't you do *that* for a change," I snap. "And for fuck's sake, go get dried out. Stop drinking so much. Stop eating so much. You're an embarrassment."

"Well, that's the pot calling the kettle black, now isn't it?" he counters, once he's done stuttering.

"You are worthless," I snarl. "I am going to start shopping around for new representation."

"Now, now, Georg, I don't think that's necessary."

"Then maybe you should DO WHAT I FUCKING ASKED." I hang up on him and head to the ice, my mood shittier than it was before our phone call, if that's possible.

I'm a total prick in practice, checking rookies right and left. At one point, Evan pulls me aside, like any good team captain should. "Hey, man, what's going on with the aggression? Like, more than usual. Are you okay?"

"Fucking Ned," is my answer.

"Really? Your agent has you this riled up?"

"He's worthless," I spit. "I'm working my ass off and he is pissing away any negotiation space I might have. Fucking sweaty bastard."

"Oh-kay..." Evan says carefully.

"And I have to start eating better. Whole special diet from Devon. Nearly passed out in the gym today."

Evan laughs. "Oh no, not a healthy diet. Whatever will you do if you can't pour vodka over cereal and call it a meal?"

"I do not pour vodka over my cereal, fucker."

"Fine," he says with an eye-roll. "Still, it's good you're taking your health more seriously. You can't stay in your twenties forever. Making changes now will help you be healthier when you're older."

"You sound like a dad," I say, annoyed.

"Good, because I'll be one soon. But you want to play for a long time, and you won't be able to sustain it if all you put in your body is cereal and alcohol."

"I thought we were talking about my piss-poor agent," I say. "Not my eating and drinking habits."

Evan puts up his gloved hands. "Just looking out for you, man. You're literally my left hand. I need you out there."

"Fuck," I say as I skate off, having had quite enough of this bullshit conversation.

But he's right. He knows I've been working out harder, trying to drink less. I do want to push my career further. I don't want to be on the trade list.

I don't want to go backward.

You think you'll amount to anything? See yourself as the next Igor Larionov?

I have to keep pushing forward for that to happen.

But are you taking things serious like you should be? No.

Wasting your talent? Probably.

Letting good opportunities pass you by when you should be grabbing them with both fists? Yeah.

Being a fucking imbecile—slaboumnyy—most of the time? Guilty.

I just have to be more than all of that.

7

shut your f#@king mouth

Pam

Somebody's not having a good day. *Georg.*

And since it's someone I care about, I can't stop my feet from taking me to the sound of his voice two hallways over. I head out of the PT suite to find him but as I approach, I see that the team nutritionist, Devon, is already at his side. Georg is screaming into his phone, mostly in Russian, but sometimes in English clearly stunted by emotion.

When he hangs up, he throws his phone at the wall with a frustrated grunt. It shatters into several pieces and Devon puts her hand on his shoulder.

"Calm down," she says quietly. "What's going on?"

"He is shitfaced," Georg snarls. "I can't even have a conversation with him. *Slaboumnyy!* He was blathering on about needing to up his game but in the same sentence says he can't do anything for me. He actually had the nerve to call me a fuck-up. Can you believe that? I helped win a fucking championship!"

"So the rehab conversation didn't go well, I take it?"

"Fuck. No, he was oblivious. Threw my own drinking back in my face."

"Well, there is that…" Devon says. At a sharp look from Georg, she pulls him to her in a hug and whispers something in his ear.

This makes me see red, for some reason. What the heck is she hugging him for? Are they really that close? I decide it's time to stop that nonsense in its tracks.

"Hey, uhm, Georg?" I say sweetly. "We've got the group PT stretching set up in the gym in a few minutes. Come join us?"

"Yes, okay," he says, pulling away from Devon. "Give me a minute. I need to change. Breathe a little. You know."

"This will help. This kind of stretching. Good stress reduction tactic…" I press gently, really hoping he'll take me up on the offer.

"Yeah, okay," he says, picking up the pieces of his broken phone and cursing in Russian as he wanders toward the locker room.

Devon looks at me. "Poor guy. He's trying to make positive changes, but his agent is not doing a thing for him."

"Oh? Sounds like he needs a new agent."

"That's why the extra workouts and a better diet," Devon says. "He's trying to attract someone else. Right now, though, he just wants Ned to represent him well in this preseason. Now is the time to negotiate performance-based stuff."

"What happens if his agent doesn't step up?" I ask.

"Any number of things. Best-case, his contract is what

it is. He plays his season. Done. Worst-case, he gets traded and no one is there to advocate for him in the trade."

"Do you think he'll get traded?"

She shrugs. "Well, who am I to say? He played really well last year. He's a wild card, though, as you have surely figured out. People have mixed feelings about him."

"Ah," I say, not sure what the right comment is. "Well, I'd better get to the gym for my session."

I wander off, brooding over the fact that this woman knows so much about what's going on in Georg's life. She's the team nutritionist, not psychologist. I mean, of course he would want to hug someone who looks like Devon. She's beautiful and clearly respected. *And why do I care?* I've already written off the possibility of any kind of relationship with Georg, mainly because it's prohibited here, but also because he hasn't given any indication of interest since last spring. *Annnd now I probably know why he's shown no interest.*

I try to put my stupid jealousy to the side as I go in to help Dale run the stretching clinic we've designed. There are six players, all on mats.

Dale talks about stretching as an integral part of any workout. He says he knows none of the Crush players stretch enough and they all laugh. He recommends yoga as a stress reducer, and a way to unfurl tight muscles that get kinked during games and gym workouts. One of the guys does downward dog and complains that he feels stupid. Another guy tells him he looks stupid too. Someone farts, and they all giggle like a bunch of middle-schoolers. *Preseason.* I shake my head, because I know this will be a completely different atmosphere once the season starts and the boys—aka elite hockey players—will actually act their profession. *I hope.*

Dale gets them back on track and the two of us lead stretches while we explain how they help protect muscles, tendons, and joints from damage.

"You don't want to have to come and see me, because being on my table means you've been injured. And being injured means you're off the ice." Hopefully they can see the logic in what I'm saying.

"Yeah, but it also means we get to have your hands on us," one of the players pipes up. "I don't think any of us would mind that, Pam."

"It's about the only way she'd put her hands on any of you meatheads," Dale says with an epic eye-roll. The guys all laugh.

This kind of light flirtation goes on through the half-hour session. I'm not bothered by it, for the most part. But as we finish up, one of the guys says, "I hope we have more of these sessions. I've just been enjoying the *nice* view down Pam's shirt the whole time. What a gorgeous rack."

"That is over the line," Dale snaps.

I level the guy with a stare that could melt metal. "Who are you?"

"Kellen," he says, a smug grin on his face.

"Well, Kellen, you just lost your right to attend these sessions."

"What are you, the principal?" He laughs. "No, you're not the principal. You're the hired help. You're here to serve us, because we're the moneymakers."

"*Serve us?* Did you really just say that to me?" I shake

my head to make sure I'm not lost in Bizarro World. I focus on him and cross my arms over my breasts. "I am definitely *not* here to take this kind of garbage, though, Kellen. I completed a five-year master's at UCLA in physical therapy to get this job, and there is nothing in my contract that says insolent comments about my anatomy by hockey players are acceptable."

"But it's okay for these guys to talk about having your hands all over them?" he counters. "I'm just adding to the conversation. And it's a compliment. So don't be such an uptight bitch."

Some of the other guys start to move out of the space, clearly uncomfortable by this exchange. Georg, who I didn't even notice, is sitting on a mat to Dale's right. He jumps to his feet and walks over to stand straight up in Kellen's face.

"Shut your fucking mouth," Georg spits. "Treat this woman with some respect. There is joking and there is being a creep. If you can't tell the difference, then you need to fuck off."

Dale chuckles and says, "Come *on*, guys. No need for combat. Kellen, your comment was well over the line, and I think maybe Google search #TimesUp when you get a minute." Snickering from the others in the room breaks the tension a bit but it's still awkward. "Just apologize to Pam and move on," Dale insists.

Kellen, eyes blazing with anger, offers up a lame "sorry" in a way that reminds me of some of the kids I babysat when I was in high school. "Not even a little bit sorry" is more like it.

"Whatever," I say with a big, loud sigh. "I've got work

to do. Next time, Kellen, eyes up here." I gesture to my face and he just stares, his jaw tightly clenched, fists balled up at his sides.

I go back to the therapy space and flop down in my desk chair. A moment later, Dale comes in and asks if I'm okay.

"I'm fine. I can handle comments like that, but I'm worried about how fast he went from joking to rage."

"Kellen?" he asks. "Yeah, he can be a hothead on the ice, but I've not seen him like that in real life. I think maybe he was embarrassed at being called out."

"Maybe," I answer, but I know I don't sound convinced.

"If you want, we can go report this whole thing to HR," Dale suggests.

"Let me think about it. I'm inclined to let it go and report it if something else happens with him."

"You're the boss." He claps his hands together. "I'll buy you a drink after work—help you calm down from this."

I give a thumbs up and he walks back out. Georg passes him in the doorway, but only steps a foot inside the space.

"I just wanted to apologize for losing my temper," he says softly.

"Oh, no biggie," I say, waving him off. "It was nice of you to come to my defense."

"Kellen's a friend, but that doesn't excuse him being obnoxious to you."

"I appreciate it, Georg. I really do. But are you okay?

You seemed so upset earlier, and your reaction to Kellen definitely escalated quickly."

"It's been a frustrating few days," he admits. "But it will be fine. I'll try to keep my temper in check. I'm sorry you had to see that."

He does a little bow and backs out, leaving me with my thoughts. He's come to my defense before. When Viktor accidentally knocked me to the ground and set off a bar brawl prior to the All-Star games. I guess I shouldn't be surprised by how he interjected with Kellen just now, but it still leaves me with more questions than answers. Why would he get so riled up if he's not even interested in me?

Is it just that he's a gentleman and would do that for anyone?

I head home more confused about Georg Kolochev than ever before.

8
i'd love to give you my number

Georg

"This is not looking like a good start to the preseason for the Crush." Kacey King is on-air in the post-game press room. "What happened out there?"

"Well, we didn't come out swinging, that's for sure," Evan says. "We were playing flat in the whole first period. I didn't see much assertiveness from our offense, and we have to skate to the puck every single time. We can't wait for it to come to us and we certainly can't allow it to be taken away once we have it. Control, aggressiveness...all things we'll work on in this preseason warm-up."

The questions keep coming relentlessly until the official press event ends. Afterward, Fiona leads everyone to the preseason "meet the press" event, where we all have to be on our best behavior and make nice for the cameras and reporters.

Kacey King, the pretty, blonde reporter who tried so desperately to break up Evan and Holly, finds me in the crowd during the event. She puts me on camera, asking a few questions about our championship season and my thoughts on how we'll recover from a loss that was so clearly on the shoulders of the team's defense.

"You're a first-string defenseman. What role do you think you have in a loss like this?" Kacey asks, playing hard-nosed reporter.

"I made sure to be where I was supposed to be about ninety percent of the time. Other times, I got knocked out of position. They were a tough team, really focused, really ready to deliver a win to their fans. We can't rest because we won the cup last year. We have to come out hungry, and we didn't do that tonight," I answer.

Kacey cuts the camera and mic and then leans forward to whisper, "On a private note, I wanted to tell you that I can really tell you've been working out, Georg. Your skating was faster and more powerful than usual. You look good."

"Aw, thanks." She's flirting again. This girl loves to stir up shit with players. And there's bad blood between us because of what she did to Holly, but right now, I have to be professional and accept her attention. *Begrudgingly.*

She reaches out and rubs her hand on my bicep. "You're getting pretty buff." Her voice is sexy, husky. "I'm hoping you'll revive your social media feeds soon and post some shirtless pics. We single gals like the eye candy."

I look across the room and see Pam and the rest of the therapy and training team talking in a small group. They always come to this first meet-and-greet in case the press wants to talk about team training or injuries in any depth. She looks over and first meets my eyes, but then looks to where Kacey's hand is glued to my arm. Her eyes narrow, but she looks away quickly.

"Well, I've got to get some more interviews," Kacey announces. "But I'd love to give you my number in case you have more to add to what you just said on camera."

"Okay, sure."

She comes in close, business card in hand, and shoves her hand straight into my pants pocket. Her fingertips graze the side of my cock just slightly as she murmurs, "We could also meet up and not talk at all."

Then she's gone, off to catch Coach Brown. I'm left feeling a little dazed by the interaction, but also marginally interested. I mean, Kacey's pretty in that too-skinny way television reporters are. I know she's a viper, from what Evan has said, but who cares. I'm not in a relationship, and I haven't gotten laid in too many weeks to count.

I look over at Pam and find her staring again. She looks away as soon as our eyes meet. I pull out the card from Kacey and see her cell number on the back. I might call it tonight. I don't really know what this thing is I feel for Pam. I'm attracted to her, for sure. Who wouldn't be? She's sexy, smart, sassy, independent. She doesn't take any shit. I like that in a woman. And she's gorgeous. A great kisser. I've certainly jacked off while thinking about her more than once, and while we didn't do much more than a little making out, I definitely wanted more. *Want* more. And I feel protective of her, more than I've ever felt for any other woman. It's like there's still something vulnerable about her under all that bravado.

I can't have my head tied up like this, though. I need to focus on my play, my team, my game. I need to think about my career so I can ditch Ned and get into a new stratosphere with a new agent. I can't drink like I have in the past. I need to work out more and eat better. But no one said I have to become celibate.

I get approached by another reporter, who brings up trade discussions.

"Do you think you'll end up somewhere else this season?" the guy asks.

"I hope not," I answer. "I really enjoy playing with the Crush. I think this game was a fluke for us, and I want to be right by Evan's side as we turn things around. We're a good team—a team that brought home the cup last year. There's no reason to mess with that."

"Well, good luck." He motions to his camera guy and they move on to the next player.

Thankfully, Fiona kicks everyone out about fifteen minutes later, and we're free to leave. I head out, Ned on the cell phone as I walk to my car.

"You'd better not get me fucking traded," I say before he can even say hello.

"You've got no worries," Ned says, placating. "No one's said a thing to me about trades."

"That doesn't mean I'm not on the short list. You need to get a plan together. Bonus structure, promise top performance. Keep me here, Ned. I'm not fucking kidding."

He blathers on about how he knows I've been upset

and how he's on my side, and I end up hanging up on him. I really need a new agent.

And I need to get Pamela Jenson off my mind.

I *need* to get laid.

So, I pull out Kacey's card and save her number in my contacts.

9
wanna do some therapeutic stretching?

Pam

Holly and I are at her cute little house, both in sweats, eating ice cream and watching post-game coverage. Holly's a bit obsessed with her job, and she runs checks on her social media feeds while making notes on how each press segment goes, how each player did in interviews. All with her big-ole belly protruding like a basketball, her tiny tank top riding up under her breasts. Breasts which, by the way, are humongous.

"Does Evan like that your tits are so big now? He must, right?"

She looks down at her chest. "He doesn't hate them, that's for sure. And they're really a lot more sensitive than they were before. So that can be fun."

I laugh at this. Holly is usually not so open about her sex life. She's always been a bit of a goodie-goodie. And she worries about me because of my "issues." I play it off like I'm kinda slutty but we both know that's my running joke. I've never explicitly told her I'm a virgin, but I think she suspects. Holly's a very intuitive friend but she doesn't pry. She's supportive and I love her for it.

"Is it weird having sex while you're pregnant?" I ask, since she's being so open.

She laughs. "It's a logistics challenge, a little. I mean, yeah. It's a little weird. But fun, too. It's good."

"You're so lucky. You won the guy lottery with Evan," I comment with a sigh.

"Well, your guy is out there too."

I give an ambiguous noise in response. "What guy is that?" But I don't want to focus on me right now, so I ask, "You happy, girlie?"

"Very. Nervous about leaving the team for the first few months of the season, though."

"They'll survive." I shrug. "Just enjoy this time with your baby."

"Yeah, I know." Then in a quieter voice, "I know. It's just...I really love my job. And I only started a year ago. I had no plans to have kids so soon. It's just...I wish I'd had more time to establish myself."

"You did, though, Holls. You came in and rocked it, and your reputation speaks for itself, otherwise you wouldn't get job offers every other week. They'll be just fine for three months. And then you'll be back to it with a fresh perspective."

"You're right," she says without conviction. "Of course, you're right."

"It's normal to be nervous in a situation like this. You're newly married, new in your career, having a baby, in a new house. It's a lot for anyone, but you're you, and that means you'll be perfect through it all."

"That's just crazy," Holly says, making a face. "No one is perfect. Especially not me. Oh look, there's Georg."

"Squirrel," I yell jokingly. But she's right, Georg is on the television screen, so I turn up the volume and we watch his short interview with Kacey King.

"He really is very handsome," I swoon after we've watched his whole segment.

"He did better on camera than I thought he would," Holly comments.

"Probably because he was ogling Kacey." I sound bitter even to my own ears.

"I do not like her. She's not a very nice person," Holly snaps. If anyone knows firsthand just how not-nice Kacey King is, it's Holly. Even as reserved as Holly is, Kacey ended up with a well-deserved slap to her conniving bi-otch face last spring after trying to break up Holly and Evan's relationship.

"Of course we don't like her. I could say more but I'll leave you to your imagination." I take another bite of my cherry vanilla ice cream and try to forget about Kacey King. "She was very flirtatious with Georg at the meet-and-greet," I mumble, my lame attempt to put Kacey and Georg out of my mind an epic failure.

"Oh, I saw that. Does it upset you?"

I shrug. "We're not together. He can do what he wants. She can flirt with him if she wants." *She can probably fuck him if she wants. And she's probably just his type. Beautiful. Experienced. Available.*

"That sounds like a yes. You're upset," Holly insists. "Why don't you just tell him you like him?"

"I don't know." My continuous dilemma is back front

and center. "I feel like if he was into me, he'd have approached me back at your wedding. And I don't want to lose my job over someone who's probably not a long-term thing. I like my job. I'm good at it."

"Okay," Holly answers. "But those things all have a way of working out, if they're meant to be."

"You want to switch gears and watch a rom-com instead?" I ask, desperate to change the subject to anything not-Georg.

"Sure thing, Pammy." *Pammy.* My mother never called me Pammy growing up. She never called me much at all, really. And not having siblings meant I was often alone, and therefore didn't often have anyone to talk to about my shit-tastic life. When we first met, Holly was cautious around me. I was insecure, sarcastic, and sometimes cruel. I hadn't seen a psychologist or accepted that what had happened to me for those forty-eight months wasn't my fault. Yet somehow, Holly had snuck under my defenses and found a friend she thought was worth loving. I've often feared that she hasn't received as much as I have in our friendship, but it's moments like these when there are no barriers, just pure acceptance and deeply rooted trust and love, that I know we're good. Holly's heart is pure and good, and her intuition, her ability to read my mood, know I'm done talking Georg Kolochev, makes me love her even more.

We end up cuddled up on the couch watching *Four Weddings and a Funeral.* The baby kicks a lot, which is totally fascinating to feel and watch. Holly requires snacks about forty times through the movie, which still amazes me. She is so not a snacker normally. Pregnant

Holly, on the other hand, is an eating machine. Where it all goes is a mystery though. She's still as thin as before except for her basketball baby belly and melon-sized tits. I know I won't be so lucky if a miracle happens and I get pregnant someday.

Evan joins us about halfway through, and it does something funny to my heart to watch her curl herself up against him. He kisses her head and rubs her back, almost absently, as if it's simply an extension of his being, to care for her.

Ugh, I want a love like theirs.

But it probably won't happen for me.

I know this.

Because I always do the same thing. I flirt and I kiss, and when it comes time to go further, I kick the guys to the curb and act like I don't care. And, usually, I don't. I've never met anyone who made me feel like I should try going any further *for*.

So why does this thing with Georg feel so unfinished?

When the movie ends, Holly is completely lights-out asleep. Evan bids me goodnight and carries her up the stairs to their bedroom. I take that perfect opportunity to let myself out, and once I'm in my car, I pull out my phone.

I bring up Georg's number and before I can talk myself out of it, I press the green call button.

"Hello, Pamela." He answers on the second ring in that sexy Russian-accented voice of his.

"Hi...I wanted to call and check in after the game. You played super hard and I thought I'd ask if you wanted to do some therapeutic stretching tomorrow."

His lengthy pause reminds me why I was an impulsive idiot for calling him.

"You called me at midnight to ask me if I want to do some therapeutic stretching tomorrow?" I can hear amusement in his tone.

"Well, I..." I'm at a loss for words. A rarity, I know.

He chuckles softly into my ear.

"I'm so sorry. God, I didn't realize how late it was. I'll catch you at the arena, whenever you want to stop in."

I hear music in the background. Georg says something but it's muffled. I realize he must be out partying. Maybe Kacey King is out with him.

"I'll let you go," I say, feeling stupid. "I'm sorry to bother you."

"No, no." His voice is insistent. "It's good hearing your voice."

It is?

"Yeah, you too," I answer after a second. I feel so pathetically stupid. *Why* on earth did I call him?

"I'll come see you sometime tomorrow. We don't practice, so it will probably be after lunch. Will you be there?"

"Yes, I'll be working tomorrow," I answer quickly, my heartbeat speeding up at the thought of seeing him so soon.

"Good. Good. Then I guess I should take you up on your offer for some *therapeutic stretching*, Pamela."

Oh—my—God. He sees right through me. I realize I need to get off the phone before I say or offer him anything worse. And it *will* happen...because I turn utterly stupid when I'm around him. "Night-night, Georg." I hope I sound like my confident self, but I can't tell anymore with him. Georg affects me differently than all other guys before him.

There's a long pause. So long that I almost think he's hung up. But then he murmurs, "I love hearing my name on your lips."

"I..." At a loss, I have no idea what to say to that comment. He has to be drunk, right?

"Goodnight, Pamela."

And then he hangs up.

At home, it takes a very long time for me to calm down enough to even think about sleep. I shower and make some hot tea. I watch some television. I write in my journal. I clean my bathroom.

With Georg on my mind the entire time.

I wonder if he's going home with someone else tonight. I wonder what he meant when he said he liked hearing me say his name. I wonder if he was shit-faced and won't remember the comment at all.

I know one thing: the thought of kissing him makes for a very heavy feeling in my lower abdomen. It makes me wet to think about him, his kisses, the way he smelled when he was close to me on the dance floor. The way his voice got a little hoarse when he said goodnight on the phone. The way he stood up for me in front of his teammates. The way he looked, shirtless, working out. None of that should matter. The kissing was less than nothing as relationships go. It was a flirtation, a distraction from my last months of school.

And now I work for the Crush and he plays for the

Crush, and there is nothing to gain from breaking team policy but a whole lot of trouble.

But as my fingers find the soft, wet place between my legs, I drive myself into a wickedly wonderful ride on the Kitty Whipping Express with zero regrets. It feels too good.

I say his name when I come.

"...Georg."

10
wake the puck up

Georg

Why did she call me? This is the question I can't get out of my head as I return to the party I ended up at tonight with some of the guys.

Pamela Jenson.

I *need* to get this woman out of my head.

But how to get said woman out of my head?

Alcohol?

Meaningless fucking?

Why, yes, that's probably a very good place to start.

There are three showgirls who've joined our group. One looks a little like Pam, with her curves and long legs and blonde hair. She sits on my lap and has me do shots from between her fake breasts. I shove cash in the front of her bikini bottoms as she grinds her ass on my lap.

The rest of the night goes by in a blur of alcohol and the smell of coconut oil. The women pay us lots of attention, helping us lick our wounds from the loss we suffered. The Pam look-alike tells me she'd like to escort me home. A song plays in the club, an old AC/DC song called *Have a Drink on Me*. We all sing along at the top of our lungs as we stagger out of the club and into the balmy, middle-of-the-night air of off-strip Vegas.

The look-alike and I stumble into my apartment at three in the morning. Where did the night go? I vaguely register the time, but pay no attention to it as we drink vodka and turn on the television. She strips naked and straddles me, still in my jeans and T-shirt. I admire her tits but don't make a move to touch them. She tells me it's five hundred for the night.

I don't even ask her name.

IT'S WELL past noon when I wake up to the shitshow of another "morning after." My head is pounding. My stomach feels like it's full of acid. My cock hurts. My wallet's empty. Like I said—a full-blown shitshow.

Definitely not my finest hour.

I don't call Pam.

I don't schedule therapeutic stretching.

I don't work out with Dale.

I show up late for practice the following day. And then we travel for our second preseason game, and I drink my way through Los Angeles, particularly because it reminds me of Pam. I find a woman with dark skin and dark hair who looks absolutely nothing like her. We negotiate her price for the night, and I spend it with her, barely able to get it up because I'm so pissing-drunk.

The game is a slaughter. I can't seem to control the

puck to save my life. Evan tells me to wake up and it only serves to rattle me. I get in a fight with someone from my own team. Coach pulls me, telling me to "get my shit together," and replaces me with the second-string. Evan manages to score, but we fail at defense and the LA team rips three shots in less than five minutes. They score two more in the third period. A five-to-one blowout and I played maybe six minutes of the game.

Evan is so pissed he won't even speak to me after. Anger rolls off him in waves as he changes and heads out to the press. Later, I watch a clip of the press conference and when a reporter asks Evan why I got benched so early in the game, I see his jaw clench tightly while he tries to control himself. He ends up saying I wasn't playing my best game, but the implication was there: I was a fuck-up. He didn't want me anywhere near the ice while I was so hungover.

I call Devon, the nutritionist, after we return and we decide to take a walk together. We just walk around the arena block, talking.

"So you were super hungover and he pulled you from the game," Devon confirms.

"Yes," I admit. "I've been drinking a ton lately. I'm not proud of it."

"Look," she says, "I'm not a counselor, but I'd say you're obviously working through something. You're not your usual, jovial self. You seem agitated, more prone to violence. This drinking…it seems like more than just partying, you know?"

"Yeah, it's…" I don't know what to say. It is different. It is darker. And I know it's not healthy. But what causes it? What's to blame? These confusing feelings for Pam? My anger about Ned? My frustration about where I am on the team? All of the above? Who the fuck knows? I know I don't.

"You know, we talked about Ned needing to consider alcohol rehabilitation, but you might want to do the same. I thought you were headed down a really solid path on your own, but maybe you need, you know, more. More help, more support," she suggests.

"Probably." Just that one word. Hard to admit. I run my hands through my hair and squint into the sun.

We head back in and she gives me a long hug, says she's here if I want to talk. Gives me her cell number in case I need support outside of work. I go straight home and douse myself in vodka before passing out on the couch with my cock in my hand.

We have three more losses, all preseason games. I've never played so badly in my life. Evan pulls me aside and asks what's going on.

"I'm not the only person on the team," I answer sharply.

"No, but you're also playing like complete shit. It's throwing off the lines, the plays. The other players don't trust you to make good decisions out there. Everyone's working around you, and that's not helpful," he says. He's being very calm. It pisses me off.

"Whatever, then." I snap. I'm bleary. Tired. Ready to go home.

"Who are you? You're not you lately. What the hell is going on?"

"I'm just fine."

"You're not fine," he snarls. "Don't fucking lie. You're not training anymore. You're not going to therapy. You're drinking more, eating less. You look like a fucking ghost. You were all hyped up earlier about not wanting to get traded, not wanting to be a fuck-up. You were looking good, strong. Even after our first loss, I could see a path for us to win, to get back to where we were last year. But now...fuck, man. I think you need to consider what it is you want in life. Because this can't be it."

I don't have a comeback for his tirade. He's right, about all of it.

"I'm not myself lately, I know," I finally say.

"Well, talk to me, then," he offers. "We're friends. I'm your friend. Not just your teammate. Not just the captain."

"I'm not into sharing feelings. No offense."

Evan rolls his eyes. "No dude is into sharing feelings, but I need to know what's going on with you."

"I'm just pissed," I answer, throwing my head back in frustration. "Ned's a fucking joke, for one. No matter how hard I work, he won't work on my behalf. I'm losing out on bonus discussions. There's trade talk that hasn't even made it to me yet. Ned acts like nothing is going on."

"Okay, that's all fair. But drinking yourself into oblivion and playing like garbage won't help that."

"I know." Fuck, do I know. *I don't want to be here. Not like this.* Not as the fuck-up. *Slaboumnyy. Talentless waste of breath.* "I started working out with Dale, paying more attention to nutrition. I've been working hard on that, you know it."

"And the drinking?"

I groan and rub my hands over my face. My fucking head hurts. "Fuck," I say. "I mean, it was good for a few weeks. Lately, though…"

"Bad," Evan finishes for me. "I can tell it's tipped beyond having a good time. And that means it's time to stop. It can't be just about your agent that's pushing you to this extreme, though. What else?"

"I mean, no…yeah…Ned's always been a fuck-up. He's never been a good agent. I kept thinking I could ride your coattails, that we'd be seen as a team. I thought Scott might pick me up."

Evan makes a noise of agreement. "He talked about it over the summer," he says. "Liked how consistent you were. He wanted to see if last season was a fluke or a trend."

"That makes me feel even worse, because now he's only seeing me take a shit out there, every game." I probably sound like I'm whining.

"Yeah, but it's only preseason. We've got a whole, long season ahead of us. Get it together; you can turn things around."

He leans in and gives me one of those sideways bro-hugs. It's awkward but whatever. He's just being a friend and a team captain.

"Get back in the gym, go back and see Devon, cut the booze," he orders. "I'll keep Scott from looking the other way, okay?"

I nod. "Yup. Got it."

"Anything else we need to talk about?" Evan asks.

"Nah."

"We don't need to talk about Pam?"

"What's there to talk about?"

"You guys had a thing, or whatever. Now she works here," he prompts.

"We hung out. It was never a thing." I rub at the aching spot thumping away inside my chest, totally failing at checking myself in front of my best friend; instead delivering a big fat tell that suggests a whole lotta otherwise. He knows I'm a shitty liar so there's no point in denying.

Evan sighs. "Sure, well, one step at a time, I guess. First up, let's get you refocused on the ice."

ONCE HOME, I sit on the couch playing Xbox through much of the day. I'm up several times to pour myself a drink, and after the sixth or seventh time, I grab every bottle of liquor in the apartment and pour it all down the sink.

Alcohol gone.

Next, I hire a cleaning service that will come and clean the place from top to bottom on a weekly basis. I had a service before, but it became necessary to let them go...as well as calling a locksmith in to change out my locks. Wasn't my fault two of the cleaners decided to join me naked in my shower with an offer to do a lot more than just scrub my marble. The fact I took them up on their offer was totally my bad. I have since learned that humping the help is never a good plan. Self-growth and all.

I also make an appointment with the tailor several of

my teammates use and set up some fittings. The NHL dress code requires suits and ties on game days—it's even written into our collective bargaining agreement—and I can always use some styling new threads. It's been a little hard to get used to the fact that I can afford to spend thousands of dollars on a new suit, but it has to be done. I'm tame compared to some of my teammates, though. The hardcore fashionistas won't even wear the same outfit twice during regular season.

I strip my bed and start doing laundry. While it's in the wash, I go online and order a shit-ton of pre-prepped meals and other nutritional supplements from the food delivery services on Devon's list so I can test out what I like the best. I toss the crap food from my pantry and clean out the refrigerator. Basically, I pull a Marie Kondo for the rest of the weekend. Once I get going though, I discover it's not nearly as bad as I dreaded it would be.

I even write a letter home and send it to my mother's email address. It's important for me that my family knows I haven't forgotten about them back in Russia. We stay in touch the best we can for now with emails, calls, and the occasional FaceTime, but it's been three years since I've been home or seen any of them. *Mama really wouldn't approve of my life right now.* I'd love it if my mother and father and sisters came here to visit me. That offer is always an open invitation, but they have yet to take me up on it since I've been playing for the Crush. My parents are traditional, so I don't push over hard, but I do insist that they're always welcome in my home here in America. My two younger sisters, Irina and Zoya, are dying to come to Las Vegas. They want to have a good time like all young college students do. I don't blame them a bit. Although, it would be both awesome and terrifying at the same time if they ever do make it to Vegas for a visit. My sisters are young and beautiful and innocent. I'd have to fuck up the asshole who even tried to mess with either of them. And these horny motherpuckers I'm around 24/7 would fucking try. They'd be all over Irina and Zoya just like the slathering dogs they are. I'd get life in prison for serial murder and that would very much suck for me.

I don't know why I chose today to start getting my shit in gear. Time to clear up my home, make it a place I like to be. *My home.* Is that it? When I'm on my own, my world is in Russian. My thoughts, my emails to my family, my ramblings. Outside of these walls, I'm Georg who plays hockey for the Crush. No one in my daily life speaks my language. No one really knows me. *Not like Evan and Holly.* Maybe it was Evan's talk, or maybe it was Devon's encouragement, or possibly something—or *someone*—else that's motivating me to shake my ass into line. Either way, it's needed to happen for far too long. I guess today was just the day for me to finally wake the puck up and get enlightened. Yep, I'm starting to feel like one big enlightened motherpucker now.

Much later, when I'm in the shower whacking off to the lovely image of a certain sports therapist I cannot get out of my head to save my life, I come to an understanding with myself.

Making all these changes?

Yeah, it's giving me mixed feelings and was fucked up at first. Change is uncomfortable sure, but I can't take any more of feeling vulnerable like I have been lately. Or like I'm teetering on the edge and one quick push in either direction will send me over; because whatever side I'm leaning toward is where I'll land.

I cannot land on the wrong fucking side. I can't piss away everything I've earned getting to this level in my career. There are guys who'd give up a testicle to be where I'm at right now in the NHL.

Still fisting up and down the length of my cock to memories of Pam, I feel my balls tighten up and the delicious hot ache that grips me as I start to come. Relief pours out of me along with the jizz, the hot water washing it down the drain along with the soap suds.

Too bad my obsession with Pam doesn't wash away as easily as the schlong juice. Nope, still there. I tried. Tried drinking and fucking her out of my mind, but it didn't work. I've haven't spoken to her in weeks. I've been a dick. *Again.* But as I've cleaned up today, I know she deserves more than that. More than me being a dick and throwing her olive branches of friendship away with little thought. In cleaning out the shit, maybe that affords a fresh slate too. *Maybe.*

11
we're all works in progress

Pam

It's about quittin' time on a Friday evening, and Holly's temporary replacement, Scarlett, comes into the therapy room. It's rare to see office folks in our suite of work spaces, but Scarlett's been an exception, as she and I have been taking lunchtime walks periodically. My first impression of her is so different from the girl I've gotten to know. Sometimes Holly joins us, because she can't sit for very long without having back pain.

We're into the official season, and the Crush have seemingly turned things around, with two solid wins at home, and Georg back on the ice and playing much better than he did in preseason. I haven't seen him in person in over a week, though. It's almost as if he's avoiding me. I was hurt when he didn't come down for therapy after we talked on the phone all those weeks ago now, but I knew I'd been stupid calling him that night anyway. You live and learn. I thought it was to do with the office fraternization policy initially, but I overheard one of the other therapists comment on how he's seen Georg and Devon having lunch together a lot recently. Guess it's just me he's not wanting to see.

He's free to date whoever he wants, I guess. And Devon is a knockout, and smart. I don't dislike her at all, even though I want to claw her eyeballs out for getting near my Georg.

My Georg. Ugh. Why do I even let myself think like that? He's obviously not *my* Georg.

"You look like you're doing some hard thinking there, friend," Scarlett comments, pulling me from my thoughts. "Don't hurt yourself."

"Oh, look who's got jokes," I retort before blowing a raspberry at her.

She giggles. "I was thinking we should go down on the Strip and have a little fun tonight. You got anything going on?"

"I do not. Sounds fun."

"Cool," she answers. "I'll text you in a bit and we'll figure out a plan."

I finish cleaning up my space and head home to shower and change. Scarlett sends me about seven texts to let me know she's starving and that we need to eat before we go out drinking. Okay, maybe not seven, but definitely a few. I decide to keep my look simple rather than risking a hangry Scarlett, slipping on a clingy pink dress, nude peep-toe heels, and a long gold necklace. I wrestle my long hair into a fishtail side-braid and throw on a little makeup. Enough to look sexy, but not so much that I'll have to worry about keeping it updated all night.

Scarlett shows up in a ride-share, looking cute with

her very long red hair trailing down her bare back. Her halter top is emerald green, low in the back and baring some serious skin. It also amplifies her curves, making her breasts look huge in comparison to a tiny waist. She wears dark skinny jeans and black heels to complete her killer look.

"We look hot," she exclaims as I open the door. "Now let's go before I eat my arm off."

"Oh, no need to do that. Plenty of real food to eat in this town." We link arms and head out to the waiting car.

Holly meets us for dinner, looking adorable in a black wrap dress and red flats. We talk about the team's week, our jobs, and the nursery Holly's been pulling together for baby Kazmeirowicz. We beg and beg her to join us out dancing but she declines. Personally, I think it would be worth the cover charge to see her get down with that big belly.

"No way," she insists, no matter how hard we beg. "I'm too tired and my ankles are already on the border of being cankles. It's like ten o'clock and waaay past my bed time."

I get a little teary as I hug her and put her in a cab home. I don't know why. I guess I'm just really happy for her. She's so beautiful and so happy and so good. I want to be like her.

Scarlett and I head to a crowded dance club, pacing our alcohol intake by spending plenty of time on the dance floor. Several men, and a couple women, try to dance with us, and while Scarlett is loving the attention, I don't feel like hooking up with anyone tonight. I think about calling it a night, but then a bunch of Crush players, and a few staff members, show up and take up space at a couple tables with a view of the dance floor.

Of course. Georg is with them, but he looks a little different. His usually unruly hair is pulled back in a man bun. His black dress shirt looks pressed and sharp. He surveys the crowd and while others head to the bar, he stays back, watching the dance floor. It takes a while for him to notice me in the crowd, but when he does, our eyes meet and it's like electric sparks fly between us.

Prince's *Kiss* comes on, and people go nuts. It is a sexy song, for sure. Scarlett is dancing with some big hunk of a guy, so I focus all my attention on putting on a show for Georg. I dance like no one is watching, feeling every beat, while Georg watches from his seat, a sexy smirk on his face.

When the song ends, he claps from his seat, still grinning. He turns to the group of people and says something that makes their heads turn. When they see it's Scarlett and me, they all wave and motion for us to join them.

We head up for a drink. Everyone is more buoyant since we seem to have busted through our losing streak. They get a little rowdy, though I notice Georg never drinks anything other than bottled water. He seems more reserved than usual.

A group of young women come to the table, all asking to take selfies with the players. They oblige, but Georg doesn't engage with them the way he normally might. One offers to buy him a shot and he declines. She asks if he wants a beer and he declines. She tries to sit on his lap and he gently tells her, "No, thanks."

Kellen levels an accusatory, "What the fuck's wrong with you, Kolochev? Hot chick wants to dance around on your lap, you should let her."

"Meh," is his only response, though his eyes are on me.

I'm only seeing this in my peripheral vision, as I pretend to be listening to one of our team's accounting officers talk about how much money went into a recent locker room renovation. But I can feel the weight of his stare, can feel it in the heat that pools between my legs. Something about having a brooding Georg Kolochev staring at me is enough to make me combust.

Several of us head back on the dance floor but Georg stays put, his eyes always on me. I dance with the accountant, though it's at a safe distance. He's a terrible dancer, goofy as hell, and steps on my feet several times. After three songs, I excuse myself to get some water. Georg meets me at the bar.

"Do you want to take a walk?" he asks. "Get some air, maybe?"

I push my lips together and give a quick nod. It's the first time he's spoken to me in weeks, and I've missed his sexy growl more than I realized. *I've missed him* even though we're not really even friends. He takes my hand and we wind through the crowd, getting our hands stamped before heading out into the night.

The Strip is filled with people and lights and noise. Georg keeps hold of my hand as we walk, not talking, until we find the fountains at the Bellagio. We find a bench and sit, watching the lights and water dance.

"You doing okay?" I finally ask. "You seem distant tonight."

"I've been sorting some shit out in my life." He rubs his palms over the stubble on his cheeks.

"Is something going on?" I really hope he'll tell me this time.

"My agent is terrible. I have always thought of him as a joke and I realized last season I need a real agent, who will fight for me. He is too wrapped up in his own drinking to care. It's frustrating."

"I'm sorry. That sucks."

"It is not just him, of course. He does not make me do the things I do. I have to change myself, too. Last year was so good. It was fun working with Evan, playing so well. But even he thinks I am in the toilet now."

"I doubt he thinks that," I say. "He doesn't seem like the kind of guy who just writes people off for having a few bad games."

"He's not," Georg agrees. "But he is unhappy with me. To say the least."

"It's his job to be unhappy with you. He's the team captain. And your good friend."

Georg laughs lightly. "Yes, yes, he is a good friend."

"Well, I'm sorry you're having trouble lately," I say, not sure how to comfort him. "I wish I could help you through this. I enjoy watching you play, and I know other fans do as well. Everyone is rooting for you to get out of this slump. You and the whole team, I mean."

He looks at me for a long time. So long that it makes me blush. And not a lot makes me blush, so that's saying something. It's the most he's said to me, and I feel...

privileged. Although, he has probably already talked this out with Devon, so my heart pauses in its inflation of this time with him.

"It's nice to know someone is rooting for...us." His eyes move to focus on my lips. He forces his gaze back up to meet mine. "Have I ever told you how beautiful you are, Pamela Jenson?"

"I...uh...n-no," I stutter.

"Well, you are. Beautiful. Smart. Sexy. Sassy. Not just tonight, though you look spectacular tonight. Always."

"I don't know what to say to that." My response is breathless, caught in my chest.

He looks away and takes a deep breath. "I am not a great man, Pamela. I wish I could say I was good, but I never have been."

"But we're all works in progress." Ain't that the wicked truth. "No one is perfect."

"Regardless. I want to be better. And I'm working on it."

"I believe that, Georg." And I mean it. I've seen it. I'm experiencing it now in this quiet moment.

He takes my hand and kisses it. The feel of his breath on my skin nearly sets me on fire.

"I'd like to get to know you better," Georg breathes against the skin of my wrist. It's painful how this one thing can fill me with so much desire.

I force myself to say real words, when I really want to sigh or moan or let out some other noise of arousal. "Me too. I'd like that, too."

He looks at me again, a lopsided grin on his face.

"How about dinner, then? We can enjoy a meal and start this getting-to-know-each-other thing."

"I'd love it."

We stand and he takes my hand in his again as we start wandering back toward the club.

"I'm a little worried people will think we…"

"Snuck off for sex?" Georg says, finishing my question.

"Well…yes." Here I am, blushing again. What is it about this guy?

"If they think it, then they think it," he says with a shrug.

"I don't want to lose my job. You know, there's a strict non-fraternization policy."

"Did you see how many staff-members came out with us tonight? Trust me when I say people break that policy all the time." It's on the tip of my tongue to ask him about Devon. Whether he's broken policy with her already, yet is wanting to spend time with me. But I can't do it. Not now. Not here. His lopsided grin is full-on naughty now, which of course, distracts me completely. "It will be fine."

We head back in to find Scarlett dancing with another player. We join them on the dance floor, Georg looking much lighter-of-mind than before. We dance close but not too close. Just the proximity of him, though—

All I can think about are the kisses we shared last spring. I want more of him and this just feels so dangerous. I don't know how I should feel about it.

Still, I throw myself into the music, the laughter. I enjoy the feel of his hands on my waist as the crowd gets tighter. We catch each other's eyes every so often. He gives me wicked and private grins that melt away any resistance I might have still held on to—into oblivion.

When he puts Scarlett and me into a cab at the end of the night, he says he'll text me about dinner.

As I wave to him through the window of the cab, I admire how truly handsome he is standing there with his eyes on me, the warmth of his lips on my cheek where he kissed me goodnight still detectable.

12
trades happen all the time

Georg

I'm waiting in the bar, sipping a club soda, when Pam walks in. She's in a red dress with a low-cut neckline. It's flowy at the bottom and not too tight, so the focus is totally on her full breasts. Her stride is confident in high-heeled sandals, her skin sun-kissed and warm, her hair in long waves around her shoulders.

She makes me want to fall to my knees. I want to beg her to make me a better man. I want to get lost in her.

I stand, leaning in to give her a peck on the cheek once she's close.

"You smell good," she says.

"Took a shower," I respond with a grin.

"Well, it's working for you. And an unwrinkled shirt, two times in a row. I'm impressed."

"I discovered the concierge in my apartment building will send clothes out to be dry-cleaned. It's life-changing."

Pam looks like she might laugh at me. Thankfully, she's distracted as we're led to our table. The restaurant is on the top floor of a high-rise casino. I made sure to reserve a table near the windows, and the view of the Strip is magnificent.

"Nicely done." She gestures at our panoramic view of the city lights. "I'm captivated."

We sit and I can't help but stare. I clear my throat and ask, "How are you liking Las Vegas?"

"So far I love it. I lucked out getting Holly's old condo and it's in a great neighborhood. I'm really enjoying my work with the team, too. I don't think it can get much better than it already is." She smiles shyly and asks, "How long have you been here?"

Oh, I can make it a lot better, baby.

"Four years?" It's more of a question than an answer. "I've lost track of time."

"You grew up in Russia, though, I know that much."

"Was it the Russian swearing that gave me away?"

She laughs. "Might have been."

"Yes, I was born in Russia. Played for the Kontinental Hockey League of Asia, or the KHL, as it's known. Went through Olympic trials and played for my home country in Sochi Olympics."

"And how did you end up here?"

"My Olympic coach connected me to my agent, Ned, and he got me a rookie contract here with the Crush. Evan and I started the same year."

"Well then, I guess that's one good thing Ned has done for you, right?" She tilts her head at me and gives me another one of her sexy smiles.

I want to lean across the table and take her mouth, but of course, I don't. "I suppose, yes. Playing for the NHL has been good fun."

"Your extracurricular activities look like they've been fun, too." Pam has a sarcastic, knowing look on her face now.

I cringe. "Some things should not be on Instagram."

"Maybe not," she agreed, still grinning. "But look, we've all got a past. We've all done dumb things and then regretted them. It's not the end of the world."

I don't want to talk about the ways I've failed as a human right now, so I change the subject. "So, Pamela, what made you want to be a physical therapist?"

She mulls this over as the waiter comes to take our orders. I'm pleased to see her order a steak and she asks, "What?" at my approving look.

"Red meat, potatoes. I like it. I thought you might order a salad or something."

"That's kind of sexist, isn't it?"

"No, not really. I've been out with…"

Aaaand I need to shut it. She does not want to hear about dates I've been on with other women any more than I should be telling her about them. I curse myself and redirect the conversation. "Back to the original question. About your chosen career?"

She gives me a little smirk before she starts talking. "Well, I started college thinking I wanted to go to medical school, so I majored in biology. I got into my junior year and had a heart-to-heart with my advisor about the cost and the number of years and so on, and she suggested I do a minor in exercise physiology and then maybe go on to get a master's in PT. There wasn't any triggering reason; I'd just always been interested in medicine, and in helping people."

"Are you glad you switched?"

"Definitely. I've never been much of an athlete myself but I did have athletes as friends, and I could see how hard they had to work to get back to their sports after injury. I liked that I could help them achieve that."

"Very admirable." I like that she's so confident about what she wants.

"What about you, Georg? Did you ever think about doing something other than hockey?"

"No. Not really. I have played since I was three. My father is a youth coach. He pretty much put me on skates the moment he was sure I'd stay upright."

"Was he tough on you?"

"He was hard on everyone," I answer. "His job is to find and train talent. Many of his players start playing in pre-professional leagues before they get to secondary education. I started when I was sixteen. But yes, I think he was harder on me, because I was his son."

She gives me a sympathetic look as the waiter brings our salad courses. We spend a few minutes eating before she says, "Is your mother still alive? Sounds like your dad is still around and coaching."

I nod. "Yes to both. My mother is a teacher."

"They must be proud of you, for getting so far in your career."

I shake my head. "My mother is maybe, and my two sisters. My mother worries I'll get injured and not have a backup plan. My sisters worry they'll never get to come to Las Vegas for holidays while their big brother is playing in the NHL. They're nineteen and twenty, and still at university. They're not allowed to travel here until they both finish school. My parents are...strict with my sisters."

"Seems like very normal things for a mom and little sisters to worry about," she says quietly.

"Yeah."

"And your father? I mean, this is what he trained you for, right?"

"My father will probably never be satisfied with anything I do," I say bitterly. *You're nothing. Talentless. Slaboumnyy!*

Pam opens her mouth to respond just as I feel my phone vibrating on the table.

"Sorry." Not sure who would be sending me texts in bulk, I pick up my phone.

Pam makes a face at her bag and pulls her phone out too. Her head jerks up and I can hardly meet her eyes

CRUSH Admin: Defensemen Viktor Demoskev and Tyler Lockhardt have been acquired.

They've picked up two defensive players. This can't be good for me. I've got to be on my way out now, for sure. I feel my jaw clench as I look out the window, at the cityscape that I have come to view as my home. I do not want to be traded.

But Pam isn't thinking about what this could mean for me. No, she instead says, "Viktor..."

I shrug. "Trades happen all the time. He's big, hard to get past. I get why they'd want him. And this Lockhardt kid's a rookie, but he looked good in preseason."

"Can you play with him?" she asks. "Or is there still too much animosity?"

"Remains to be seen, I guess." What I'm thinking is that animosity seems likely, but I doubt we'll have to play together anyway.

Ugh. I feel sick.

Our entrees come but I can hardly eat. Pam tells me about her upbringing but I'm hardly able to focus on what she's saying. Her mom got divorced several times, I guess? She never met her real father and is an only child? These are important revelations, but I simply can't find my way past how devastated I feel knowing the trade is about to come. Also knowing I'll probably not be able to see much of Pam once I'm playing and living somewhere else.

This fucking sucks.

When the waiter comes to offer dessert, Pam looks at me expectantly.

"I'm not feeling all that well." My tone is apologetic. I hand my credit card to the waiter and he heads off to settle the check. "Pam, I am so sorry, but I think we'll have to take a raincheck on dessert. Is that okay with you?"

"Of course, it's okay. I'm sorry you're not feeling well. Do you think it was something you ate?"

"No, I don't think so." How can I tell her that I'm worried that this means I'll be shipped off to some other team soon, that there is no point to us even exploring this thing that's between us? Everything about this news sucks. And now I have a headache on top of it. I'm not even lying when I tell her again that I don't feel well suddenly.

Once I sign off on the bill, I walk Pam to the elevator and out to the street to hail a cab. She reaches out and touches my cheek and I can't help but put my hand over hers. We just stand there like that for what seems like a long time.

"You look troubled. Can I help?" she asks, her pretty eyes searching for answers that I don't have right now.

"I'll be all right. And I promise I'll make this up to you another time."

"Sure, of course. Feel better, Georg." She drops her hand, and fuck I want to pull her to me. She's hot and I want to fuck her, but right now it's a different need I have. *For once, I saw more.* I'm living cleaner, playing stronger, and I believed Pam could complete a different want. Something decent. *Good.* She gives me a little smile and a wave after I put her in the cab. I force a smile, attempting to suppress my anger and disappointment.

Once again, something good in my life is turning to shit. *This is so fucked up.*

When trade deals are announced there's usually no more than a day or two before you're on the ice in a new city wearing a new team jersey. If something indeed goes down with me, I'll have time to pack a bag and that's about it.

I watch Pam's cab drive away, the pit in my stomach twisting painfully. This could be the last time I have with her...and I just sent her home.

Tak trakhkav!

13
let's try that again

Georg

Saturday and Sunday were spent feeling like I was having a heart attack. All of my "enlightened motherpucker" bullshit from last week has evaporated in the span of time it took to read the texts from admin. I finally called Evan, who calmed me down somewhat and convinced me I was only anxious about Viktor joining the team. It was a rare weekend without a game or practice, which meant I had far too much damn time on my hands.

Now we're back on the ice for morning practice. Evan and I are working our drills hard, trying to show Coach Brown and whoever else is watching that I am still in this game, still 110 percent committed to this team.

"Have you seen or talked to Demoskev since LA?" Evan asks.

"Why the fuck would I want to do that?"

"I'm just bloody asking," he answers sharply. "Don't get your knickers in a twist."

"It's a fucking stupid question," I snap back. "It's not like we're mates. Never have been."

"Fine," Evan says, turning my short pass into a hard shot toward the practice goal. "Forget I asked. But you're going to have to work with him. He's coming, whether you like it or not."

"What the fuck was Bud thinking?" I say, irritated with the topic. "He saw the bar fight footage. He saw you get wrecked in that game against New York last year. Why would he want that douchebag on the team?"

"He was probably thinking he needs an enforcer since the rest of our defense seems to have its collective head up its collective ass," Evan answers.

"I resent that," I say, only half joking. "You should be telling them to stick Demoskev where the sun doesn't shine. He knocked the crap out of you last year. Dirty bastard."

"Well, I'm just calling it like I see it," he pushes. "And whatever. It is what it is. We'll have to let bygones be bygones."

"I hope you two get along great, then," I say, knowing I sound like an irritable child, but who cares at this point. "He can be your wingman, and I'll be playing for whatever shitty team they trade me to."

"Has Ned confirmed this is the plan, G?"

"Negative." As if the lazy bastard is actually doing any work. *Mudak.* "The fucker is probably asleep in drool and leftover donuts. He is not working the best deal for his client at the moment."

Evan sighs. "Why don't you call Scott?"

"Your agent." I purposefully phrase it as a statement,

because I want to be certain of Evan's blessing before I consider approaching his agent. We respect each other too much to go behind the other's back. That's not what friends do.

"Yeah. I mean, tell him you're drying out, fully committed, really need someone on your side. Offer him a more generous cut than he usually gets. Ask him to do this one thing for you and see how it feels, if he thinks a longer-term relationship might work. Tell him it's okay if he wants to walk away after, but you really need big guns on this." Evan nods. "And tell him I gave you his number."

"Thanks, man," I say as the whistle blows on practice.

We head back to the locker room to shower and Evan asks if I want to grab lunch in the pub downstairs in between our two practice sessions.

"I do," I say, "but I need to run down to therapy real quick, first."

"Why? You hurt?"

"No. I took Pam out on Friday and it started out great but it went to shit after we got the text about Demoskev."

"Oh, I forgot she got knocked to the ground during that scuffle," Evan says. "I wouldn't blame her for feeling nervous about him coming here."

"It wasn't really her. She didn't seem all that fazed, actually. It was me who was a twat about it."

"Oh," he answers. "Tough lady, that Pam."

"She is. Anyway, I really need to apologize for taking a dump on a nice evening. I'll meet you in the pub."

I head down and find Pam looking sexy-as-fuck whilst

munching on an apple, her feet up on her desk with a magazine in one hand.

"Working hard, are we?" I ask, grinning.

She sits upright and puts the magazine on her desk. "Lunch time. I don't have anyone scheduled until one."

"I just came down to apologize, because I bailed on a nice evening the other night. And I also came to cash in that raincheck."

"Oh you did, did you?" She tilts her head, a wicked little grin curling over her lips. "Who says I even offered you a raincheck?"

I give off a nervous laugh, hoping it sounds more like cocky and confident even if I don't feel that way. "Well, I know Friday was about as fabulous as it gets, but I can do better. I'm hoping you'll give me the chance."

"It wasn't totally shitty, Georg."

I can't help the laugh that escapes. "So that's a yes to a do-over?"

She pushes her lips to one side. "I suppose...on one condition."

"And what's that?"

"You'll let me cook for you at my place? We'll keep it simple."

"Done." I want to throw up a fist in triumph. "Tomorrow night?"

"Sounds good. I'll text you."

I give her two thumbs up and retreat while I'm ahead. As I step out of the therapy suite, I call back, "I'll bring some Russian caviar."

"I said keep it simple." She wings her magazine at me.

It hits the door frame. I chuckle as I see her get up to retrieve it, and I run right into Devon.

"Sorry, Devon. I wasn't looking where I was going."

"No worries. You look good today."

"Feeling good. About to grab lunch with El Capitan."

"Evan then?" she guesses, smirking.

"Yes. The bromance is real. At least for me it is."

"Well, make sure he eats something that isn't complete shit, will you? I think he's sympathy eating with his pregnant wife. He's put on ten pounds since last spring."

"Whoa," I shout. "I knew it. I can't wait to hold that over his head."

"I mean, it's probably muscle weight, to be honest," she says. "He's been training pretty hard with Dale."

"Nope, I'm going with baby weight. Much more fun."

Devon rolls her eyes and puts her hand on my bicep. "I wanted to check in with you anyway. You okay with Demoskev coming here? I know he's not on your list of favorite people."

"He certainly is not, nor Evan's," I answer, curling my lip at the thought of the big Russian being in such close proximity again. "But I've never seen him check one of his own teammates either, so as long as he gives me space, we'll function just fine. He won't be the first asshole on a team, and he won't be the last."

"Any word from your agent?" she asks more gently. "Do you think it means anything that the team is bringing in two defensive players?"

I shrug. "Hope it doesn't mean anything. No word out of Ned. I'm calling Evan's agent shortly."

Devon starts rubbing her hand up and down my arm. Out of the corner of my eye, I see Pam through the glass windows of the suite. She's wiping down an already clean therapy table, but I can tell she's watching this whole scene. And more importantly, now wearing a frown where a sexy smile was a minute ago.

"Well, I've got to run, Devon. Evan's waiting for me."

"Come down later if you want to talk," she says as I retreat.

14

the pretty kitty

Pam

First, Barbie needs to get her hands off *my* Georg.

Second, I am really enjoying the view of his backside from this angle.

Third, holy cow, did I just offer to cook him dinner at my place tomorrow night?

As Georg withdraws from whatever conversation he just had with Devon, I watch him leave and can't help the thoughts that creep in. He has access to any woman he wants. He could probably walk outside and have a hockey honey waiting to go right home with him. I honestly have no claim on Georg Kolochev. We kissed, we danced, I fell asleep in his hotel room after the bar fight. That's about it. And is he even the kind of guy I should be seeing anyway? He's a loose cannon. Maybe on his way to another team.

And why me? Devon is gorgeous. She obviously likes him. He obviously likes her. They hang out at lunch sometimes. Maybe they've shared a few dinners together at nice restaurants where they're away from the workplace and able to do whatever they want. And maybe they already do, and I'm just an extra girl to flirt with. *Because I'm not sure I'll ever be more than that to anyone.*

I should just face it. I'm one woman in a big crowd of women who find Georg attractive. And I do find him attractive. His body. His face. His hair. The way he plays when his head is in the game. I like his honesty. And I freaking love his English/Russian accent. When he speaks, his speech comes across as a captivating mix of very formal English with some street-talk thrown in. I could listen to him for hours. It seriously does something to me.

And I hope he likes crappy food, because I cannot cook to save my life.

"HEY THERE," I say, welcoming Georg inside my condo. He waves a bottle of red wine at me and plants a kiss on my cheek. His lips feel warm and his beard stubble remarkably soft against my skin. "What's this?" I ask as I inhale a delicious whiff of him. He smells so good I want to lick him. I wonder how that would go over if I just leaned in and swiped my tongue up his neck. I picture myself doing it and feel my body flush with heat.

Lord Jesus. Get ahold of yourself, girl.

"I forgot the caviar," he says, handing me the bottle, "so I grabbed a nice red for dinner instead. Couldn't come here empty-handed."

"I thought you were off the sauce?" I immediately

regret asking when I see the shadow that falls over his handsome face.

"A glass or two with dinner won't be a problem. It's the overindulgence that gets me into trouble." He shrugs with a half-smile. "Though I don't have to drink, if it makes you uncomfortable."

My heart melts a little at this, for some reason. I shake my head. "No, you're a grown-up. You can make that choice for yourself."

His half-smile turns into a full-blown grin as I take his hand and lead him into the kitchen. Holly gave me a chicken recipe that's supposed to be super easy, but that remains to be seen because I've never made it before.

Georg sees everything all over the counter and says, "I'm thinking I better help you."

He's wearing a crisply pressed, white dress shirt and dark jeans. I very much admire his look tonight, from the slim fit of the tailored shirt to the five o'clock shadow on his chin and cheeks. He looks good enough to eat.

And don't forget...lick.

"I'm thinking I may have forgotten to mention that cooking is not one of my special skills," I tell him sheepishly.

"So you invited me over to your place for dinner but don't really cook?"

"Yeah, pretty much, but Holly assured me the chicken recipe she gave me is foolproof...and it sounded like a good idea at the time." I shrug and smile at him, waiting for his reaction.

He doesn't hesitate even a second. "Not a problem for me. I have a whole phone full of places to order from." He holds up his phone and toggles it. "But you should know I am somewhat capable in the kitchen as well...thanks to my grandmother who lived with us when I was a boy."

"Hmmm...ordering in or braving the perils of preparing Holly's chicken recipe with Georg," I tease out loud with my palms up.

He stands before me and folds his arms over his chest like he's posing for a lineup on *The Dating Game*. Hot. Very, very hot with his muscles flexing under the white dress shirt. Straight up arm-porn going on there.

Before I can change my mind, I grab an apron from one of the kitchen drawers and push it over his head. "Looks like we are cooking our dinner tonight," I say as I tie up the back for him.

He glances down and busts out laughing. I've given him an apron bearing the outline of a female torso in a pink flowered string bikini. A joke gift that I received at a bachelorette party in college.

"I look good in this bikini."

"It's a nice look on you, I agree." We both laugh and it feels easy...*right* this time. Even if our dinner sucks, I'll enjoy the hell out of Georg's arm-porn while he chops and dices.

I pour two glasses of wine and we get to work following Holly's directions. It's a one-pot meal, so once all the prep is done, we just need to wait for it to cook. I've got the bread and salad already on the table.

The music is playing from my phone—just a light, jazzy Spotify playlist that I put on for background noise sometimes. Georg seems to like it, though, as he pulls me into his arms. We dance and it's kind of silly, each of us taking breaks to sip wine, or refill our glasses, or to check on the food.

It's not like I haven't danced with Georg before. I have. But here in my kitchen, with no one watching, there's something more intimate about it. In spite of the silliness. In spite of the breaks to drink and stir the pot. And he must feel the same because there's an electric minute where we simply stop. Everything stops, and we look in each other's eyes. And then his lips are on mine. *And they're even softer, sweeter, more delicious than I remember.*

I feel his heat everywhere. He's so tall, and he envelops me, even though our lips are the only part that touch.

A chaste kiss that nevertheless has me swooning against him as he holds my face in his hands.

I don't want the kiss to end but gather my strength and turn from him anyway. My cheeks feel hot where his hands were touching. I know my skin must be flushed bright red. I make a show of checking on dinner and pull myself together in the kitchen before calling out to him, "I declare this dinner ready to eat."

"I can't wait to taste it," he calls back cheerfully.

Georg is grinning wickedly at me as I deliver the plated chicken scaloppini to the table. My stomach does its own little flutter-dance at the sight of him sitting at my table waiting for me.

I don't want chicken. I don't want salad. I don't want bread. I only want the taste of Georg on my lips again.

But we do eat, and it's actually really good.

"Pamela, this is excellent. I give you five stars."

"I agree, and thanks for the five-star rating, but we really have to thank Holly for giving me the recipe. Not that she had much of a choice because I was desperate."

Georg laughs and shakes his head at me. "I'm still charmed by the fact you invited me for dinner but don't cook."

I grin sheepishly and shrug. "I almost ordered a pizza."

He laughs again. "I like pizza. It would have been okay."

"Devon probably wouldn't like you eating pizza, though." I can't keep the bitter, jealous tone from my voice. I try to cover by saying, "I mean, I know you're on a stricter food plan these days."

Georg studies me for a second. "There is nothing between me and Devon."

"I didn't..." I shut my mouth, take a big breath. "I didn't say there was."

"Of course you didn't," Georg says innocently. "I just wanted to make it clear. In case you were wondering." He smirks and looks down at his lap.

I stab at my food while I try to think of what to say, but Georg changes the direction of the conversation, and asks if I have any brothers or sisters.

"No, it's just me. My mom doesn't stay married long enough to start a family with anyone."

"Do you have a good relationship otherwise?"

"It's okay," I say. "She's my mom, so..."

"It's complicated?" he suggests.

"It is."

"My father and I are also...complicated."

"What was it like growing up in Russia?" I ask in an attempt to steer the conversation to something easier. I've become a master at that, because talking about my mom, about the strained relationship we've had, especially for the last eight years, is something I avoid at *all* costs. *Knowing she wondered if I was really innocent . . .* No, not going there. Not now. Probably not ever. "Do you go back to Russia very often?"

"I don't know how it would compare, really. I spent a lot of it in an ice hockey rink."

"That doesn't sound like much of a childhood." I never thought about how much he might have given up, or how long he's really been dedicated to this sport.

"No, I had a fine childhood," he answers. "Much better than many."

My wine glass is empty, so Georg pours more for us both.

"Do you enjoy other sports, other than hockey?" I ask as I take a drink. "Any other hobbies?"

"Motorcycles. I have three Harleys. I like working on them and riding, of course. My contract prevents me from going near them during the season though. I like movies and television, and I play basketball sometimes."

"And you like to party," I blurt, sounding far too judgmental. *Damn my mouth.*

Georg blinks at me. "I have been known to indulge in all that Vegas has to offer, yes, but I've been trying to rein in that part of my life of late."

I feel stupid for calling him out like that. I bite my bottom lip before taking another drink. "I'm sorry. It's none of my business and that wasn't a nice thing to say."

Georg pushes away from the table and stands. I worry he's going to leave but instead, he takes a few long strides and holds out his hand. I take it as he pulls me up.

"It matters," he says quietly. "Your opinion of me matters. But I cannot change my past."

I keep biting my lip as I get lost in his green eyes, not sure what to say.

Georg puts his thumb on my lip. A shot of heat blasts straight through to my core.

"You keep biting this." He leans in and swipes his lips against the skin right next to my lips. Again, just below my ear. Then again, back near my lips. "It must taste good."

I let out a sigh. It's totally involuntary. Totally embarrassing. Georg just grins and says, "Good girl." His lips meet mine.

Maybe it's the wine. Maybe it's the way he smells, like soap, and this dinner we just made together and red wine. Maybe it's the way his tongue politely begs for entry as it swipes my bottom lip. Maybe it's the feel of his whole body lined up against mine. Or the way his biceps feel as I grip them with my hands, like my life depends upon hanging on. Or how his hands find their way to my lower back, his fingertips just grazing under my flowy, white top.

Whatever it is, whatever the reason, I open for him. Our tongues meet and then kissing him is like breathing. His mouth is on mine and then it isn't, because it's on my jaw, my neck, my clavicle.

His hands move to my ass as he picks me up, my legs encircling him as he starts to walk. Up the stairs, still kissing. Into the bedroom, still kissing. I'm on my back. He's between my legs, his erection rubbing my most sensitive places despite the two pairs of jeans between us.

My shirt? Gone. I'm in my jeans and my white, lace bra and even though I'm mostly clothed, I feel totally bare. Georg's lips are all over me, his breath hot as his teeth graze my nipples through the thin fabric of my bra.

"You are so beautiful, Pamela. *Krasivaya.*" I love the way he calls me "Pamela" in his gorgeous accent along with the Russian words, whatever they mean.

I push my hand between us, feeling the hardness of him through his jeans. He moans and grinds against my hand. I push back, rubbing him harder, my hips rolling in circles, my back arching as he pushes my bra down, exposing my nipples. He groans before bringing his lips to them.

God.

The feel of his lips and teeth on my sensitive nubs as he sucks and pulls with gentle bites is like nothing I've ever experienced before. I don't want him to stop.

It's purely indescribable, possibly enough to get me off if he kept at it. As I writhe beneath him, the heaviness of his body against me sends me into another realm of consciousness. I know my panties have to be wet.

I want so much more.

And it's time for his jeans to be gone.

I fumble a bit as I unbutton him but he helps me push the jeans away from his hips. He's wearing black boxer briefs, tight enough to show the bulge of a big hard cock I can't wait to meet. I rub him some more through the fabric and he twitches in response.

"Touch me," he murmurs against my breasts. "*Kosnites' yego.*"

"You don't know what that Russian does to me," I say, dipping my hand down between his skin and the fabric. I grip him and slide my hand up and down the silky-smooth skin. He pumps his hips and fucks into my hand.

"*Tak khorosho,*" he moans. "Feels so fucking good."

As if he can't take any more, he jerks away from my grip, scooting down, his hands focused on getting me free of *my* jeans. I shimmy out of them, feeling so very naked as his eyes go dark. He buries his face between my legs, his mouth hot through my sheer pink panties. Quickly, though, he looks up at me, desire all over his face.

"You smell so good…like dessert. Sweet. Let me taste you?"

I gulp, meeting his eyes. I nod and relax my legs, wanting nothing more than to feel that wicked tongue, those talented lips on me.

His hands work quickly and my panties are gone in an instant, tossed aside somewhere, my fresh wax-job on full display for him. *Thank you, Ellie at The Pretty Kitty.*

His hands grip between my thighs and spread me open as he groans again. "Bare pussy. Fuck, Pamela, you're so gorgeous."

Then, Georg's mouth is there. His beautiful, kissable lips are there, sucking, his tongue delving in to find my clit. My hips push up, the build beginning as he uses his fingers to push my pussy apart, that magical tongue of his flicking against my clit with abandon.

When he pushes his tongue deep inside me, I nearly

lose it, crying out. The reverberation of his sexy chuckle against my clit cranks me a notch closer.

"So close, Georg," I say, barely able to speak. "Please."

Then the wicked, wicked man backs away. He gives me a lopsided, ornery grin and shakes his head as he pulls away his boxer briefs, freeing his thick cock. He strokes it a few times, just to make a point, and then reaches out and pulls my hand there, too.

Together, we stroke him. Our eyes never leave each other's. It's so erotic, and that heavy feeling of want builds between my legs again. I need to come.

I need it so badly.

I open my mouth and watch his green eyes widen for an instant as he gets my meaning. He scoots up, slowly inserting himself into my mouth. He's slow. Gentle. He makes sure I can handle it. He pumps, only a little at first but then goes deeper. I have to force my throat open in order to take his length but I want him in all the way to the hilt. He fucks my mouth slowly over and over, sighing heavily each time he bottoms out at the back of my throat.

I'm so lost in the moment that I barely notice when he turns his whole body. I keep sucking on him, wanting nothing more in the moment than to make him come. But then his lips are between my legs again, his wicked tongue back to ply me into a spectacular orgasm. *God, yes.*

He licks me all the way down to door number two. Wha? Now *that* was unexpected, but sinfully pleasurable, much to my shock. I don't have time to dwell on it though, because his busy mouth trails its way back to where he started and picks up the pace. His tongue delves deep as his fingers work my clit. I know I'm making nonsensical noises, but I don't even care. Moans and groans fall from my lips as the orgasm I need so badly grows closer and closer. I want him to come with me though, and so I stroke the area underneath his balls as I suck him even deeper. He grunts in response and I can feel his cock grow harder in my mouth. He's close too.

As soon as I feel myself fall over that cliff face, my body tensing beneath his tongue, he starts to spurt warm and salty into my mouth. Simultaneous oral orgasms. Say *that* three times fast. Except I'm pretty sure I won't be able to even say my name for an hour or two. The climax hits both of us hard as we cry out in that delicious instant of perfect pleasure. I swallow everything he gives me as he kicks his cock deep into my mouth to finish, at the same time licking me to completion.

Wow.

When he nestles beside me, upright again, I'm still clenching with aftershocks down below. He kisses my neck, his hand on my belly. I push it down and he inserts his middle finger as my hips move. His palm grinds against my clit and I feel the buildup once more, falling into a second, longer orgasm that literally takes my breath away.

I'm unable to do anything beyond turning onto my side and resting my head on his chest. He runs his hand through my hair and holds me close. Years pass. Maybe a century, even. It doesn't matter because I suddenly feel the need to do something that I've never wanted to do before. *I've never trusted anyone before, which is mind-*

boggling, because this is Georg Kolochev. Curious Georg. Hockey playboy bad boy. Yet I trust him... and I've never felt this comfortable with a man before, as if we're equals. Kindred spirits, even though the concept sounds ridiculous. But there is more to him that the outside package. *I just hope I'm right.*

"I want to tell you something." I can hear his heart thumping inside his chest against my ear. I love the way our bodies feel pressed together.

"You came?" he asks playfully.

"Well, that, too, but actually...I—I am a virgin."

He stops breathing. A heartbeat thuds. Another. "What the fuck?"

"I'm...I've never...had intercourse." He tenses underneath me. I've never been given an orgasm by another person, either, but I keep that one to myself. "I've shocked you."

"I guess? Yeah, I just assumed...a woman in her twenties...that you would've..."

"No. Close, but never penetration. I've just—it's complicated. But I was never ready."

"I am glad we only did this foreplay, then." He kisses my hair.

"Why are you glad we didn't do...more?"

"Because if I were to be your first, I'd want it to be very special. I'd want to make it special for you...when you were sure you were ready."

My heart melts at his sweet words. "Well, this was really good. A really good start."

He kisses the top of my head again. "I may not be here though," he says. "If I get traded—"

"You won't," I answer firmly, feeling my chest clench at the thought of him leaving.

"I might."

"Well, I don't want you to go."

He's quiet for a long time. So long that I think he might have fallen asleep. I start to nod off, comfortable in his arms. When he finally speaks again, I'm almost sure it's a dream.

"I don't want to go either," he whispers. "I want to stay here. With you, *krasivaya*. With you."

15
one big motherpucker

Georg

Our first practice with the new guys. Viktor is as intimidating a physical presence as he's always been, and some of our younger guys are clearly in awe of the big man.

Mikhail goes right up against him and gets shut down quickly. Viktor's an enforcer, and there's a reason the Crush wanted him on the team. Mikhail, cocky as always, just keeps trying, getting more and more angry with every check against the boards. He finally throws off his helmet and spews his frustration at Viktor in Czech. Viktor, for his part, looks bored. He's certainly heard worse.

"That is one big motherfucker..." Evan says as we watch the whole exchange go down.

"Shouldn't you be stopping them from coming to blows instead of commenting on the guy's size there, Captain Crush?"

"I'm just saying..."

"Sure, he is big, but he looks worse against Mikhail."

"True," Evan agrees. "All right, let me get in there between this little spat."

He skates over and breaks it up. Mikhail is not as large as some of the other players on our team. He's just over the six-foot mark, and wiry with muscle, rather than bulky. He's quick on his feet and quick-tempered. I hated him the first half of his rookie year, but he's grown on me a bit since then. And even though he's a hothead, I know Viktor could, and would, smash him like a bug if he stepped over a line. I'm just not sure what that line is at this point.

I get paired with the rookie, Tyler, who was the "add-on" to Viktor's trade. He's young, blond, tatted-up, and all over the fuckin' place. We take turns blocking shots from one of our second-string forwards and though he's quick on his skates, his passing accuracy is for shit and his blocking is inconsistent. I leave the feedback to the defensive coaching staff and try my best to make nice with him.

"How you liking Vegas so far?" I ask as the coaching staff resets for a new drill.

"It's good."

"Not pissed about the trade?" I ask.

He shrugs. "I just wanna play. Don't care where."

"Why the quick trade, though?"

"It was too quick for me to get pissed." He lets out a grunt of frustration. "I'm too rash. Not disciplined enough. Need more mentoring. Whatever the fuck that means. Pretty sure the NHL wouldn't have picked me up if I wasn't good. They should just play me."

I'm not sure what face I'm making, but I'm shocked

he's being so open about why he got traded. "I mean, sure, yeah, I don't know why someone would take you on only to trade you," I say.

"I played first string varsity hockey for Minnesota. Hot prospect," he says with another shrug. "Barely had time to get to know the team. Barely got ice time in the preseason. Fuck 'em anyway."

I chuckle at this. "I think I like you, kid."

"Yeah?" he asks. "That's cool. You're the guy who got in a brawl with big Brutus over there during All-Star weekend, right?"

"You call him Brutus?"

"Not to his face," Tyler answers. "I like my teeth in my mouth."

"Ha!"

"Looked like you pummeled his ass."

I definitely like this kid. Yes, I do. "I put him down, that's for sure. I was surprised he took the blame for that whole thing."

"From what I heard, he was the dick who started it. Fuckin' deserved it. I'd have had your back if I was there."

"You don't like him?" I ask.

"I like him just fine. He ain't done nothin' to me, but I'm always down for a good brawl." He gives me a cocky smirk.

"Fair enough. Well, we've got some history. Goes back a few years."

"Figured as much," he says.

We go back to work and for whatever reason, practice is way more interesting than it's been all season. This kid will probably get next to zero playing time this season, but he's fun to talk to anyway.

After an extra-long practice, we head back into the locker rooms. Coach talks about what he's seeing out there, and actually says we're looking pretty good. We've all gotten notes and feedback, but this is the first practice where he's had anything positive to say. I'll take it.

As everyone starts for the showers, I pull Viktor aside. Evan is hanging a few steps back and the new kid Tyler is flanking my other side.

"Viktor," I say flatly.

"Georg."

He's so huge. Tan. Crazy muscular. Military-style haircut. Intense eyes. I'm not afraid of him but damn, he's like John Cena, for fuck's sake. Personally, I think he tries to be like John Cena. I've heard that he does underground MMA fights in the off-season.

"I wanted to see if we could put our shit into the past, work together now that we're on the same team. I appreciated that you fell on your sword after that bar fight last season. It was a gesture that didn't go unnoticed."

"That night I was plastered," he answers, his English good but his accent thick. Much thicker than mine. "I barely remember my words."

"You insulted my wife," Evan chimes in from behind my left shoulder.

"She was not your wife then," he says. "But yes, I was offensive to the ladies that night."

"It's not like that's the first time your mouth has gotten you in trouble, Demoskev. Let's be honest."

"This is true," he concedes. "You are no saint, either, Kolochev. Two drunken assholes, we are. It's a wonder we are not friends."

Why is he being so agreeable? I'm leery, but I don't want to press too much. I just say, "Don't see that happening, but I'm willing to let the past go. You?"

He holds out a hand and we shake on it. And that's the end of it. The big brute wanders off to shower and I turn around and make a face at Evan.

"That was totally anticlimactic," Evan comments under his breath.

"Fucking pussies," Tyler mutters as he grabs his shower caddy and stomps off.

"What the fuck?" Evan muses as he stares after Tyler.

"He's a character. Have fun getting that little shit in line."

"Great," Evan groans as he wanders back to his locker.

THE NEXT NIGHT, we're back on the ice and on the road. The first period is flat on both sides. Not much energy, a fact that both Evan and Coach Brown focus on during the period break.

In the second period, Evan is practically on fire, scoring three goals in about a six-minute span. The momentum is enough that Mikhail manages a score, as well, and we head into the third period with a three-goal lead.

Viktor and I are on the ice together in the third, with Mikhail and Evan on the warpath to score again.

Anaheim has other plans, though, and they come out taking shots on goal like it's nobody's business. It's all we can do on the defensive line to keep the puck away from our keeper, let alone make sure it gets to our wingers.

Frustrated, one of Anaheim's defensive players plows Viktor into the glass—a truly ugly check that starts a battle on the ice. But Viktor actually uses his words like a big boy—even though they are nasty Russian curses—still, it's not at all how I expected him to react.

The Anaheim player swings at him, knocking his helmet off his head. I skate over and get in between the two of them, pushing them apart, telling them both to simmer down. The ref joins us and sends the Anaheim player to the penalty box, putting the Crush on a power play.

Viktor gets benched for the last few minutes of the game and the rookie Tyler comes in. We make the most of the power play as I end up with the puck. Anaheim knows Evan and I work as a unit, so they focus their entire defense on him, leaving Mikhail uncovered. I whip the puck over to him and he strikes, scoring his second goal of the night.

With a five-one win, we leave Anaheim feeling the beginning of a good thing happening. The slump we had in the preseason now seems like a distant memory.

In the locker room, I get a head-nod from Viktor, a thank you for coming to his aid in the game. I nod back, feeling some of the tension of our past melt away.

Tyler suggests a group of us go out for drinks to celebrate. Evan, of course, declines. His days of partying are over. Holly is due in just a couple weeks, and he wants to FaceTime her and make sure she's okay. I haven't been drinking much these past weeks, but I do want to go out. I feel antsy, with pent-up energy from our game. Pent-up energy after the night I spent making Pam cry out my name as she came on my tongue.

I hate to admit how much I want her. It scares me. I've certainly dated, but nothing has ever felt serious. And I don't know if this thing with her is serious, but it certainly feels different from other flings. It feels like a much deeper connection. I want to know her...and please her.

I want to be her first.

I'm still actually floored by her revelation. There's certainly more to the story of why she's still a virgin. *Damn.* And strangely, I hope we get to the point where she wants to tell me all of it.

At the last minute, Viktor decides to join our group and we end up walking from the hotel to a small dive bar. Classic country music plays on an old-school jukebox as we sidle up to the bar. Viktor draws a lot of looks from his sheer size. When he opens his mouth and a thick accent comes out, he draws more than looks. Two attractive women, probably a bit older than all of us, make their way over to ask us where we're from. Tyler's South Boston accent is just as much of a hit, and the two guys flirt hardcore, both clearly in need of some physical release after a fast-paced game.

I pace myself, joking that I'm the "party dad" for the night. I alternate between sipping a beer and putting more money in the jukebox. I have a thing for Garth Brooks—don't fucking judge—and I play all the songs they have of his, starting with the classic *Friends in Low Places*. Of course, everyone in the bar sings along.

"You remember that junior league game where Kuztnetsorov broke his ankle?" Viktor asks me after his third or fourth beer. He's slurring a little, definitely feeling pretty loose.

We've moved from the bar to a booth, and both Tyler and Viktor still have the rapt attention of the two women from earlier. I've only just started on my second beer and pretty clearheaded. I do remember that game. "It was crazy. The most violent game I've ever played in, hands down."

"I think only his skate prevented his foot from coming off." Viktor laughs. "It was gruesome."

"Sounds awesome," Tyler chimes in.

"In the way disgusting things are awesome," I answer. "I think I got a black eye in that game. It was a joke."

"The after-party was no joke, though," Viktor recollects. "Champagne. Women. Crazy sex. I think there were seven people in that room. Naked. You were there, yes?"

"Uhh," I groan, making a face as the other three at the table go wide-eyed. "I *may* have been."

"You were," he says with a knowing, amused look. "Your scrawny ass was tits-up with at least two women that night."

"I plead the fifth."

"There is no fifth in Russia. Admit you were a wild one."

"Okay, I admit I was a wild one," I say reluctantly.

"And admit you liked it. It was fun," he orders.

"I admit it was fun…"

Viktor looks satisfied. "And Sochi…" he says, his eyes glazed with alcohol and nostalgia.

"I hated you in Sochi," I say. "You were like that blond dick in *Rocky IV*."

Viktor howls at this. "You were just jealous I was so pretty."

"Yes, that's totally what my issue was," I say with an eye-roll that makes everyone laugh.

"It's my job to be an asshole," Viktor answers, still laughing.

"Well, so far so good, then. Awesome job."

He gets serious for a moment, his eyes narrowing. "You know, I did not mean to hurt your girlfriend."

I meet his stare and contemplate. "I know. I don't know if she knows, though. And she's not really my girlfriend."

"She's working for the team now, yes?"

"Yes, she is a physical therapist for the team."

"I will apologize. Tell her I am working on my temper. Working on being better."

"I'm sure she'll appreciate that…after she gives you a tongue-lashing," I say. "She's a tough lady."

"You are not with her anymore?"

"We weren't really together. We went out a few times, then we didn't talk. We had dinner the other night, though."

"Romantic dinner or friend dinner?" he asks.

"Hey," I say sharply. "Pamela is off limits to you, fucker."

He puts his hands up and grins. "She is very beautiful. I had to ask."

He then makes a big show of making out with the brunette who's all snuggled up to him. Tyler and the blonde disappear into one of the restrooms, and I'm left thinking about Pam. *Wanting* Pam.

I excuse myself and make the quick walk back to the hotel. I undress and flop onto the bed, turning on the television and flipping through the channels before deciding to text her.

Georg: Hey sexy. I miss you.

Pam: Well hello to you, too. Good game tonight.

Georg: It was a good win. Maybe I will make it another day on the team.

Pam: I hope so.

Georg: I need to see you when I get back.

Pam: Oh?

Georg: Naked. I need to see you naked when I get back.

Pam: You're making me blush.

Georg: Your body is so perfect.

Georg: Luscious, full breasts that are totally real. Perfect nipples.

Georg: Tiny waist. Legs for days. Gorgeous ass.

Georg: Don't get me started on your bare pussy. I can still taste you.

Pam: Well then, Georg. You certainly know how to rev a girl up.

Georg: Are you turned on?

Pam: Yes...

Georg: Can you touch yourself?

Pam: Oh yes...

Georg: What are you wearing?

Pam: Only a T-shirt. No panties. I'm so wet already.

Georg: Spread that pussy apart, Pamela. Dip your fingers into all that wet honey.

Pam: What are you wearing, Georg?

Georg: Nothing. I'm alone in my room. My cock is in my hand. So hard.

Pam: Are you stroking yourself?

Georg: Yes. Of course. Though I'm imagining your mouth on me.

Pam: Yes. I liked that. I liked having you in my mouth...

Georg: Are you fingering yourself?

Pam: Yes...yes

We go back and forth, the sexy texts hotter than

almost any encounter I've ever had. I ask her to send me a picture, and she does one better by FaceTiming me. She gives me peeks of her gorgeous tits as she twists the nipples in her fingertips. She even gives me a shot of her wet pussy as she slides her fingers in and out while arching back on her bed.

She is fucking beautiful.

She wants to watch me jack off, so I give her what she wants, and when we're both close, we focus on our faces, making sure we have the chance to see each other orgasm. All I see are her brown eyes as I start to come, making a right mess all over the sheets of my hotel bed. I'll be sure to leave something extra for housekeeping when I leave. It must suck having cum-cleanup as part of your job.

It takes us both a moment to calm down before we can talk again.

"That was fun," she says after a few long moments, "but I'd rather it be the real thing."

"Me too." I drape the sheet over my lap and talk to her again. "I...I need you, Pamela. All the time I think about you."

She gives a soft smile that makes my stomach do a weird flip thing. She bites her lip. "I feel the same, Georg."

We talk about dumb things, meaningless things, until the wee hours of the morning when we finally hang up.

But instead of feeling relaxed, I feel my heart might beat its way out of my chest. It's anxiety. Will I get traded? What is this thing between Pam and me? Is it fair to start something I probably won't be able to finish? I told her I wanted to stay and I do, but what could there possibly be between us in the long-term? I am not Evan. I am not the man who plans elaborate ice-skating dates and long summer holidays in the mountains. I am not the man who rushes home to his pregnant wife. I do not know if I want a wife. Or a family. I only want to get through the next day. That's all I can do at the moment.

I am not the right man for her. She deserves more. She deserves the world.

I am no good, no matter how hard I try. *You'll never be enough, or good enough, for hockey or anything else in your life. Anyone. Vy takoye razocharovaniye. Such a disappointment.* But even though I know it's the truth, I still want her.

I still want her.

16
mafia hockey players?

Pam

There's been no word on any trade talk related to Georg, but his role in the solid win at Anaheim certainly can't hurt his case to stay. The Crush are back home for three games in a row this week, and I've seen many of the players on my therapy table as they work through their various pains, injuries, and preventative processes.

I was surprised to see Georg go to Viktor's aid in that last game. I mention this to Georg while I help him stretch out in the hours before the game.

"He apologized to me for being an ass and I forgave him," he says. "He still owes you an apology, though, and he knows it. I think he was going to try to get in your good graces and then ask you out."

"Not my type," I answer as I work a knotted muscle in Georg's calf. "I have my sights set on someone else."

"Oh, do I know him?" He gives me a smirk, green eyes flashing in classic Georg fashion.

"Maybe you do, maybe you don't," I answer playfully.

"Well, he'd better be good to you or he'll have my fist to answer to."

"I'll keep that in mind," I say with a laugh.

We finish up and just as Georg gets off the table, Viktor walks in. Well, more like he looms in the doorway and stares. He's a really big dude.

"Comrade," Georg says, giving Viktor a silly, mock-salute. "We were just talking about you."

"About how attractive I am?" Viktor asks in his thick accent.

"About what an ass you are, actually," Georg answers, deadpan.

"I have never claimed otherwise." Viktor turns toward me and gives a slight nod. "However, Pamela, it has been my intent to tell you I did not mean to harm you during our skirmish last spring. I am sorry for my actions and for losing my temper."

"Thank you, Viktor, I appreciate that but it wasn't just your actions, it was also your words. You were a bit of a pig that night."

"I was," Viktor says, his head bowed. "Please accept my sincere apology."

I must admit he apologizes nicely. Viktor Demoskev might look menacing but he seems sincere, and I can't fault his method for making things right. "Okay, apology accepted. Thank you. Now, are you my next appointment?"

"Yes," the big man confirms. "I am having some shoulder pain."

"Let's work it out then," I answer. "Time for you to beat it, Kolochev." I point my thumb at the door and wink at him.

Georg makes a face. "Fine. I'll go, but you tell me if this guy bothers you. I know people."

He turns and leaves, a bit of a spring in his step. Viktor just laughs.

"Face down on the table please," I tell him, hoping like hell he doesn't break it.

SCARLETT and I are having drinks at a club a few blocks down from the arena. The Crush just won their second home game and are seemingly back on track after a rocky preseason. We watched most of the game from the stands but left in the middle of the third period.

"I can't decide which one is hotter," she's saying as her fingertip slides through the condensation on her wine glass. "Viktor or Tyler. I mean, Tyler is cute in a young way. Like, an American boy way. You know? But Viktor is, like, a grown man. You know? Like a very big, hulking man. He probably has a big penis."

"Big man, big hands..." I say, taking a sip of my beer. "It seems okay to speculate on that one."

"Do you think he's in the mob?" Scarlett's on her third or fourth drink and even though we've been stuffing ourselves with fried appetizers, the food can't keep pace, so she's definitely feeling the effects of her alcohol.

"Who, Viktor?" I ask.

"Or Georg," she says. "They might both be."

"Mafia hockey players? That's just dumb, Scarlett."

"It's not dumb," she insists. "I have a second job as a

server in one of the casinos and there's been all these scary-looking Russian men in gambling every night since Viktor started on the team."

"Probably just here on holiday like a million other people. Besides, hockey players can't be involved with gambling. It's forbidden in professional sports."

"I don't know 'bout that," Scarlett answers before letting out a little hiccup. "I mean, the players don't have to gamble to be part of the mob anyway. The Russian mafia has tentacles everywhere. And how else to explain there's all these scary-looking Russian dudes appearing suddenly, just when Viktor arrives on the scene?"

"Oh, I don't know, coincidence maybe? I'm sure he doesn't travel with an entourage of mobsters, Scarlett," I say, heavy on the sarcasm.

"Well, he's pretty scary. And they do call him The Mad Russian." She takes another drink and seems to think for a moment. "He is kind of hot though."

"You have an unusual definition of hot."

"That's true, actually," she says with a big nod of affirmation. "It gets me in trouble sometimes."

"Why do you have a second job?" I feel like a change of subject is needed.

"Oh, I mean, my job with the Crush doesn't pay very much. A little more while I fill in for Holly, but not enough. I have some money I have to pay back." She sighs heavily. "Long story. But listen, I know a mobster when I see one."

"Wow, okay," I say carefully. I assume the money she owes and the mobster comment aren't connected. At least, I hope they aren't.

"Hey, did you hear about Daisy?" she asks.

"Daisy?" I can't place the name.

"She works in the cube across from Holly," Scarlett explains.

"Oh, yes, Daisy. No, I hadn't heard anything about her. You forget I work in the therapy and training dungeon. I don't know most of the office scoop."

"Well, she and her boyfriend broke up, and I guess he wouldn't stop calling the office. He sent a bunch of flowers, then he called a lot, and then he sent cookies. It was nuts. Fiona told her to tell him to stop it or she'd be fired," Scarlett says. "It's not Daisy's fault, though. She didn't ask for all that."

"Well, I'm sure Fiona's just trying to keep the office drama to a minimum."

"Fiona's uptight," Scarlett says. "But Daisy told him to stop. She said he cheated on her and she kicked him out of the house. He was trying to get her back. She's super embarrassed and angry that Fiona threatened to fire her."

"I'm sure she is." But I don't know Daisy, so I don't really care about this story, so I have no problem changing the subject. "How's the job now that the training wheels are off?"

"Well, Holly might be resting at home, but she still checks the social media feeds a million times a day. And her plan is so specific that I think a monkey could do it. It's more like I'm executing her vision, not actually managing the social media for the team."

"It is still her job," I answer sharply, feeling defensive for my friend. "I mean, you're doing it in the interim, but she'll be back. And she worked super hard to get the following the team has. She won't want to risk that when she's only going to be out for three months."

Scarlett, even in her drunken state, must see that she's close to crossing a line. We may be work friends, but Holly is my *best friend*. She's like a sister to me.

"You're right, Pam. Of course, you're right. I'm looking at this the wrong way. It's a really good opportunity to learn."

"Holly's really good at what she does."

"She is. Really, really good. How much longer before the baby?" I decide Scarlett is a sloppy but sweet drunk.

"A week, maybe? Not long."

She grins. "That's so exciting. That's gonna be one cute baby. They're both gorgeous. He's a hunk. Ugh. She won the husband lottery."

I nod. "I can't disagree. He's really sweet to her. It makes my heart hurt to watch them together."

"Why can't we find amazing, hot guys like him?" Scarlett whines. "I mean, the list of deadbeats I've had in my life is like a mile long."

"Same," I say. "But I kind of liked it that way. Easier to push them away once I got tired of them."

"Oh, I don't push them away fast enough. I always get sucked in. I always imagine whatever loser I'm with is my prince. I always fall hard and fast. It's a sickness."

"Daddy issues?" I ask gently. "Realize my question is coming from a girl who's never met her own daddy."

"Of course." She nods into her drink. "I love my dad, totally a daddy's girl, but he started it all. Gambler, big mess of a life. And I'm the one always there trying to peel him off the floor."

She empties her glass of wine and heads off to the bar to order another. She gets a lot of male attention while she's there and one guy buys her a drink. They flirt for a minute and then she waves me up to the bar.

Reluctantly, I grab my beer and scoot out of the booth. She puts her arm around me as I near the group. The guys are good-looking, not gorgeous, but passable. The one who has his eye on Scarlett has shaggy, brown hair and retro-looking eyeglasses. His friend is a total hipster with thick reddish-blond hair in a man-bun. He has one of those big beards, and he's wearing skinny jeans. I'd bet someone money right now that they work on computers or something equally nerdy.

"So, you two work for the Crush?" Retro-Glasses asks.

"We do," Scarlett says. "I work in social media. Pam works in physical therapy."

"I'm Rowan." Big-Beard holds out his hand. "You're Pam."

I nod and take his hand. "And this is Scarlett," I say, hitching a thumb toward my friend.

"And I'm Brett," Retro-Glasses says. "We're in town for a tech convention. We own a software company."

Boom. I am the champion. Tech guys for the win.

We chat with the guys over the next round, but I'm bored by the time my bottle is empty.

"Scarlett, I've got to run over and check in on Holly before it gets too late. Share a cab?"

She nods, but types her number into Brett's phone. I resist the urge to roll my eyes.

We hop in a cab. Scarlett's apartment is on the way to

Holly's house. She babbles about how cute and nice the guys were and asks why I didn't give Rowan my number.

"Not my type," I say with a shrug.

"Are you still pining over Georg Kolochev?"

"Not pining, dear."

"But you do like him, though."

"I do," I admit. "I doubt there's a future there. And I'm not supposed to date him anyway—not if I want to keep my job."

"Just fuck him and get it over with. You totally should."

"Nice potty mouth." I smack her playfully in the arm.

Scarlett breaks into giggles. "I think I'd like to fuck Viktor Demoskev," she blurts before slapping a hand over her mouth and blushing ten shades of red.

"Yuck. I mean…seriously, Scarlett?" I shouldn't judge. While Viktor isn't my flavor, he obviously appeals to Scarlett. A lot.

"Not yuck," she insists, shaking her head almost violently. "Yum. He's yum. It would be so hot with him, even if he is in the Russian mob."

"Go home, drunk, you're Scarlett."

Scarlett finds this inordinately funny. She's very drunk, I realize, so I make sure she gets into her apartment safely and then have the cabbie take me to Holly's.

"WAIT—YOU'RE telling me Scarlett suspects Viktor

could be in the Russian mafia? Oh Jesus, she did *not* say that."

I think Holly is more dumfounded than anything. And I didn't even mention the "fuck-not-yuck" part. Some things are best left alone, and the thought of Viktor and Scarlett doing it is definitely something I am leaving alone.

"She was drunk, so who knows, but yes. I think she really believes he might be connected to the mob. She also thought Georg might be, which seems downright crazy to me."

"There's something peculiar about our girl," Holly says from the couch, where she's resting with her swollen feet up on a stack of pillows. "I'm not sure I want her poking around in my job over there." Her belly looks like a beach ball underneath her pink and white striped T-shirt. She's adorable, but I don't tell her that. I know she doesn't feel at all adorable while being so uncomfortable in her last days pregnancy.

"That sounds like A-type hormones gone wild," I respond. "As your friend, I'm telling you that you need to relax and enjoy this baby. Don't worry about the Crush's social media work. You made a plan and she's going to carry it out. And you'll be back in no time, wishing you'd had more time with your baby."

"You're probably right," Holly agrees, throwing her arm over her eyes with a dramatic sigh.

"She's definitely right," Evan shouts from the kitchen.

"Traitor," she yells back. "You're supposed to be on my side."

A few moments later, Evan pads in, wearing his flannel pajama bottoms and a T-shirt. He is a gorgeous specimen of a man, I must admit. He leans over the back of the couch and plants a thorough kiss on her lips.

"I'm always on your side, baby," he says softly, grinning. "But you really do need to let go and just enjoy this time off. You've worked hard and you deserve it."

"Oh, don't try to butter me up," she snaps, but she's fighting a grin.

Evan sets a pint of ice cream and a spoon on her big belly and says, "I wasn't trying to butter you up. Not even a little."

Holly gives him a huge smile and scoots herself up, ready to ravage that little pint of ice cream. "Okay," she announces as she shoves a big spoonful in her mouth. "You're forgiven. For the moment."

"You guys are giving me a toothache," I comment. "I might need to leave before I lose all my teeth."

"Marry Georg and you, too, can be sickeningly sweet," Holly says.

This makes Evan laugh. "That seems like putting the horse behind the cart, or whatever that rubbish expression is."

"Putting the cart before the horse," Holly corrects through a spoonful of vanilla bean.

"Whatever." Evan sticks his tongue out at her. "They're not even dating." He turns toward me with a curious expression and asks, "Are you?"

I shrug. "We had dinner out one night and he went home with a panic attack. Then he apologized and we made dinner at my house. But since then? A few flirty texts. A few words at work. Otherwise, nothing."

"Do you think he's spooked?" Holly asks.

"He likes her for sure," Evan says. "But yeah, probably. A little. I mean, he's worried he's going to get traded. He's trying to do the clean-living thing. And his agent is a flake. So, it might not be a good time for him to get in a relationship."

"Has he ever been in a relationship?" Holly asks.

Evan thinks about this. "Not in a long time. Nothing serious, anyway."

"We're alike that way," I say. "Which makes me think that this may have just run its course."

"It doesn't always have to be like that," Holly argues. "Sometimes you can tame the beast."

Evan refills my wine glass and his own. He winks at Holly and she blushes. They're married and she's nine months pregnant, and she's blushing when he winks at her. I feel like I'm intruding in some kind of weird foreplay.

"But if he leaves for another team, then what's the point anyway?" I ask, my head falling back against the comfy chair I'm occupying.

"Are you falling for him?" Holly asks. Great question.

Am I? I've never been in love or thought I'd get there either. But I told Georg something I've hidden as if it was a dirty secret. And instead of laughing at me or thinking there was something wrong with *me*, he treated my virginity as something sacred, and *that* wasn't expected. I'm not sure I've ever met someone like Georg before, and given how much I think about him, sexting or not, that scares me.

"I mean...yeah. I think I am," I admit. "Which sucks."

"Well, I think you should tell him," she says. "Just tell him. And if he feels the same, you can make it work."

"It's not that simple, Holls."

"It *is* that simple. Even if he gets traded, you can still do the long-distance thing. Or get a job closer to him. You're good at what you do. You can go anywhere and do it."

"Babe," Evan says softly. "Calm down. They have to figure out their own thing. Just like we did."

Evan's sitting at the other end of the couch with her legs in his lap. Although he's got a wine glass in one hand, his other is gently rubbing her thigh. I love how they can't seem to keep their hands off one another.

"I'd better head home," I say, standing up. "It's super late. Thanks for the drink and the talk."

"Call me tomorrow," Holly says.

I nod and head for the door, plugging in a request for a driver as I do. I have a feeling those two are still finding ways to have sex, even though that baby is about to come out. They're so happy and their happiness makes me both sad and hopeful. Holly was really hurting from her breakup with soccer boy at the end of college. She was sure she'd never find love again. That she'd never be happy again. And then Evan fell into her life and she tried not to love him. But here they are, married, happy, moving their lives forward.

Could I be so lucky? After the abuse when I was

young, and then the years of pushing men away before they got too close, could I ever find someone who loves me the way Evan loves Holly? Who looks at me the way he looks at her?

And could I ever open myself up enough to let him in?

17
no good deed goes unpunished

Georg

"Ned, this is Devon."

"Nice to meet you, Ned," Devon says extending her hand.

Ned, for his part, looks a little dazed by the gorgeous woman in front of him. He takes her hand to shake it but can't seem to come up with anything coherent to say. She's used to it, I'm sure.

We're at a small restaurant off the Strip. It's a comfortable Italian place that has tall, private booths. I picked it because it's time for an intervention. If I'm honest, I didn't want to do this, but Devon is both soft-hearted and logical. She believes in second chances, and even though the man in front of me has pissed me off more than pleased me in the last few months, I'm trusting in her judgment on this one. I need better handling to reach my goals...and maybe he does too. And if there is any chance of having anything with Pam, I need to stay in Vegas.

We sit and order a light lunch. Ned orders a double Scotch on the rocks.

As we wait on our meals, I say, "Ned, I want more than what you're doing. You get that, right?"

Ned nods. Beads of sweat have formed on his forehead. He uses his napkin to wipe at them, messing up his combover.

"You're not sober, and it clouds your ability to do your job," I say. "Devon is the team's nutritionist and she's been helping me clean up my act."

Ned looks around wildly. He looks like a trapped bird. "I don't need—"

"Don't tell us you don't need rehab," I start. "You used to have a great reputation but your athletes are going to other agents."

"Are you?" he asks.

"Maybe. Probably. You got me this gig, and I'm thankful. I want to help you."

"Ned," Devon says, "do you have a family?"

He pushes his lips together and frowns. "They don't speak to me," he admits.

"And why is that, do you think?"

"Because they say I drink too much, ruin stuff." He straightens up a bit. "Look, I'm not perfect but I do okay. I don't need to go to rehab." The man is delusional, but a part of me gets it. Before we won the cup, I didn't believe I had a problem either. I thought I could do my job and drink and fuck to my heart's content. I'm not an alcoholic, but the dark side of drinking wasn't far from what I craved daily. *But not anymore.* Ned's got a team of people who could handle his business if he went away for a while. Whether he'd consider doing that is up to him.

"You may not think you need rehab, but from my side, watching you offer shit all in meetings, you do. You've got Len and Rosemary who can run your business while you're gone. But you'll lose it all if you keep going as you are." He's sweating and shaking his head, but there's something in his expression that makes me believe he's listening. Maybe he's hit rock-bottom and we're just a voice of reason at the right time. God, one can hope. "It's up to you, Ned."

Our food comes and Ned grasps his drink like it's a life raft. We let him have it, talking about my career goals as we eat. Ned frowns the whole time, and I can tell he's not comprehending everything I'm asking him to do. It's only when we're almost done eating that he says, "I can't provide all of that."

"No, you can't," I agree. "That's the point. I need an advocate. I need someone ownership will listen to, who they respect. It may have been you at one point. Heck, I owe it to you for getting me onto the team in the first place. But now?"

"Ned, I know you don't know me, and don't have to listen to anything I'm saying. But I've worked with men with high-stress jobs and have seen alcohol ruin lives and careers. The ball is in your court here." Devon's voice is soft and calm, but also commands attention. It makes sense given her dual qualifications of psychologist and nutritionist.

Ned sits for a long time, hands gripping that glass of Scotch so tightly his knuckles turn white. Finally, he nods. "I don't agree I need rehab, but I could take a look at a place...if you've heard of somewhere. But I need to call my team first."

"Yes, you do," I say. "Devon has a clinic she's referred people to before, and she rang them before we came here. They'll meet you today." He doesn't look completely convinced, but he has his cell phone out.

"Right, well...I need to call Len, and then...then I guess I could take a look."

Ned sits for a long time, hands gripping that glass of Scotch so tightly his knuckles turn white. Finally, he nods. "Fine. I'll go."

We square things with the restaurant and load Ned into Devon's car. There is a rehabilitation facility about twenty minutes outside of Las Vegas, and we drive him there, help him check in before riding back to town.

"Do you think I should have stayed with him?" I ask.

"What? No." Devon shakes her head.

"I mean, do you think I should have checked in there, as well?"

"Hmm..." She seems to choose her words carefully before she continues, "I feel you know your own body and your own heart, Georg. And if the desire to do all of those things you talked about at lunch with Ned outweighs the desire to drink, then I would have to say no."

"Good." I breathe a sigh of relief. "A very good answer. Thank you. And thank you for helping with Ned."

"It's what friends are for," she answers. "You did a good thing today."

"GEORGIE," Bud says as he ambles toward me in the hallway. His beer belly stretches out the Crush polo shirt he wears. "How's it hangin' today?"

"Good. I'm glad I ran into you, though. I'd like to sit down with you and Max and whoever else. I keep hearing trade rumors and I just put my agent into a rehab facility, so I'm on my own to manage things right now. I'd really like to talk about this with you all before a decision gets made."

"Oh, well," Bud stammers. "You know, those decisions are complicated. Budget and distribution of talent..."

"I helped take this team to the championship," I say. "Evan and I work well as a team. No one knows his style of play like I do."

"Well, I hear you, I really do, but I can't stop a moving train," he answers, his face turning red.

"So, does that mean a trade is imminent, Bud?"

"It's on the table, yes." It's the most direct thing I've ever heard him say.

"Well, I want to see Max," I say.

He sighs heavily. "I'll try to set something up for you."

I know he's just trying to placate me. Probably trying to get away from this conversation as fast as possible. "I'm serious," I say sharply. "I deserve a meeting before a decision is made."

He nods. "Okay, yeah. I hear you, big guy."

Big guy? I want to fucking puke right here in the hall.

He must see murder in my eyes because his face goes

an even deeper shade of red. He blinks. "I'll get something on the books."

And then he's gone, toddling down the hallway, probably off to tell Max I'm a nut job who needs to be gone yesterday.

I make my way to the locker rooms, ready to suit up for our third straight home game. My head is all over the place.

"You okay there, bruv?" Evan asks.

"Just a lot on my mind right now," I say. "I'll be fine once we hit the ice."

"What's going on?"

"A trade in the works, and I just put Ned into rehab."

"Did you call Scott?"

"I did. He was out of the country and said he'd call me back when he gets back next week. Might be too late then."

Evan swears and then tells me it will all work out. I want to believe him. I choose to believe him, at least for now, since my team needs me to have my head in the game.

After pre-game rituals, we skate out on the ice. The lights are crazy and the crowd is wound up and loud. They're happy to see us winning again. The sound of a full house really puts my mind in the right place, and my play reflects that.

Coach has Viktor and I out on the ice together, now he knows we can play together without killing each other. We play well off each other, working hard to protect our goalie from another team that just comes out lobbing shots on goal like a machine. Coach chose to play three defensemen and two offensive players, so Viktor and I flank Tyler in the middle, while Evan and Mikhail play up top.

We are stopping every single shot. Nothing is getting by us, and the crowd is crazy for it. The game is mostly defensive for us, up until the third period, when both Mikhail and Evan score two goals each. We win four to nothing, and the sound in the arena is enough to make us go deaf.

In fact, my ears are still ringing when I walk into the post-game press conference. Evan handles most of it, as he usually does, and he gives big props to the defensive line. The questioning goes to Tyler and Viktor, who are asked how they feel about getting traded to the Crush. They're both gracious, happy to be playing with the defending champions. Then they turn to me, saying there's a lot of talk I might be traded soon. I only answer that I'm hoping to stay, that our line is really gelling, and that I think it would throw off our balance to trade now. I talk about how hard I'm working for the team, how I'm in better shape than I've been in a while, and how I'm totally committed to being a strong player, no matter what.

Evan pats me on the back, so I know I used the right catchwords. Near the end of the conference, though, I see him check his phone. He looks at me, eyes wide, and says, "I gotta get out of here. I'm about to become a dad."

The press folks go nuts, and Evan races out the door to head to the hospital. As Fiona closes things out, Kacey King approaches me. She's in a tight purple dress and high heels and looks like she's moving in for the kill.

"You played really well tonight, Georg."

"Thanks."

"I got all dressed up hoping you might want to go out for a drink?"

"I'm good," I say. "Not really drinking these days."

"Oh. Well, we could grab a bite to eat. Or, cut the preamble and just head back to my place?"

"I'm not...available right now, Kacey. I've got a lot on my plate at the moment and no time for socializing. Sorry."

Kacey's face looks like she just sucked on a lemon. She takes a big, dramatic breath, flips her blonde hair and says, "Well, call me if you change your mind."

I definitely won't, but I don't tell Kacey that.

Only one person can calm the absolute fucking anxiety I have about being traded. I need to hear her voice even if it's just for a minute.

Once I'm in my car I pull up Pam's number and press the green call button. She sounds sleepy when she answers, but the words that come out of her mouth are golden. "Yes, Georg?" I do love it when she says my name.

"Did I wake you up?"

"Evan did just a few minutes ago. Holly is in labor so I guess I'll just stay up now and wait for news that I'm an aunt. I'm giving them their space at the hospital right now, but as soon as that baby arrives, I'll be heading over there to meet the little master or miss."

"He got the call in the postgame press conference. It was quite the scene. I can't believe Evan is going to be a dad. I'm sure it's on all the sports news channels as we speak. Didn't you watch the game?"

"I fell asleep in the second period, I must confess," she says, yawning softly. "Did we win?"

"We did." I chuckle a little. She's cute when she's half asleep. "Lightning struck in the third. The first two were boring from a scoring perspective. I might have fallen asleep, too."

"Sorry," she says with a sexy, hoarse laugh.

"No need to be. I worked hard. No need to have anyone cheering me on."

"Oh, don't be a baby. I'm sure there were a hundred women out there, cheering just for you."

"Only one I was interested in, though."

"Oh."

"Pamela, can I take you out again?"

"Umm... Sure?"

"Is that a yes?"

"Yes. I'd love to."

"Tomorrow?"

"Okay."

"Perfect. Sweet dreams, lovely Pamela."

18
linq'd & licked

Pam

" I can't believe we hit that," I exclaim on a stifled yawn. I didn't get much sleep once I knew Holly was in labor at the hospital. Evan was over the moon like all new parents must be. God, I can't even imagine how I'd be as a new mom. Adulting is hard enough on a good day, but add in another human being you're now responsible for meeting their every need on top of their very existence? Off-the-charts-terrifying.

But Holly took it all in stride like a pro she is when she delivered their baby girl in the early hours of the morning. They named her Danya, which is very Russian and also the name of Evan's grandmother. I'm predicting she'll be a great beauty and Evan and Holly will have their hands full in about thirteen years with all the boys lined up to be her special "friend."

Tired or not, I had no intention of canceling our date. After that sweet phone call from Georg last night asking me out? No way. I've missed him.

As we take our winning chips to the counter to cash out, I ask, "How much did we win?"

"Three thousand," Georg says. "You are the roulette queen."

"What's next? Blow this money on tattoos?"

"I'm down." He gives me one of those mischievous grins of his that should be illegal and says, "But, I have something else to show you first."

He looks at his phone and nods to himself. "Yes, the timing is good."

We walk a few blocks. The night is balmy for Las Vegas. People are everywhere. There are women in wedding dresses, people in costumes, tourists with fanny packs. The Strip really hits the jackpot if you're into people-watching.

"Have you been on the LINQ?" Georg asks.

"No, I haven't."

"Great," he says, taking my hand and leading me toward the big Ferris-wheel thing. It's not a traditional Ferris wheel, though, as it has dangling, glass pods that allow riders to remain comfortably inside while getting a great view of the city.

He tells me to hold on a minute, and then about ten minutes later, comes back and takes my hand again, leading me through the crowd. We're ushered into one of the pods, our only company a young man in a tuxedo.

"I feel underdressed," I comment, gesturing to my short black skirt, houndstooth flats, and sleeveless, black top.

Georg gestures to his own dark jeans and blue,

untucked dress shirt and laughs. "Don't mind him; he's not paying the bill for this thing. We can wear what we want "

There's a table inside the pod, set with a variety of finger foods. A bottle of wine chills in a bucket. There's some sexy-sounding music playing. I don't recognize the band, but it mixes heavy electric guitar with an electronic bass drop that literally makes me want to sway in Georg's arms.

"Can I pour for you?" the young waiter asks.

"Sure, thank you," I say. "Georg, did you rent out this whole thing for us?"

"I did," Georg says. He gives me an adorably shy grin. His cheeks even look a little pink. "I wanted to make up for flaking out the last time I planned a romantic meal with a view."

I smile back at him. "That's really sweet."

The waiter pours our wine and then, surprisingly, steps out of the pod. Shortly after, we're alone and the wheel is moving.

We each make a plate of food and then head to the glass, taking in the view as we rise higher and higher into the sky.

"This is breathtaking," I say. "Thank you for this experience."

"You're welcome."

"Any news on the trade talk?" I ask after a few minutes.

"I think my performance has been good enough that I will stay. I have talked to Bud and requested a meeting with Max about it. They know I want to stay, that I'm committed."

"That's a relief."

"Well, no relief yet. But I'm hopeful."

"Me too," I say. Georg puts his arm around me and I lay my head on his shoulder as we take in the lights of the city below. After a few, long moments, I ask, "What do you love so much about the Crush? Why do you want to be here, specifically?"

"I love this city. I love my teammates. We are like brothers...the good, the bad, and the ugly, you know? We have each other's backs. I don't want to have to recreate that again, in another place, with another group of players."

"I hadn't thought of it like that. I guess I've always imagined it would be kind of fun to pick up and move. To meet new people, try new things. But I can see your point."

"You did that here, though your best friend was here, too. Security blanket of sorts. Imagine moving across the country and knowing no one."

"Yes, it was easier because Holly was here. But I would have done it either way."

He smiles softly. "I have moved many times for this game. There comes a point when it feels time to settle down a bit. Put down some roots, so to speak."

"That seems reasonable, certainly." There's a brief, awkward silence between us. "So...I heard there was a bit of prank the other day..."

He chuckles. "I totally stole the idea from YouTube.

There's a joke about Tyler, how he spends a lot of time doing his hair. So while he was in the shower, I kept sneaking more shampoo on his hair, so he could just never quite get it all out. And he couldn't see because he wears contacts and he had them out after the game. He was so pissed. It was hilarious."

I can't help but laugh because it's such a silly prank, and Georg is so gleeful as he tells me about it. He's like a big kid. It's one of the things I love most about him.

Like. Not love. One of the things I *like* about him.

Okay, changing gears seems like a good idea, and I know just the thing that'll do it.

"I have a weird question for you, Georg. It's so bizarre there's no way to ask it without just being really direct, so please forgive me in advance."

"I am intrigued, Pamela."

"Scarlett was talking about some shady Russian guys who've been around the casinos a lot since Viktor started with the team. And she'd had a bunch of alcohol, so this is probably really stupid, but do you have ties to the Russian mafia?"

I feel my cheeks go flaming hot. What a ridiculous thing to ask him.

Georg's eyes go wide. "Wow. That's not a question I was expecting."

"Sorry," I say, rueful.

"No, no, it's okay. I thought it was going to be about my drinking. But no, I don't have ties there. In Russia, especially hockey, there are certainly very powerful influences and people, but I left all of that behind when I came to the United States. I am in no way connected."

I let out a breath I didn't know I was holding. Georg faces me and takes my hands.

"I'm not a perfect man, Pamela. You know it. I know it. I'm trying, though. I'm no longer getting drunk. Taking care of my body and my career as best I can. I'm trying to be better. I want you to trust me, to know that I want to be good for you."

"But you don't owe me a thing."

"I know but...that's not the point. Owing. What does that even mean here?"

"I'm just saying that we've only hung out a few times."

"So? That means nothing to the fact I care about you."

I turn away because I don't want him to see the tears in my eyes, the way my face contorts as I swallow back the lump that's formed in my throat. I know he cares about me. I can see it. But he's Georg. And I'm me. And neither of us is any good at making anything that will really last.

He puts his hands on my shoulders, forces me to face him again. He hunches over a little to get in my face. "Pamela," he says, "Please. Talk to me."

I look up and he's so earnest. Everything about his expression is open. The way he calls me "Pamela" feels so intimate and special.

The song that's playing, one I realize later is called *I Feel Like I'm Drowning* by Two Feet. It's sexy, thick with desire and hurt. *I feel like I'm drowning. You're holding me down and...you're killing me slow...so slow, oh no...* It's perfectly sexy. Perfect for whatever is happening here.

I can't speak, so I just lean in and kiss him. At first, it's just a sweet meeting of lips. But then his arms are around me and that heat is between us again, burning between my legs. My mouth opens, his tongue slides in. Our bodies are completely aligned, and I feel him hardening as the desire for more overtakes me.

We're in this glass bubble, hundreds of feet in the air and exposed for all the world to see, and I want nothing more than for him to touch me. *Indecently.* And he must read my mind because he obliges, putting his hand beneath my skirt, eagerly pushing my panties aside, dipping between my legs, feeling the want there as I clench around his long fingers.

He falls to his knees, then. We're very high up. I think we're on our second or third rotation now. I've lost track of time and hope we stay in here forever.

He pushes my skirt up, his hands on my rear as he pulls me forward, pushing my hips toward him, his face pressing between my legs, his tongue exploring up and down my pussy. He's like a starving man, his noises carnal and gruff. His fingers dig into my backside roughly. He's way more intense than the other time he did this.

I come without warning, and quickly. I cry out and sag against him as the orgasm shoots deliciously through my body. I'm tingling. I can hardly hold myself up. I can barely remember my own name.

When the aftershocks subside, he stands, grinning like a cat, pulls my skirt back into place, and kisses me on the lips, my scent all over him. I like it.

"That was…unexpected," I say shakily.

"Spur-of-the-moment decision." He's still grinning.

"Proud of yourself?"

"Very," he says smugly.

I don't know what else to say, so I grab my wine and hide my returning smile behind my glass.

We have maybe four rotations of the wheel. During the two hours we're in that bubble, I manage to repay the favor to Georg, who swears a blue streak in Russian when he comes in my mouth.

So hot.

I'll never look up at the LINQ again without blushing.

We exit the wheel, thoroughly relaxed after our orgasmic ride together, and are immediately approached by three young women.

A brunette in bright pink booty shorts asks, "Don't you play for the Crush?" She looks barely above her teens. The other two look even younger.

"I do," Georg answers.

"I knew I recognized you. You're the defensive player, the one who's friends with Evan Kazmeirowicz."

"Georg. And yes."

"Oh my gawd!" she squeals. "I watch every game. Can I get a picture with you?"

"Sure." He gives an ambivalent shrug, looks at me and says, "Forever to be known as Evan's friend."

The girls hand me their phones and line up. I take a few quick photos but on the last one, the brunette licks Georg's face. He laughs but pulls away quickly, wiping where she licked him with the back of his hand.

The girls thank him and run off. He looks at me, and I can see he was blindsided by that girl just now, but it still irritates me to have to see it happen. "That was gross," he says, clearly annoyed.

"A little," I agree. "No, actually a lot."

He looks around and says, "I'm going to go wash my face and hands after that. Be right back."

I nod, pulling out my phone while I wait. I pull up Instagram and scroll through the feed. I'm shocked when I see a photo of Devon, planting a kiss on Georg's cheek. The caption reads, "This guy!" followed with three heart emojis.

My heart sinks into the floor. *Why did I believe him so easily?* He had chuckled that day. He'd looked me in the eye, but with a smile, and said, "There is nothing between me and Devon." And I'd believed him. The lunches. I haven't spoken to Georg every day and night since Anaheim. Far from it really, so he's had a lot of time on his hands... *God, I'm so stupid.* This photo was taken two days ago. And she's very beautiful... Very together... *And not me.*

Suddenly, breath won't come. My heartbeat is not what it should be I'm sure. Clammy. *I need to get out of here.*

I should have known. Should have known that this wasn't real. Wasn't more than flirtation and making out. Should have known he wouldn't be able to be committed to just one woman. Should have known that I will *never* be enough for a guy like him. Even the misbehaving teenage licker pissed me off and he wasn't even into her. Devon is a whole different story.

As much as it hurts admitting to myself, I know I can't do this with Georg Kolochev.

I don't think about what I'm doing, because it's automatic behavior for me when I feel scared. I do the thing I always do in a relationship that starts to get messy.

I run.

I run as fast as I can and jump into the first cab I see.

19

remember to count
to ten

Georg

"So, wait," Evan says. "You gave each other oral on the LINQ and then she jilted you?"

"Yeah," I answer, still perplexed by the whole thing. "It was so strange. We had a *great* time together, both of us—umm—enjoyed ourselves. It was all very sexy and then...poof...she was just gone. Won't text me. Won't pick up my calls. It's fucked up."

"Did you do something?"

"No," I say, offended. "Nothing."

"Well, something must have spooked her. Was there anything weird on social media? Any past girlfriends or sex partners who might have messaged her?"

"I don't think so." No girl has really chased me enough to be a problem. I've always told them the score, and no one would even know about Pam yet.

"Hmm," he ponders. "Well, from what Holly tells me, Pam has some messed-up stuff in her past and she's never really been in a serious relationship. So maybe her baggage just got in the way."

"Yeah, maybe..." I say, but I'm not so sure. "How is Holly? How's the baby?"

Evan gets a very sappy look on his face. I almost think he might cry. "They're good. Holly's a champ. Having a baby is no joke. It requires a superhero, I swear. I had no idea."

Holly had their baby, a girl, just days ago. Little Danya looks like a very tiny, very angry old lady in the photos he showed me, so her name fits since she was named for Evan's Russian grandmother.

"Why are you even here, Dad? Why not take a game off to be home with them?"

"The team needs me," he says. "And Holly told me she'd burn my favorite T-shirt if I didn't come and support the team. I tried to stay home."

I laugh. "She's the best."

"Yeah, she really is."

We play San Jose tonight, a team that has been losing all season. It should be an easy win but it's obvious from the first few moments on the ice the team is desperate. They're sloppy and aggressive, and on the first period break, Evan tells everyone to look out.

"Play smart and pay attention," he orders.

"These guys are out for blood. Don't bleed for them," Coach Brown adds.

We head back out on the ice and Mikhail scores quickly, the first goal of the game. Our home crowd goes wild, but I can see it on the San Jose players' faces that things are about to get ugly.

I've got the puck at about seven minutes in, and a San Jose player comes out of nowhere, high sticking me to the neck, knocking my helmet off and sending me straight onto my back. I see stars immediately, and I think I might throw up. My vision is wonky, but big-ass Viktor comes to my aid, checking the player into the boards.

Annnnd then all hell breaks loose.

I'm struggling to get up. I roll to my side, then force myself to my knees. No one is paying me much attention, because there's a melee going on against the glass. Everyone is fighting, even Evan, from what I can tell. I stumble to my feet, but I'm woozy as I make my way to the big brawl. I end up getting elbowed in the temple before someone swipes my legs out from under me. I land at a really weird angle, my right leg and foot pinned up under my body. I can't get up a second time.

As the fight is broken up, the officials send the whole first string to the penalty box, and I'm still on the ground. It's only then that anyone realizes I need some help, only then that the medics make their way out to me.

"Can you get up?"

No.

"How many fingers am I holding up?"

Don't...know.

Things are blurry as I'm loaded onto a stretcher. The noises hurt my head. The lights of the arena are too bright.

Eventually, though, everything gets quiet. *And dark.*

I WAKE up in a hospital bed. I try to read the white board on the wall to see the date. I have no idea how long

I've been out. My head feels like I got hit by a sledgehammer. My tongue feels dry and swollen. If I didn't know better, I'd swear I was just totally hung over. But my leg is in a big brace, too, and I've got an IV in one arm and a heart monitor attached to my chest.

"Well, fuck," I say, my voice sounding hoarse to my own ears.

"That about sums it up," a familiar voice says from somewhere.

I look around and see Coach Brown sitting in a chair, reading the paper.

"Hey, Coach," I say weakly.

"Strained ankle, torn knee PCL ligament, mild concussion," Coach says.

I sigh. "Length of time for recovery?"

"Six weeks is what they say," he answers. "The docs will be in soon to review with you. Light rehab can start in one week. We'll play the rest by ear."

"I'll be back on the ice in three. I promise."

"Hold your horses," he says. "I want you out there healthy. Don't push it."

He tells me we held San Jose and that Evan scored two rapid-fire goals after my injury. "He was on fire, super pissed," he says proudly. "I haven't seen him fight like that in a long while."

"I couldn't follow what was happening," I say.

"Yeah, 'cause you decided to get up from the first blow and insert yourself in the mess. You wouldn't be here if you'd just stayed down, you idiot."

"Sorry, Coach."

He makes a face and folds up his paper. "Well, just

wanted to catch you awake. Take your time getting better. We need you out there, Georg."

EVAN VISITS A BIT LATER, and while he's here he calls Holly on FaceTime. She tells me to get well soon, and shows me baby Danya, who is still a tiny thing but much cuter than in the immediate hours after she was born.

"That was such a wickedly cheap shot," Evan says. "What a bunch of fucking tossers."

I nod. "True."

"What hurts the worst?"

"Head," I answer. "Worst hangover ever."

"Ugh," Evan groans. "Sorry. I saw it coming...tried to get back to you, but it was too late. Viktor leveled the guy, but it was a chain reaction. Craziest fight I've seen in a long time. In any game. We're still all over the highlight reels."

We talk for a little bit longer but after a dose of pain medication, delivered by a distinctly not-nice nurse, I feel myself slipping into sleep. Evan gives me a fist bump and tells me to feel better soon.

When I wake up, someone is holding my hand. I blink a few times, my vision blurry. But there she is, blonde and pretty and smelling so fucking good. She's also crying.

"Hey, now, I'm not dead."

She gives me one of those ugly cry-smiles. "I'm sorry. I don't know why I'm crying, really. I just hate seeing you hurt."

"I'll be fine. Nothing some time with a really good physical therapist won't cure." Thank God she's actually speaking to me. She had gone completely radio silent. But at least she's touching me...

"I am up to the task," she says with a nod and a swipe at her tears. "That's actually why I came by."

I'm sure it's just the injury or the medication, but that statement really hurts. "You just came to talk about rehab?" I can't hide the hurt in my voice and don't even try.

"Well, I..." She shuts her mouth and looks out the window. "I am here in an official capacity, yes."

"Oh." I pick at the blanket with my other hand. "Well, let's talk about the plan then."

We meet each other's eyes and I can see hurt in hers, though I can't figure out where it's coming from. I haven't been able to work out why she bailed on me at the LINQ.

"What did I do, Pamela?"

Her jaw clenches. She lets go of my hand and backs up, sitting in the chair and pulling out her work notebook and a pen. "The concussion is the trickiest," she says. "Let's give you a week to alternate heat and ice on the ligament and ankle. The hospital will recommend a thousand milligrams of Ibuprofen every six hours, and I'll concur. No need for heavier-duty pain management. Especially not since you..."

She stops mid-sentence but I know what she was going to say. "Have dependence concerns? Am possibly an alcoholic? No need to give me more shit to get addicted to." I sound bitter.

Pam looks sad. She opens her mouth and shuts it

again. She takes a deep breath. "Yes. It seems too risky. And frankly, I know you'll want to get back on the ice as fast as possible and opioids will dull your reactions and thought processes. You don't want that in a game like this."

"Okay. I agree." I'm abrupt, and so fucking ready to be finished with this conversation.

"With a concussion, it's hard to know how long it will take for full recovery. I saw the video. You got your clock cleaned pretty good, but that the concussion was fairly mild. I'm sure your doctors will tell you that, on the hopeful side, it might be forty-eight hours, but it could also be weeks. Limited brain activity, big decision making, exposure to electronics...will all help the healing go faster."

"Well, I don't use my brain all that much, so it should go pretty fast," I say with a laugh, which instantly hurts my head and makes me cringe.

Pam barely laughs. She'll barely look at me. "The ligament and ankle, we can start with electric muscle therapy, heat, and ice. We'll do some massage work on the muscles and then work our way back into stretches and strength. Sound good?"

"It all sounds fine." I stare at her and wait.

Finally, finally, she looks up and meets my gaze. Her eyes are still watery from crying. I can feel that my mouth is set into a deep frown. "Pam, what happened? I thought we were becoming closer? Now you're all professional and whatever that was the other night never happened? I don't get it."

She's quiet for a few moments, then says, "It killed me

to see you get hurt, Georg. I watched it on television. I wanted to come straight here. To crawl into bed beside you."

"So why didn't you?"

"Because I thought maybe I'd have to wait in line," she answers in a whisper.

"Wait in line?" I ask, not comprehending. "I mean, Coach was here. Evan came by. Is that what you mean?"

She shakes her head and bites her bottom lip, looking out the window for a long moment. She seems to settle herself and with a big sigh, looks back at me once more. "So, now you're on the IR—what does that mean for a trade?"

Great. Now she's changed the subject once more. I let out a sigh that's equally weighted to hers. Let her see I'm frustrated, too. Damn it, I'm the one who's hurt here.

"No one wants an injured player added to their rosters. I'll be off the table for trades for now," I answer flatly. "It's a good thing. And Coach said he needs me out there, healed up, so I feel like I'm on the other side of all of this trade talk. I really do need to get in there and get something in writing, though."

I hate this. I hate that she won't talk to me.

I look up at the ceiling, count to ten...and then push her one more time.

"Pamela." I wait until she lifts her sad brown eyes and looks at me. "*Please*, will you fucking tell me what happened the other night?"

20

that's one way to hold off a trade

Pam

I put my hand up over my mouth, as if to forcibly keep inside everything I want to say to Georg. He looks so pathetic in the hospital bed, hooked up to wires, his gaze somewhat unfocused. His expression is confused, hurt, even a little angry. There is longing there, too. He's wearing it all right now, I think because his injury prevents him from controlling himself like he normally would.

He's never had a very good poker face in the first place. When he feels silly, he looks silly. When he's happy, it's obvious. When he's mad, you know it. Georg really feels whatever is on his face in a given moment. Or rather, his face shows what he's feeling in a given moment. And right now, I know I owe him an explanation.

"I'm sorry I ran out the other night," I start. "I really am. It's just that I saw Devon's Instagram feed and there was a picture of you two together. Hearts and such in the caption. It was like a blow to the stomach to see it."

"What picture?" he asks. He seems genuinely confused.

"It looked like you were in her car or she was in yours," I say. "Taken not too long ago. I mean, I knew you were friends but I...well, we had just done something very intimate and I just—"

"You got spooked thinking I was two-timing you?"

"It's not that—it's impossible to two-time someone if you're not in a relationship with them," I say sadly. "We've never defined this thing between us, and it's fine if it's just casual. I just...I don't know. I work with her. I don't want there to be weirdness between us."

"Devon is my friend, yes, but she's *just a friend*. She helped me do an intervention with Ned. We drove him to a rehab facility. The only picture I know of is one she took right after we dropped him off."

"I still don't understand why she would caption it like she did. It says 'this guy' and has a string of red heart emojis. Like she wanted people to know she was with you. That you were special to her." I know I sound jealous and petty, but I can't help it. I feel the tears bubble up again and choke them down.

Georg just shrugs. It's a really frustrating habit he has. "I don't know what to tell you. She's my friend. She helped Ned. She's helping me. But there is nothing else between us. I already told you I'm only interested in one woman, and she is you."

Just then, Dale comes in. He gives me a fist bump as he strolls past to appraise the patient.

"Got yourself into a bit of a pickle, hey there,

champ?" Dale asks cheerfully. "That's one way to hold off a trade."

"*Yebat' sebya*," Georg growls in response.

"Yeah, I looked that one up, buddy," Dale says. "That's not very nice. Also physically impossible."

"You're so loud," Georg says, teeth gritted in annoyance.

"He does have a concussion," I point out. "Maybe take it down a notch. We were discussing his rehabilitation plan. It'll be a few days, I suspect, before we can start any real work. And maybe one or two before some light work in the gym with you."

"Guess I was late to the rehab party," Dale says, only somewhat more quietly. "But really I came to wish you a speedy recovery. You've been playing great lately, and I hate to see you on your ass."

"Thank you?" Georg's response comes out more like a question.

I rehash the plan with Dale with the doctor in the room, but as we talk, I can see Georg nodding off, so we head into the hallway. Once we're all in agreement, Dale offers to take me to get some coffee.

We head to the hospital coffee shop, and when I take my first sip of my mocha latte, I close my eyes and make a sound of satisfaction.

When I open my eyes, I find Dale grinning at me. "That good?"

"Better than I expected from a hospital. And much needed. Thank you. This was a good idea."

"You're welcome. So, are you and Georg a thing or what?"

My eyes about bug out of my head. "What? No. No, we've hung out a few times but we're not...he's not..."

I'm stammering. And Dale is smirking. "He's not what? Not your boyfriend? Not interested in you? I have to disagree. He can't keep his eyes off you when he's around you. Not that I blame him. I've been trying to get your attention since day one. Are you not into guys? Please tell me you're a lesbian or something, so I can feel better you haven't noticed me yet."

"I'm not a lesbian, Dale."

"Damn."

"I do care about Georg, though," I say, not sure if I really should admit that to Dale. I'm not blind, and I have noticed that Dale is interested, but the mutual attraction just isn't there? I know I'm not supposed to fraternize or whatever, but we started hanging out before I worked for the Crush. I don't know if it can go anywhere, as I don't perceive him as a guy who settles down, though he's told me it's what he wants. He wants to stay and play here, settle in for a while."

"Well, that's what he wants for his career," Dale argues. "It doesn't mean he's ready to settle down in other parts of his life."

"I get that," I say. "And I've never been a settling-down kind of person either. I don't even know if I want that, specifically, with him. But I'm interested in figuring it out."

"So...you're saying I have no shot?"

"I didn't know there was a shot requested until three minutes ago."

"Well, I'm shy. I was scared to ask you out."

I give him a massive eye-roll in response. "Whatever. Your heart's not that broken."

"You're right," he says with a cocky grin. "But I do think you're smart and sexy. When things crash and burn with Georg, I'll be here to soothe your broken heart."

"I'm pretty good at protecting my heart," I answer with wink, standing and tossing my cup into the nearest trashcan. "Boom. Two points."

I walk away knowing he's watching, knowing he sees a confident woman walking away. But it's a façade. I'm a fraud. My heart has already been compromised by someone who makes me feel anything but confident that it will ever work out between us. It's not that I think Georg is a liar, but he's been proudly single for a long time now, and I'm not sure if I'm the girl who could truly bring about such a change in him. *I'm only interested in one woman, and she is you.* I want to believe...

I so want to believe.

21

pour some sugar on me

Pam

"I can't watch this," Evan says. "I'm feeling seriously sick watching this shit."

The Crush are playing like total garbage. With Georg out on IR and Evan on a brief paternity leave, the team is relying heavily on Mikhail and Viktor, and they just aren't playing well together. Viktor is an enforcer. He's big and solid but he's not a strategic player. He's not quick. And Mikhail is struggling without a solid defenseman at his six.

I'm watching the game at Holly and Evan's house, and while Holly assures me that little Danya could sleep through a hurricane, I'm still nervous every time I yell at the television. This game is brutal.

"What the hell is going on with these refs?" Evan groans. "Seriously bad calls in every period. I shouldn't have taken this much time off."

"What, you being there would magically make the refs call the game better?" Holly asks.

"No, but I could be there to help Mikhail. It's like he's all alone out there."

"Well, he needs a lesson like this, babe," Holly argues. "He thinks he's hot stuff and it's good for him to see holding down that level of play is not as easy as he thinks."

"I suppose," Evan says dubiously, "but this is just painful."

Holly gets up and stretches. "I'm going to get a snack, anyone want anything?"

"I'm good," I say, looking down at the sleeping baby in my arms. She's a beautiful little thing with a button nose and a head of dark hair.

"Can I have a beer, my love?" Evan asks.

"Sure thing," she says as she heads toward the kitchen.

Danya starts to fuss a bit and before I can even try to calm her, Evan has swooped in and taken her from my arms. He puts her on his shoulder and pats her back, planting a kiss on her tiny head.

"Sucker," I mutter.

"Yep. I am totally whipped," he admits cheerfully.

Holly comes back in with a container of hummus and a bag of carrots. She puts Evan's beer on the coffee table and gives him a lopsided grin.

"Back to healthy, are we?" I ask, eyeing her snack. "No more ice cream or fried cheese?"

"Ugh," she says. "I'm so glad those cravings are gone."

"Got her an awesome new jogging stroller," Evan announces proudly. "She'll be back to doing half-marathons by summer."

The doorbell rings and I head over to open it. It's Scarlett, who's in tears.

"They're really sucking out there. And people on social media are being really mean," she says as she plops down in a chair.

"Well, social media feeds don't control game outcomes, for one," Holly says. "And second, don't take it personally. They need a common place to vent their frustration."

Scarlett turns to Evan and asks, "Why aren't you out there tonight? You played like three days after the baby was born…"

"Evan is allowed to take time off, Scarlett," I jump in, my tone sharp. "He deserves to take time off to enjoy his family. It's not a one-man team, so the team should be able to function without Evan for a couple of games."

"And Georg. It feels like there's no team without you two," Scarlett wails. "Ugh. I can't wait until everything goes back to normal, and I can just go back to prepping press passes and writing press releases. This is too much stress."

Evan now has the baby in his lap and is cooing softly. At first, I don't realize what he's saying but tune in when I hear him say to Danya, "You're the baby here but that girl's acting like a baby, too. Who's the bigger baby?"

This makes us all laugh, even Scarlett, who apologizes, her cheeks turning as red as her hair.

"What's the prognosis on Georg?" Holly asks.

"He'll be fine as long as he avoids his Xbox while his concussion heals. We've got a good plan and he's in better shape than he's ever been, so I think he'll be back on the ice in no time."

"And the prognosis on your relationship with Georg?" Scarlett asks with a smirk.

"There isn't one. Not really." Scarlett is sweet, but there are times when she rubs me the wrong way. Like now. She has no clue how hard it was for me when I saw the picture of Devon and Georg, but I'm not exactly an open book. And judging by my knee-jerk reaction *and* the tears in the hospital, clearly my heart is so much more invested than I believed. So, for once, I'll offer her more. "We had a great date and I bolted when I saw a picture of him on Devon's Instagram page. He's explained when the pic was from, but the heart emojis? I don't know..."

"Well, he said it was nothing, and he wants to be with you. So, do you believe him?" Holly asks pointedly.

"Do you?" I return sharply.

"I do," Evan says, still making silly faces at the baby. He looks up at me and says, "I *know* him. He cares about you, Pam. Devon is not a conversation we've ever had."

"Maybe you should ask Devon," Holly suggests. "Get it out in the open. If she has feelings for Georg, you'll be able to tell."

"It's just a big messy disaster." I flop back against the couch cushions. "What good would it do to talk to Devon about this?"

"Well, if they are just friends, you can put it behind you," Scarlett offers.

"And if they're not?" I ask. "I'll feel like a big idiot."

"But at least you'll know," Holly says.

Yeah. At least I'll know. And then my heart will be

ripped to absolute shreds, because I'm not the long-term girl. My mom's blood runs in my veins, and surely no man will ever want to get that close to me.

WHAT ARE the odds I run right into Devon on the day I'm supposed to start therapy work with Georg. Nothing like facing your fears whether you're ready to or not.

"Good morning, Miss Pam," she says cheerfully, balancing her coffee cup, keys, jacket, and bag as she steps toward her office door.

"Morning," I say. "Need a hand?"

"Oh, thanks." She hands me her coffee while she unlocks her door. "Like the rest of my life, my morning ritual is perpetually overcommitted."

I put her coffee on her desk for her and make to leave but decide to just get the question out into the open. Sometimes you just have to rip off the Band-Aid and bear it. At least it's over quickly. "Are you and Georg Kolochev an item?"

Devon's eyes go wide at first, then crinkle at the edges as she lets out a hearty laugh. "No. No we are not."

"I just saw the picture you posted on Instagram and thought maybe..."

"Oh, I was just really proud of him that day. He had to do a hard thing, asking his agent to go to rehab. He and I have talked a lot this season, mostly about his commitment to his own health. But there's nothing romantic there. I mean, he's cute and all, but no."

Now I feel stupid. I can feel my cheeks going hot and

Devon appraises me further, tilting her head. "Are you in love with him?" She gentles her tone quickly, "Don't worry, I won't tell the fraternization police."

No sense in lying, right? "We've spent time together and I really do like him. I just didn't want—"

"To get your heart broken? To find out he wasn't a one-woman guy?" She's nodding at her own statement and I can see something in her eyes. Pain, maybe? It's distant, but it's there.

"Yes," I say simply.

"Well, for what it's worth, he's a really good man. He's not always acted with the most maturity but he is loyal to those he cares about. And he's evolving, every single day. I think he's worth your time."

I push my lips together and nod, taking in a big breath, letting it out. "Thanks, Devon."

THE BUTTERFLIES in my stomach are having a field day as I eye the clock. It's nothing new. I've been feeling this way all day long. Because Georg is coming to see me today. He's my last appointment. And I'm a freaking wreck waiting for him to show. I don't know what to expect at all. We haven't resolved anything between us since he was injured. Although that's partly because he was barred from using technology while recovering from his concussion, so we couldn't really text or FaceTime. I've spoken to him twice on the phone, but mostly to check in from an official standpoint, so we could coordinate his physical therapy appointments. He's been doing everything right to get healthy and back on the ice, and my job is to support him in any way I can, helping him to meet that goal. I have to remember that.

Through the big glass windows, I see him in the hall accosted by a teammate who claps him on the back and chats him up for a minute. People are happy to see him up and around. He has been very much missed by a lot of people.

"Welcome back," I say after he steps into the therapy suite. He looks gorgeous as usual with his hair pulled back in a tie and that happy expression he wears on his handsome face much of the time. Georg is a beautiful man. Whatever else he is to me, whether it becomes something more between us or it doesn't, he will always be remembered as he is right now in this moment—a funny, sweet, beautiful man, smiling at me mischievously, suggesting he's up for anything a little naughty. Or probably a lot naughty is more like it.

I'm so screwed.

"Thank you, Pamela. It's really quiet in here today."

"That's just because it's the end of the day. You're my last appointment."

"Ahh. Well, how do you want me?"

I'm at the instrument table when he says this. I can't see his face but I'm positive I heard innuendo in that statement. I turn slightly, just enough to give him the side-eye, and find him standing with hands on hips and rockin' a cocky grin on his handsome face. *Gah.*

"Start on your back on the table, please." I do my best to sound professionally aloof, but I don't think it's working. Because when I turn back towards him, the cocky bastard is standing there with his shirt whipped off. All that glorious arm-porn I love so much is on full display to distract me. *Send help.* I look to the chair where he tossed his shirt, and then track slowly back to where he's standing next to the table. Wearing only a pair of flip flops and some black athletic shorts. I resist the urge to swallow and fail miserably. Twice. "Umm, Georg, I am not aware of any upper body injuries, so you can probably put your shirt back on."

"But I want you to have something nice to look at while you work."

Smiling widely up at me in typical Georg fashion, he's far more than a "nice" sight with that sexy body stretched out on my work table, but I don't tell him that.

I push my tongue into my cheek to keep from returning his smile. "Well, I won't be paying attention to anything other than your injury, so I guess it's just the ghosts who will enjoy the view of your pasty white chest."

He sits straight up. "Pasty?" he objects, mock-hurt in his tone. "I am not pasty!"

I let loose a smile, and we meet each other's eyes. There it is—that spark of chemistry, immediately rendering me hot and wanting him again. That's all it takes.

He lies back down and I begin my work. The whole time, we tease each other, our verbal jabs sharp and ruthless, but also very funny. It makes the hour go quickly, so when I look at the clock and realize his session is over, I'm shocked.

"Well, Georg, that's the end of our session today. I'll see you again on Thursday?"

"Back for more torture? I can't wait," he says, sitting up. "You're mean, by the way. The way you opened up those tools, like a serial killer trying to decide which tool to use to cut off my appendages."

I'm suddenly very focused on just one of said appendages. In his thin athletic shorts, I can clearly see the outline of his cock, and he's semi-hard. He notices my gaze and gives a lopsided grin. "Your hands were all over me. How could I not be turned on?"

I look around. There's nobody left here. Everyone has gone home for the day.

"Are you thinking what I'm thinking, Pamela?"

I bite my lip.

"You are," he exclaims. "You sinful little fox."

"This is my work space, Kolochev. And I was thinking no such thing—if whatever you're thinking is dirty— which I know it was," I lie. How can I not? I get hot just looking at him, let alone having my hands on him for the past hour.

"I was thinking a very dirty thing and you should just fess up, because I know how you look when you're turned on. There is no one here. Go close the blinds, and I'll make you come until you scream my name."

I gasp. A big, audible gasp that's filled with surprise and delight...and so much want.

I turn away and head to the windows to the suite. We have blinds because sometimes our guys want privacy while we work on them. As I reach out to close them, my hands are shaking. I shouldn't be doing this. It's so risky. What if someone walks in? I could lose my job. But damn, I'm so aroused right now, it's painful. I don't know what it is about Georg, and how he makes me feel like this, so turned on that I feel I might explode.

My steps back to him are slow. As I near him, he reaches out from his perch on the therapy table and pulls me to him, his lips on mine before I can even process what's happening. *Thank God.*

The kiss is fast and rough and hot. And then he hops down from the table and says two words, "Get naked."

I don't have to be told twice.

I watch his eyes grow hooded as I perform a strip show for him. He's in a mood to watch apparently, because he doesn't help. Off go my shoes and socks. His dick grows bigger with each item of clothing I toss aside:

Crush polo.

Khaki shorts.

Front-clip red bra. He licks his lips and swallows hard when that gets tossed.

Matching panties. A sexy groan erupts out of him before he tells me to get on the therapy table, face down.

I don't know what to expect, but it's not the massage he gives me. He uses my therapy oil and gives me a nice back massage first, then works his way from my feet up my legs. When his hands caress my inner thighs, I relax and let him spread my legs. I know he's staring at my pussy.

He massages my ass, casually spreading my cheeks, running his fingertips down, down, down, just grazing my aching sex.

He's got me so worked up, that I'm so wet it's probably getting on the table. When he flips me to my back, he pushes my knees apart and leans in to place one kiss on my clit before turning his attention to my breasts.

He massages, getting a few licks and nips in when he can, a devilish grin on his face the whole time he works on me. His eyes shine with mischief as his hands work themselves lower, to my belly and my hips.

Georg's thumb finds my clit, working a slow but steady rhythm. My hips buck involuntarily, the telltale start of an orgasm already building in my lower abdomen. He picks up the pace, his face lazily entertained as I push my hips up wildly, my motions growing more crazed with each increase of speed and intensity from his thumb.

I'm letting out crazy, nonsensical noises as the orgasm starts. "Yes" is the only thing that sounds even remotely like a real word. He keeps working while my pussy clenches, my body overcome by pleasure. He continues his efforts as the aftershocks roll through me, and it's only when I lay boneless does he let up.

Then, he crawls up on the table, on his knees, and pulls me to him so I straddle him, the only barrier between us his thin shorts. His hard, long cock rubs at that swollen nub, and I feel the want building again as I ride against him, pushing my clit against his hardness.

Georg's fingers slide down my ass and find my pussy, wet and gaping. He pushes his fingers deep inside of me as I rub myself against him. His lips find my neck. I kiss his forehead.

"Yes, Pamela. Yes, just like that. Yes. Come for me, baby."

"Georg," I manage to breathe. "Yes. Yes, Georg."

And then the world is gone. I come and come, the longest and best orgasm I've ever had.

Georg asks for nothing in return. He just pushes me to the edge, over the cliff, his body strong as he holds me, his breath hot as he kisses me. He whispers, "I want you so, so badly, Pamela. So very badly."

"I want you too, Georg. I want to be with you. I want—you—to be my first."

"Ty chti mne moyu lyubov'."

I have no idea what the Russian words mean but it sounds beautiful when he repeats it several times, holding me possessively as the orgasm rocks me into another universe.

He kisses me for a long time, still holding me against him like he won't ever let go.

I realize I don't want him to.

I'M TOO scared to do such a thing ever again. I've had major anxiety about it, worried somehow we'd be caught on camera. And while what we did was literally the hottest thing ever, I've forced myself to return to professionalism when he's around. We still tease and flirt, but he understands when I tell him I think we need to be more careful. He knows I loved it, but I also love my job.

Georg does well in his therapy and training sessions with Dale and me. So well, in fact, that he's back on skates in just four weeks. He's not yet cleared for competitive play, but he is allowed to practice and suit up and be on the bench.

Evan is back, too, and while the team is winning, it's not without struggle. Not having Georg on the ice has definitely exposed a weakness in the team's defense, a weakness that has attracted the attention of Evan's agent, Scott Rose, who offered to take on Georg as a client. This is really big news, because Scott is a kingmaker. He's well known for making huge financial deals for his clients, and Georg has sent me about a hundred texts to tell me how awesome this new development is.

Dale and I meet with Coach Brown, Max Terry, Georg, the team doctor, and Scott in a big conference room near the owner's suite. I've actually never been up on this level of the arena. It's almost intimidating, but also kind of funny, as there is eighties rock music playing softly. I think it's a Def Leppard song called *Pour Some Sugar on Me*. Totally cheesy but catchy as hell.

Georg is really into it, though, singing along softly, drumming his fingers on the table. I have to force myself to keep from smiling.

"He's working super hard," Dale is saying. "All season he's been focused in the gym. He's very fit, so it's been no problem getting him back up to speed on my end."

"And in physical therapy?" Coach Brown turns his attention to me.

"Same," I say. "Georg is working very hard. He was diligent in following concussion protocol and the injuries to the ligament and ankle are healing really well. His range of motion on the ankle is about ninety-eight percent right now."

"He can play next week," the doctor announces.

"Great," Coach says. "Thanks, team."

It seems we're dismissed, but Georg and Scott are asked to stay behind. He catches my eye as I stand up to leave, a wicked gleam flashing in his greens. It goes straight to my belly. We've been texting back and forth like high schoolers, but we haven't had any more *personal* encounters since the wild one in the therapy room a couple of weeks ago. My body misses him.

Dale puts his hand on my back as we walk out into the hallway. I hear Georg clear his throat. It's a definite sound of warning.

I can't hold back the grin as Dale quickly drops his hand.

22

my first time at a dude ranch

Pam

I don't usually watch the Crush games from the stands. Some of the home games, I'm on call to assist with light injuries, cramps, etc., so I watch on a monitor in the therapy suite. Otherwise, I just get too nervous to watch live, so I watch from home or with Holly at her house.

But there is no way in hell I would be any place other than in the stands tonight, while Georg is making his return to the ice. I send him a text.

> Pam: Good luck out there, hot stuff. Make a touchdown or whatever.

> Georg: Ha ha!

> Pam: Seriously, though, sub out if that leg bugs you.

> Georg: Yes, boss.

> Georg: You in the stands tonight?

Pam: No, I'm naked and touching myself in bed right now.

Georg: That is not a way to keep me focused on the game, Pamela.

Pam: Kidding. I'm in the stands. Fully clothed.

Georg: Thank goodness.

Georg: If we win, I would like to request nudity later.

Pam: Deal. Go sink a basket now.

Georg: I'm rolling my eyes at you right now.

Pam: You know there's an eye-roll emoji, right?

Georg: Did not know that.

Pam: Have fun out there! XX

Georg: XXX is more interesting.

Pam: Focus.

Georg: On you. XXX baby!

I grin the whole way through the pre-game rituals. They play a video of Georg's best moments and make a huge deal out of his return to the ice. The crowd goes nuts when he comes out with the team, and I actually become teary at all the fan love for my guy.

Georg is back on the starting lineup and he looks around the stands as he takes the ice. When he finds me in the stands, he gives a cocky wink before taking his position.

The game is so much different from the games during his absence. He's on fire out there, getting the puck to Evan so he can score two times in the first period alone.

The opposing team comes out swinging in the second period, though, firing shot after shot on goal, so that Viktor, Tyler, and Georg are stuck protecting the goalie. They score only once, despite more than twenty shots on goal.

A third period check sets Tyler into a rage. He starts a huge fight that results in him in the penalty box and the other team on a power play. They make use of it, scoring quickly, narrowing the gap. Mikhail responds, though, with a goal of his own, and then Georg and Evan pull out a fourth goal in the last minute of the game.

The crowd is electric in this arena. My ears feel like they might bleed, it's so loud in here, and Georg and Evan's faces are prominently displayed on the jumbotron, heroes once again, a dynamic duo that absolutely cannot be replaced.

There is, as always, a press event after the game. I hang back with Scarlett while the press interview Evan, Georg, and Mikhail.

Kacey King, the queen of evil, barges up to the front of the press pack. Her black dress is skin-tight and so low-cut I wonder how the heck her bosses let her on television dressed like that. Her long, blonde hair is straight down her back and her eyeliner is crazy heavy. She looks like she's ready to go out to a club more than to do her job reporting on sports.

"Georg, Georg," she says, cutting through the questions from the press corps. "How did it feel on the ice tonight?"

"It felt great. I was ready to get back out there and I proved it tonight alongside these guys."

"Those were serious injuries," she says. "How were you able to come back so quickly, and looking so strong out there?"

"I had a lot of special attention from my physical therapist." He gives the camera one of his signature grins.

There's a lot implied in that statement, so much that it makes me blush. Scarlett notices, coughs, and elbows me, hiding her face behind her clipboard while she giggles.

"Well, he must be a miracle worker," Kacey comments.

"She," Georg corrects.

"She?" Kacey asks, confused.

"Yes, Pamela Jenson is my physical therapist. She."

"Oh, well," Kacey attempts to save face by turning away from him and zeroing in on her next target. "That's wonderful. So, Evan, how has being a father affected your play out there?"

And with that, Georg has shut down whatever play Kacey was making. He looks over at me and bites the inside of his lip. He's not smiling, but his eyes are alight with their usual mischief. He's nearly bursting with energy, his legs bouncing under the table, his fingers drumming on the table again. This is crazy Georg, silly Georg, *and* naughty Georg. He's back, and I am incredibly happy for him.

This is the Georg I love.

Love.

Did I just say "love?"

Yes, I did.

I'm in love with Georg Kolochev.

After Fiona shuts down the press event, Georg finds me at the door. He takes my hand and I get a pointed glare from Kacey. I don't care, though. Georg is here. He's healthy and strong. There is no way he's getting traded.

And now I know that I'm in love with him.

We walk to the player's parking area where he opens the door of his BMW for me, planting a kiss on my cheek before I get in. We don't say a lot as he starts the engine and makes his way out of the stadium and onto the street. We didn't explicitly make plans, so I'm not sure what to expect. Another night in the casinos? Another dinner with a gorgeous view?

Georg cranks the stereo as we drive, an eighties station playing on XM. Eurythmics' *Sweet Dreams* is the first song that comes on, and Georg sings along with every word. It makes me smile. A lot. We drive for nearly an hour, Georg happily singing, headbanging, and otherwise being his silly and adorable self.

When we pull into a quaint little ranch, I'm stunned. There are horses munching on grass along both sides of the long, dirt driveway. The house is simple, two stories, with a big front porch complete with a porch swing.

"What's this place?" I ask.

"It's a horse ranch but also a bed and breakfast. A friend of mine owns it."

"I have to say, I was *not* expecting a dude ranch when we got in the car. Also, I packed nothing."

"All part of the conspiracy," he says, grinning. "If you recall I requested nudity later if we won and you agreed. I have the proof right here on my phone. You said 'deal,' and we *did* win tonight, Pamela, and it is definitely *later*." He's so cute when he's like this.

"Well, aren't you the clever kidnapper? Look at you, Georg Kolochev, plotting out a way to have a night of sin with me." I'm teasing, but suddenly completely aroused as I squirm in the seat and clench my thighs together. I've missed being intimate with him. It's been a long time coming with his injury and all.

"*Weekend*, baby. I need a whole weekend to do all the sinning I want to sin with you." He gives me a knowing look, his green eyes dark and gleaming from across the seat. I understand completely what will be happening here tonight. And I also understand I'll no longer be a virgin after this weekend.

I'm finally going to have all-the-way-sex with Georg.

Oh.

We pull up to the house and get out, the door opening immediately. A portly older woman says, "Yes, it is our Georgie."

Georg holds out his arms and says, "Miss Louisa, good to see you," as he pulls her into a hug. They embrace, her silver bun coming loose as he spins her around. She's smiling broadly as he sets her down and gestures to me. "This is Pamela Jenson. Pamela, this is Louisa Stone. Her husband, Jim, owns an establishment in town as well as this ranch."

"That's a nice way to put it," Louisa says with a laugh. "My husband likes two things: horses and naked women.

So I stay here to help with the horses, and he manages the naked women."

I think my eyes might bug out of my head. This makes Louisa laugh. She throws an arm around Georg's waist and they wander into the house. Georg reaches out his hand to me and tows me along with them.

Inside, the house is gorgeous, clearly recently renovated to include the shabby chic décor one would expect of a farmhouse with lots of modern furniture, dark wood, and other pretty features. Louisa shows us around the main level, which includes a living room featuring a crackling fireplace, a spacious kitchen with a gorgeous, wood-topped center island surrounded by four stools, a powder room, and an amazing library stocked with floor-to-ceiling bookshelves.

Upstairs, there are two main suites. Both begin with a sitting room complete with television, comfy-looking couches, a coffee and wine bar, and a fireplace. Further back, a massive bedroom and en-suite, complete with an oversized soaker tub and huge, walk-in shower.

"This is so gorgeous," I say, in awe. "I want to live here all the time."

"So glad you love it," Louisa says with a wide smile. "I spent a lot of time thinking about design when we decided to renovate and make this into a B&B. Jim couldn't understand why the living room first, but I figured it gave an extra buffer of privacy in each suite."

"Great idea," I agree. "But it's also just really comfortable and warm. Really gorgeous."

"Well, there are no other visitors tonight, so you have the place to yourselves. I'll finish up the food downstairs and then head home. Be back in the morning to make breakfast."

"You don't live here?" I ask.

"Oh, no. Jim and I have a house about a half mile back on the property, closer to the horse barn. So you've got the place all to yourselves. All night long." She gives us a knowing wink. "There are robes, fresh linens, and a few clothing items in the closet, so help yourself to anything you need."

As Louisa leaves the suite, I stare at Georg, dumbfounded. "You had all this planned out?"

"Of course," he answers. "I had a lot of time to think while I was recovering. I wanted to get out of the city, have some time to ourselves. Celebrate."

"What if the team had lost tonight?"

"But this is not a celebration of the team, Pamela." He steps close...closer...until our bodies are nearly aligned and his hand is on my cheek. He leans in, his lips brushing mine so softly. "This is about us. About you and me."

"Us?" I almost forget to breathe and feel a little weak in the knees as I stare into his eyes.

"You must know I'm in love with you, Pamela. I love you."

"But I—I didn't know you felt that way about me."

"How could you not? You don't feel it in every smile I give you? In the way I look at you? You can't feel it in the way I touch you?"

"I—I was blinded I guess...by my own feelings..."

I can hardly talk, and feel incredibly overheated all of a sudden.

He kisses me again, slow and deep, and then pulls back, still holding my face in his hands. "I am not a great man, not nearly good enough for you. But I poured every ounce of my love into each stroke of your clit, each pulse of my tongue against your sweet, sweet pussy. Did you feel it, Pamela? Can you feel it right now?"

If it were possible for me to melt into a puddle of mush, it would be happening right this instant. Right now, when my breasts are heavy and aching, my stomach filled with butterflies from wanting him so badly. It would happen now, when I can think of nothing else but the way his long hair falls lazily into his eyes, the way his mouth curves like a bow, the way his breath feels on my skin, the way he just told me he loves me.

"Yes," I breathe. The arousal I feel is almost painful. I want him. All of him. Inside me. "Yes, I feel it, Georg, I feel you."

And I love you, too.

His lips find mine again, his hand inching its way down my lower back to my backside. He cups my ass cheek and pulls me to him roughly, the hardness of him evident through his jeans. His tongue begs for entry and I open to him, sighing against his mouth.

When he pulls away, I'm positively electric with want. Georg, however, seems intent on prolonging my misery. "Come on, *krasota*," he says softly and then leads me out of the suite, down the stairs to the kitchen, where a beautiful tray of food awaits.

We each find a stool and pull up to the island, sampling the array of cheese, meat, and fruit.

"So, Pamela," he says as he pops a grape into his

mouth, "before we do anything more tonight, I need to know how is it that someone as beautiful and amazing as you are still a virgin."

I feel my heart sink a little at the question. In all these months, he's never asked and I haven't wanted to tell him. I still don't, not when everything feels so good and perfect. But this is part of who I am, and if we are to move forward and have a real relationship, then I do need to share this dark part of my past with him.

"Well, I was..." I start but I can't quite figure out how to give voice to my past. I feel the tension on my face. I know it's there, because Georg's playful expression turns more to concern.

"You can tell me, baby. I want to know all of you. Everything...the good and even the bad."

I swallow back the lump that forms in my throat and take a deep, centering breath. "My mother has had a lot of husbands. I think I told you that, right?"

He nods.

"Well, one of them...when I was a teenager...he—"

"Raped you?" Georg's voice cracks.

"No, no." I shake my head. "He touched me, though. Did other things. Gross things. And I'm okay now. I've been through therapy and whatnot. But I think it...I think it made me feel like damaged goods. And it made it hard for me to trust men. So, I always only allowed things to go so far before I ended them. I've never had a real relationship. Nobody had ever given me an orgasm before you came along, Georg."

I feel my cheeks turn to flame as I look away, ashamed to verbalize my past like this. I won't cry, though. I decided a long time ago that I wouldn't shed one more tear over that piece of garbage. I'm a victim, sure, but I refuse to live my life as if I've been victimized.

When I feel Georg's hand on my shoulder, I look back and he pulls me into a fierce hug.

"You are not damaged," he says against my hair. "You are perfect to me. And fuck that *zasranec*. I'll kill him someday for hurting you."

"Believe me, I've thought about it myself," I say, pulling back to look at him. "But he's not worth a second of my time, or yours."

Georg's expression is soft, emotive. "You are one of the strongest women I have ever met. The way you are so independent and take care of yourself. How you stand up for yourself. You are so perfect to me, Pamela."

"I so love the way you call me Pamela, but I'm not perfect. Not by a long shot."

"No one is," he says softly while covering my hand with his. "I am not, either. But for me, you are. I am *svoloch'* for not saying it sooner."

"Any sooner might have been too soon," I answer. "I am very good at pushing people away. It's good that things were...looser...for a while. More casual."

"I tried not to want you," he says. "But the heart can be stubborn."

"I tried not to want you, too, but it didn't work at all."

And here come the tears. Not for my past, but for the present. Happy tears, I suppose. Georg uses his thumb to wipe them away as they fall, his face soft, supportive. Loving. I bite my lip and try to give him a reassuring smile.

"We don't need to focus on sad things," I say. "You're right; we're here to celebrate."

"What are you celebrating, Pamela? I told you what I'm celebrating."

He meets my gaze, his expression hopeful. I suck in my bottom lip, fighting the fear I feel in admitting this feeling. But right now, I'm still reeling from the fact that I told Georg about *him*. And when I did, he held me...*fiercely*. No one has ever stood up for me—supported me wholly—like that. That hug communicated love more than words ever could, and now I see hope and love in his eyes rather than disappointment and disgust. *Love. That's what I'm celebrating.*

"I'm celebrating you, Georg Kolochev. Us together, because I love you too. I don't know how you managed to be the one to steal my heart but you did."

His face splits into a wide, glorious smile and he pulls me to him again, his lips in my hair as he showers me with kisses. The kisses move to my forehead, my cheeks. My ears, my neck. Finally, he lingers at my lips, softly kissing me, his hands on my face. It feels so right, so good.

"I want you, Georg, tonight...all of you. I am ready to be *wholly* yours," I whisper against his ear. This time, the implication is so much more. My body is heavy with it, aching. All I can envision is the two of us in the act, him buried deep inside me, fucking me into oblivion. God, I want to experience that with him.

"I was hoping you'd say that," he answers, standing and moving the tray of food farther down the counter.

He lifts me up so I'm sitting on the wooden counter.

We kiss again, urgently. Our teeth click together. I bite his bottom lip. I'm still in my Crush T-shirt and he kisses the logo before pulling it over my head, exposing my simple, white lace bra.

"I'd have picked sexier underwear if I'd known about this plan."

"No matter, baby. It will be on the floor before you know it."

And he's not joking. He reaches around, unsnaps my bra, and tosses it. The air in the house is comfortable, but there might as well be freezing cold air on my skin, the way my nipples pucker, standing at attention, jutting shamelessly.

"These fucking gorgeous tits want my attention," he says, tracing his fingertips over the pebbled nubs. I arch my back, sighing with pleasure at this small act.

He leans in and kisses each nipple, first lightly, then returning, his tongue making lazy circles, tasting me, his hands fondling. I could come, I think, just from this.

"Do you want me to touch you, Pamela? Will you be wet if I do?"

"Yes," I breathe.

"Yes, what?" he asks, pushing my breasts together, his breath hot on my skin.

"Yes, please. *Please* touch me."

He puts a hand between my legs, up my skirt, his fingertips grazing my very wet panties. The amount of wetness makes him chuckle. He pushes the fabric to the side and dips his middle finger right inside me. My hips buck instantly and I nearly fall back onto the countertop.

"As fun as it would be to take you here on this kitchen

counter, it is not at all what I had in mind. Come with me."

It's jarring when pulls himself away from me, but I take his hand and we practically run up the stairs to the bedroom suite. Georg hurries into the bathroom and runs a bath, complete with a minty soap. As the water runs, filling the air with fragrant steam, I follow him, still only in my skirt, my breasts bared and feeling heavy with desire. I watch him as he removes his shoes and socks and then lights several candles placed around the ledge of the tub. He turns on some music. A sexy-sounding woman sings, *I've been a bad, bad girl. I've been careless with a delicate man.*

"I don't think I've ever heard this song," I admit.

"It's Fiona Apple," he tells me.

"She's sexy."

"That's the point," he says with a wink, dancing in a way that I think it supposed to be sexy, but actually ends up making me giggle.

I'm shivering, teeth chattering, but it's definitely not cold in here. I'm nervous. Georg senses this and comes to stand in front of me. He rubs his arms over my bare upper arms, causing my skin to erupt in goosebumps. My nipples tighten up once more.

"Take a deep breath, Pamela." He places a single kiss on my collarbone. "I want this to be so good for you."

He divests me of my shoes and socks and then my skirt and panties before pulling off his own shirt and jeans and handing me a hair tie. I pull my mass of hair up into a messy bun while Georg stares hungrily at the whole length of my body. His green eyes start at my breasts and then trail down below. He definitely appreciates the waxing. He's told me several times.

I take a minute to admire his body as he drops the last of his clothes to the floor, the black boxers making a soft noise as they land on top of the growing pile of discarded clothes. He kicks the messy pile out of the way with his foot and looks at me.

The two of us completely naked facing each other.

It's extremely intimate. Just the two of us baring ourselves. No words are spoken, because I think we both understand a moment of silent admiration is what's needed. I certainly need it. I haven't had nearly enough naked time with him. Not that it's even possible to have enough naked time with Georg. He was a beautiful man even before I fell in love with him. Now that I know he loves me too, I want to look at what's mine.

I take in every muscled line of him, from his sculpted chest and arms down to the V below his cut abs that renders my normally sane mind to utter mush, and below that, his beautiful hard cock that I'm dying to feel moving inside me. I think I might die if I don't feel it soon.

He lifts his hand and coaxes me toward the bath, stepping in first and then helping me into the tub. We both sit, facing each other, and when he squirts some soap onto a big sponge, I scoot forward, pushing my legs over top of his. There are scant inches between us and it is incredibly sexy. The water is warm and aromatic, the candles dance around us. Georg takes the sponge and sweeps it over my shoulder and down my arm. He repeats the process on the other side and works the sponge around to my back without taking his eyes off me. It's a very sensual experience, being washed by another person. I can't wait to do the same to him.

He moves the sponge around to the front of me, giving attention to my neck, chest, and breasts. As he massages and caresses, I arch into his touch, feeling more and more aroused by the second. Eventually I take the sponge from his hand and repay the favor, washing him, and feeling his erection grow longer and thicker for me. I scoot closer, nearly straddling him, his hardness lined up against my folds.

My hands find his shoulders, his neck, as we kiss. His hands rest at my lower back. Our kissing is slow and exploratory, but there's a point when my hips begin to move against him, that hard length of his cock hitting the small nub of my clit right where I want it. I let out tiny sighs against his mouth, becoming more needy by the second.

"Turn around," Georg whispers.

I do as I'm told, sloshing water up out of the tub as I turn. I position myself between his legs and lean back. He leans into my back and kisses the side of neck while his fingers massage my inner thighs. Slowly, his fingers work their way to that aching spot between my legs. A thumb finds my clit while two fingers push inside of me. Georg's free hand cups one of my breasts, pinning me back against his chest. I can't help but buck against his hand as he finds my nipple and tugs on it. One thing's for certain: I am completely and totally in his care and couldn't stop even if I wanted to. I'm his to do with whatever he wishes in this moment, and I realize that I have never trusted anyone like I trust Georg.

"You are so beautiful, so precious, *krasota*. I love everything about you." *I feel that. His love. His.*

"I love you too."

He continues to make me feel beautiful, precious…his everything. I have no idea how long we make out in the tub, but it's long enough for me to have orgasmed and for the water to chill.

What we've done is sinful, sexy, and scorching hot. But I still need more.

More of my Georg.

I want *all* of him.

23

sin-shots & cannon blasts

Pam

Dripping wet and giggling like a couple of teenagers, Georg pulls us from the cooling tub and starts drying me off with a fluffy white towel. He is careful and doesn't rush, which makes me realize this is all part of his secret plan. His tender care is something I could definitely get used to, and I think he's making a point of letting me know what I've been missing all this time by denying us being together.

Once I'm dry, I reach for another towel and take my turn drying him, enjoying every inch of his finely formed body. I take a moment to admire him and nearly forget to breathe. Christ, he's a beautiful man. His cock is so—big —and hard. So hard. And it's for me. The sexy image of what he'll be doing with it soon makes my knees go weak.

But I keep my sinful thoughts to myself as he leads me into the sitting room. He flips a switch on the wall and a fire blazes to life in the fireplace. A soft, fluffy rug adorns the floor in front of it.

"I have been dreaming of seeing you spread out on this rug." He gestures to our little love nest in front of the fireplace.

"Well, let me make that dream come true for you, then." I stare at him as I calmly pull the elastic from my hair. It tumbles down around my shoulders and down my back, delivering a little tickle that makes me shiver involuntarily.

Georg watches me like a hunter stalking his prey. Silent. Waiting. Patient. So very ready to pounce.

I lower myself to the floor slowly, stretching myself out onto the soft rug for him. The warmth of the fire radiates onto my bare skin as he tracks my movements. His eyes stare at me darkly, taking in every bare inch of my body as he strokes his cock. It turns me on to see him, his shoulders wide, his muscles sharply defined. The light patch of hair on his chest, the matching happy trail lower on his abdomen. His thighs and calves are muscled, strong. But it's his face I enjoy most, the lazy smirk he wears on those cherub lips, the sharpness of his cheekbones, the disheveled hair. It's all of him, I suppose.

"Bring your sexy self over here," I say, dipping a finger down between my legs to touch myself. "I'm cold and lonely."

"I do not have to be told twice." He finds a spot next to me, propping himself and watches me. "Does that feel good when you touch yourself, baby?"

"Hmm," I groan, biting down on my lower lip.

"Does that mean yes?"

"It's never as good as when you do it."

He puts his hand over mine, helping guide and

intensify the touch as my hips roll in circles. He moves his hands to push my legs apart, spreading me wide open with a firm touch.

Putting me into position to accept him inside. *Finally.* All I can think of is that I am completely and totally ready for this with him.

An unspoken agreement passes between us—one that Georg makes sure I don't miss as he inserts two fingers inside of me. His mouth works against my neck as he pushes in and out, fingering me to the brink of a magnificent orgasm.

"Oh, God," I gasp. "Oh, God...oh, God, I'm going to —come."

"I know. And as you do, I'm going to be inside you. Okay?"

"Yes, yes."

He rolls on a condom quickly before focusing his fingers back where they belong. He picks up the pace, speaking in Russian and telling me how sexy and soft and beautiful I am with him like this.

I can't think beyond the immense feeling of pleasure that takes over as I find my climax, the sounds more animalistic than human coming out of me I'm sure. I feel the wide tip of his cock press into me, hot and hard.

He doesn't hesitate.

The whole long length of him melds into the pulsing aftershocks of my orgasm as he pushes all the way inside me. I'm so wet that any resistance is obliterated by our need to fuck, so much so that the burn only lasts an instant before melting away. It's been such a long time for us coming to this point. We both cry out in that moment of full contact. I still beneath him, the realization of what's happening overwhelming me for a quick second.

"Breathe, Pamela...and look at me."

I open my eyes to find him hovering over me, a smile on his lips as he studies me. I'm full of him, but the sense of fullness is something very welcome and very wonderful. It feels...complete to have Georg inside me, the heavy weight of him pressing into my curves, claiming me in the most primal way.

He starts with a slow thrust and asks if I'm okay, kissing my lips, his eyes never leaving mine as he makes love to me slowly.

So carefully at first.

Then sweetly.

Then the newness of him moving inside me blurs into something a lot less sweet, and a lot more like sin as his strokes into me grow more focused and deep.

Glorious—thrilling sin. Sin I don't ever want to end.

The intensity builds with the increasing rhythm of our bodies as I wrap my legs around him, pulling him in deeper still, aligning our flesh as close as I can. The hard slide of his cock striking around my clit sets me off again, the tingle of orgasm unbelievably beginning once more.

"You feel so—fucking—good," he tells me on hot, hard, thrusts of his driving cock into me. "I've been wanting you like this for so long."

"I know. Me too...oh God, I'm gonna come again." I allow myself to ride the wave of extreme pleasure that's coming for me as Georg keeps right on pounding his beautiful cock into me.

"Wait for me, baby, wait for me," he says, his eyes

becoming hyper focused on mine as his face takes on a dreamlike expression. I can feel his cock swell as he starts to come, his movements slowing into hard jerks, drawing out every last bit of the climax that's gripped both of us.

He puts his forehead against mine as he stills. "*Ya tebe lyublyu*," he breathes. "I love you. I love you. I love you."

He kisses me—a hard, passionate thing full of emotion and intimacy. I certainly feel that. I feel so much that I never dreamed I'd experience. It honestly feels like I've been waiting for *him*. That only Georg could love me in a way that made me feel so whole and free.

"I love you, Georg," I tell him as he holds me in his arms, our bodies tangled together among the sheets so closely.

He loves me.

I love him.

So why does this still feel so terrifying…like I'm chasing an impossible dream?

Georg

IT WOULD NOT BE a stretch to say that making love to Pamela was as close to catharsis as is humanly possible. Every sound she made. Every pulse of her tight cunt around my cock. Every kiss she gave. It was unlike anything I've experienced.

Maybe it was the fact that we both admitted our feelings. Maybe it was the place, and the hours it took to finally get to where we were ready for the act of sex itself. When I plunged inside her I was lost. What I would have given to be bare inside her when I came. We still have a lot to talk about but it can wait. Right now is for enjoying each other. And the fact we've made it to this point. She's fully mine now, nobody can deny it, not even her. I have the proof.

The knowledge of how beautiful she looks when my cock is buried deep inside her and she's about to come is mind-bending really. Hearing those three little words come sailing from her lips to my ears. She's the first woman to tell me those three words. I'll have to experience it many more times before I'm even remotely satisfied, but at least I know now how that feels.

I know what it's like to have her naked in bed with me, still coming down from the high of some really spectacular fucking. I know how her body feels against mine. I know the flowery scent of her skin. I know that she gets quiet after she comes. I knew that already, because making her orgasm is something I've managed to do every single chance I've been given, but hasn't been all that often. Pam is so skittish about us being seen as a couple because of that stupid non-fraternization policy management has. Finding any sort of private time together has been a rare thing for us so far.

That will have to fucking change.

Right now, though, I know she's thinking about what we just did. I hope it's not *over*thinking, because with Pam that can be a problem. Admittedly, I am completely surprised at her comfort with sex, despite what was done to her by that sick fucker. My girl is beyond amazing. And

I can't believe she loves me too. Neither one of us have a solid track record with past relationships. Hell, I've never even had a past relationship last this long unless I count Miss March from one of my dad's old Playboys. Miss March was a smokin' hot blonde, not unlike Pam now that I think about it. She was my thirteen-year-old self's fucking wet dream. Quite literally. I had legit plans to marry her someday.

"So, how do you rate your sin-shot, Pamela?" I ask this as I trail my hands all over her flushed skin. I don't want to stop touching her now I have her beside me. Naked.

"Excuse me, my what?" She gives me side-eye and readjusts her body so she can face me, halfway propped on my chest, her soft curves settled against me like perfection.

"Your sin-shot. Your first time?" I know I'm smirking, but I can't help it. I love teasing her as much as she loves being teased.

"Oh that," she says nonchalantly, as if she's forgotten what we just did. "I might need an encore before I can say for certain, but it was a pretty wonderful start, Mr. Kolochev."

"Mr. Kolochev plans to give you many encores just as soon as you're ready for more."

"You're so considerate of me. One might think you've done this sin-shot thing before..." She sounds shy now, her eyes focused intently on curling a piece of my hair around her finger.

"Well, let me assure you that I haven't. You are my first sin-shot. I have never been with a virgin before." I pull her up to meet my lips and kiss her slowly. "I've never done a lot of the things that I've done tonight with you."

She pulls back just enough to see me, her big brown eyes flashing. "You haven't ever told anyone before…that you love—"

"Nope. You are my first." I cut her off because I sense this conversation is getting way too heavy for the both of us. We took it so slow for so long but now things feel crazy fast. I give it a few more minutes before getting up to deal with the condom in the bathroom. I see robes hanging on the back of the door, put one on, and bring the other one back to her.

"Come on, sexy, let me take you downstairs and feed you." I pull the sheet away and reveal her all luscious and naked wearing nothing but the after-sex glow I put there. I love that she's never shy about being naked with me. I fucking love it. God, she has a beautiful body, lying there on the bed all flushed and soft after being fucked by me for the first time. A body that was made for fucking. Correction—*made for fucking me*. She's quiet as she lets me wrap her in the robe, first one arm and then the other. "Everything okay?" I ask as I pull her up from the bed.

She nods and looks up at me, all mysterious and beautiful, but doesn't say anything. She just smiles at me, a mix of shyness and boldness that only makes me want to have her again. But she needs a break first. There's all the time in the world for the countless, X-rated things I want to do with her.

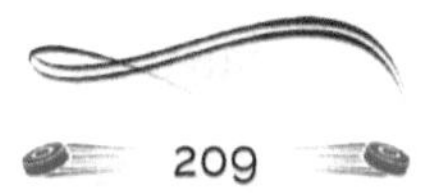

"I THINK I AM TRULY FAMISHED," Pam tells me as we load up two plates of food, and grab seltzer water from the fridge.

"Burned off some calories," I joke, giving a playful smack on the ass.

"We could burn off some more. You did say something about this kitchen island earlier...maybe we..." She trails off, running her finger along the line of the countertop.

I feel the corners of my mouth twitch...right along with my cock.

"Perhaps I could make an appetizer of that sweet peach between your legs. How 'bout that?"

Pam doesn't have to be told twice, hopping up on the counter and leaning back on her arms. I slide my hands up under the robe and split it open; running my fingers up her long legs and urging them apart. She's like putty in my hands the second I put my mouth on her. I grip her ass, my tongue licking at her sensitive clit, the sweet juice coating my lips as I pull her against them. Her hands tug on my hair as she goes wild for more, bucking against my busy mouth, falling apart to what I'm doing to her.

Fucking hot.

She's so responsive. It's one of the many, many things that turns me on about her. It's always a pleasure making her come. And when I do, she cries out my name and falls back on the counter, glowing and breathing heavily, gorgeously naked with the halves of her robe flung open on the kitchen counter of Louisa and Tom's ranch house getaway.

So fucking sexy as she stares up at me.

Quietly...thinking? I don't really have any idea because she doesn't say anything except my name.

"Georg." Softly whispered on a ragged breath with the orgasm I just gave her still racing through her bloodstream. I want to have her like this all the time. Tonight is just the beginning.

I watch her recuperate, trailing just a fingertip along her bare skin, over her nipples, enjoying as they turn into tight buds that I *know* are begging to be sucked.

"Want to head up and watch a movie?" I ask once her breathing goes back to mostly normal.

"Yes." She sits up and ties her robe closed again. "If I can walk up the stairs after that."

"No need. You hold all the food, I'll carry you."

"No that's not what I..."

Too late. I sweep her into my arms, laying a proper kiss on her soft lips before turning her to where our food and beverages await on the other side, untouched due to our appetizer distraction. She loads everything up, laughing, and we head up the stairs. It feels good to carry her.

I've never had such a good time doing nothing. Literally. We eat and have fun feeding each other while watching completely lame television. We talk about silly things like, if you could be a fictional character, which one would you choose? Me, *Tony Stark*. Pam, *Lara Croft*. She is a badass at heart and it's one of the things I love about her.

"What movie scared the shit out of you as a kid?" She's on her side facing me, her head propped up by an elbow...with her robe gaping open. I can see plenty of side-boob and the edge of a nipple; and while spectacularly hot, it takes me a moment to organize my thoughts enough to form an answer to the question.

"Any film that Eli Roth has ever made. Christ. Let's just say that I never have, and never will step foot in a youth hostel. You?"

"*The Sixth Sense*. That movie freaking terrified me. I will never watch it again even though I know the big twist at the end." She shakes her head with a shudder, which has an extra nice effect on her tits. I wait for more information but she's already on to the next question. "Who was your first kiss?"

With her eager to change the subject, I don't press her to elaborate, completely content to enjoy the visual feast of her tits framed in her gaping robe. *Crazy hotness this girl in bed.*

"That's easy. Svetlana in the bushes at the park when I was nine. Afterwards, she told me she was moving away and my tender young heart was shattered."

"Awww, that is sad. At least she didn't harm you. My first kiss was a teammate on my soccer team at six, but I can't remember if his name was Forrest or Fletcher." She tilts her head and taps her temple. "Might have been Finley, on second thought."

"Must have been some kiss, then," I say, oddly jealous of the six-year-old boyfriend for knowing six-year-old Pam. I'm glad she can't remember the little fucker's name.

"Well, I couldn't tell you that either, but I do remember the time when I accidentally kicked him in the nuts during a game that benched him for a week."

"Ouch!" I cover my cock and balls with my hands in mock horror.

"It was an accident, Georg. *Ac-ci-dent*," she insists, laughing.

I could do this forever, I think. I don't know what it is about her, but she's so easy to talk to. So easy to be with. So much fun. Being with her makes me happy.

And, yes, did I mention that she fucking turns me on every time I'm around her? I can't help it. My need is off the chain when I'm with her. Or on the phone talking. Or texting. Or FaceTiming.

We come across a porno—a *Lara Croft* animated one —and watch it for a few minutes. At first it's funny, totally ridiculous, over-the-top cartoon fucking. "This is why you would be *Lara Croft* for your fictional character, isn't it, Pamela?"

"Ha. Hardly. I didn't even know *Lara Croft* pornos existed until five minutes ago."

"A likely story."

We make up our own lines for the actors—the few there are beyond grunts and sighs and endless moaning —but then…

Pam is on my lap rubbing her tits against my chest, her mouth hot on my ears and neck. She's rocking her slit back and forth along the shaft of my dick, and in about thirty seconds I'm rock hard again.

Fully on top of me now, she aligns my cock and impales herself all the way down on it. No condom. I nearly nut at the feeling of being bare inside her. She starts to ride me, throwing her head back as she finds her rhythm. God, she is so beautiful, her tits shaking every time she punches down with a hard grind.

I hold her hips, just watching her take pleasure from my cock. To think, this is the first time she's ever done such a thing. It turns me on knowing I'm her first like this. I realize something else as well.

I want to be her last.

As her orgasm squeezes around me, she moans my name again. "Georg…"

Hearing her say my name while she's coming does something to me.

It sets me off instantly and I unload. Inside her. I let it all go despite knowing we haven't discussed this at all. Birth control—sexual history and test status—the whole shebang of awkward but necessary topics.

Gasping as the last of the shudders of orgasm are worked out of my cock, as it's still pulsing deep inside her tight heat, I say, "Ah, Pam…"

"I'm on the pill," she says, blushing shyly at me. "It's fine, and I know you're clean because I've seen the tests at work. I was a virgin until tonight, so I know I am…I just know…it's okay for us to do this without condoms…if you like." I decide that adorably shy Pam is my new best favorite.

"Oh, *I like*. I like everything about you and my dick spending close personal time together."

She lets out a giggle and says, "We should probably grab a shower. I feel a little, um, dirty." Her cheeks turn pink at her teasing. God, I love this woman.

"You are thoroughly dirty, but it's very sexy to know I'm the one who made you that way." I pull her down for a slow kiss. "Either way I'd be happy to help you get clean before bed."

We step into the oversized shower, and while I want nothing more than to take her slowly against the marble-tiled walls, she's probably sore, so I gently massage that sensitive place between her legs. She still sighs and closes her eyes.

"Why is it I can want you so badly still?" she asks, sagging, her head against my chest as my fingers dip inside her once more.

"I feel the same," I answer, kissing the top of her head.

I don't take her there in the shower. Instead, I help her shampoo her hair and then we get out, dry off, and head into the bedroom.

"This is a really comfortable bed."

"It is," I answer, still semi-hard and thinking about how wet she still was in the shower. Even after several orgasms and sex twice.

"Aren't you sore?" I finally ask as we get under the covers together.

"A little," she says with a big yawn. "But it's a good sore. I like it. I like being sore from you."

My heart jolts at her words. Like an electric shock or something. I can see she's tired. And we have time. So much time, I realize. "Close your eyes, lover."

She curls up next to me, her head in the crook of my arm, her arm draped over my stomach. I watch her sleeping until my eyes will not stay open any longer.

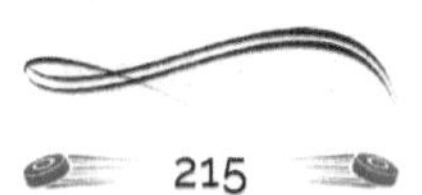

I WAKE to the ring of my phone.

"Hello?"

"Hey, champ, it's Scott."

I sit up. Pam is on her stomach, deep in sleep, so I get out of bed and head into the sitting room. "What's up, Scott?"

"Sorry it's early. Did I wake you?"

"It's fine. What can I do for you?"

"Well, it's more like the opposite really. Or what I have done for you, more like. How do you feel about money?"

"I like it very much, Scott."

"Well, as your new agent, I felt it was important to impress upon the powers that be just how important you are to the operation. The team's performance has been lackluster at best with you out on IR. Even Evan's play isn't as sharp without you on the D. So, I reminded the owners and it didn't take too much arm-twisting to get you a new contract offer."

"Really?" My heart is beating out of my chest.

"Yep. It's a far cry better than what you had going before. I think you'll be happy, but take a look at it and let me know if you need to me to go to bat on anything. It's in your inbox."

"Okay, I'm out of town right now but I'll get to it as soon as I'm back this afternoon. Call you then."

"Great," Scott says. "Talk to you later. Great game last night, by the way. Fucking awesome to see you back in top form."

He hangs up and I have a pang of sadness as Ned comes to mind. I feel more than a little badly, but Scott

Rose is the agent I've needed for a long time. The agent I've deserv— No, I haven't deserved Scott until now. It wasn't long ago that my team taunted me with vodka breakfasts and hockey honeys. And as I look back at *that* man, he's not the one who deserved an agent working hard for him. He wasn't working hard for himself or his team. Not then. *But I am now.* And I've proven myself

Sleepy Pam comes out wrapped in the bed sheet and plops onto my lap, her head on my shoulder.

"I woke up and you were gone," she says in a pouty voice.

"Sorry," I say quietly, stroking her hair. "I got a call from Scott, Evan's agent."

"Your agent now, too."

"Yes. My agent now, too. And really glad about that, because he said he got me a great deal."

"Oh?" she asks, perking up a bit.

"I haven't seen it but he thinks I'll be happy. It's in my inbox."

"Well, we should get back so you can take a look at it, then."

"It's okay, I told him I'd look this afternoon. Let's get some breakfast, take our time."

I pull away the sheet as she stands up and smack her ass playfully. "You should walk around naked all the time."

"So should you," she says from over her shoulder as she heads back into the bedroom.

I follow right behind her thoroughly enjoying the view. She looks around like she's searching for something. "I think we left my shirt and bra downstairs in the kitchen."

"Guess you'll have to go tits-out for breakfast then," I say with a shrug. "I don't mind."

"Louisa might, though." She sounds worried.

"Well, Louisa's husband owns a gentleman's club. I would guess she's seen a fair share of tits in her lifetime."

"You don't think she goes to the clubs, though?" She wrinkles her nose at me and I want to kiss it.

"I think they've been married a very long time and while he enjoys the sight of naked women, he has only ever made love to his wife."

"No way."

"True story. He is faithful and they are kinky. Don't let her trick you, because she is a minx."

Pam grins and shakes her head. "Well, I still need a shirt."

I manage to find mine and she throws it on. But the outline of her tits against the soft fabric of my shirt is so tantalizing, that I decide I can't let her leave the room just yet. I trace her nipples through the fabric and she arches into my touch. So responsive to every touch.

Needing to be fucked...

It's the truth. She needs it. I certainly need it.

"I'm gonna fuck you now," I nearly growl. "You okay with that?"

"Yes, please..." Her breathless whisper is the only answer I need to hear.

In a second, I have her on the bed, legs spread wide so I can have a good long look before sinking my cock into her. *Fuck hot.* I hold her open with one hand and line my cock up with the other. I don't give it to her soft this time.

The sounds she makes only spur me on. She wants more...

So, I give it.

It's at least an hour before we finally make it downstairs for breakfast, but I've already had my feast.

24
decisions, decisions

Pam

Two weeks later.

Georg: How is my sexy woman doing?

Pam: I'm good. I have a meeting in a few, but it's slow times around here when you guys are away scoring touchdowns and homeruns.

Georg: lol. I wish you could travel with us.

Pam: Because you miss me.

Georg: Because I miss you.

Pam: Ha ha! JINX

Georg: jinx

Georg: See? We think the same.

Pam: Tonight I'll be watching you play while naked in bed touching myself…per my usual.

Georg: Niiice. FaceTime after?

Pam: Even nicer.

Georg: Ha! I can't wait…ILY

Pam: ILY2. Heading into my meeting so bye for now, hot stuff. xo

Georg: Laters, baby.

I'm grinning as I step into Bud's office, imagining what antics Georg will be up to when we FaceTime tonight. He never disappoints. I miss him more now when he's away than I did before. It's different when you've accepted that you're really in love with another person. But it's my first time even remotely close to feeling this way, so I'm used to fighting the doubts that creep in. Georg is confident enough for the both of us he says. I can't wait until he's back from on the road. The Crush are away on the East Coast for a series of three. If they win all three games, they'll clinch a playoff spot. It's important that Georg keeps his head in the game and focuses on playing his best. For that reason, we decided to keep our relationship a secret until the season ends. It just makes the most sense to set healthy boundaries from the start. Plus, I work on his team members, touching *their* bodies, but he trusts in me to know there would never be anything other than professional behavior from my end. I keep him happy off the clock, and he can remain focused on his job on the ice. We'll have the summer to come out as a couple and can go from there letting management in on the news.

"So, Pam," Bud says, visibly uncomfortable, his forehead sweaty and his leg shaking. Also, he won't make eye contact.

"Yes, Bud?" I ask, looking around his office.

All training and therapy staff members report to the GM, which is a little weird. It really means we don't get much supervision at all, because Bud is often in his own world most of the time. I guess there used to be a manager for our area, but he quit to go work for the team in Nashville. Bud decided they'd save money and he'd manage this team. Which is a joke.

"We haven't touched base in a while," he begins.

"Ever, actually. We haven't touched base since I started working here before the start of season."

"Ah, yes." Bud pulls a handkerchief out of his pocket and rubs his forehead with it. "Well, I'm sorry about that. I hear good things about the team down here, so I leave you guys to it. For the most part."

"Well, it's good to see you, I guess?" I answer, not sure why he called me in today.

"Yes, yes," he says. "Of course, it's good to see you, too. And thank you for doing such a good job this year. It's just that…well, I've heard through the grapevine that you may be violating our fraternization policy. I have on good authority that you have engaged in a relationship of a sexual nature with Georg Kolochev."

All breath leaves my lungs.

"Excuse me?" I ask, barely audible.

"I've been alerted that you and Georg have been seen several times in public together. I realize that many of our staff do join players for nightlife here and again. But there were other allegations, Pam, that are harder to ignore."

"And those are?"

Bud actually turns beet red before he speaks. A pit forms in my stomach.

"One of the therapy room computers was left on. The camera was left on. There's only visual of one of the other therapy tables, but there is audio. It is, uh, quite graphic. And it follows your first therapy appointment with Georg upon his return after injury."

I have no idea what to say. The words are twisted in the back of my throat. Throwing up in the trash can by Bud's desk might be the next thing I do.

"Pam," he says, his tone ultra patronizing, "you won't have been the first to fall prey to the sexual desires of one of our players. They're alpha males. Virile. But you're supposed to be a professional. And whatever happened between you two should never have happened, certainly not in the professional space."

Mortified to the depths of my soul, I will myself to keep my ass planted in the chair, because my very first instinct is to run out the door and keep on running until I get to my car. Somehow, I find a way to make words come out of my mouth. "I wish I had something profound to say, sir. I lost myself in a moment of weakness and I—I really love this job. I'm sorry I acted so very irresponsibly."

"I am going to have to ask you to consider if your love for the job can outweigh your libido, Pam. The only way this can work is if you agree to stop seeing Georg Kolochev."

"But we're in a—but I—but I care about him," I stutter pitifully, trying to plead my case. "We have grown to care about each other. I know we can keep our relationship away from the team. We can certainly be more private with it."

"You do realize that Georg Kolochev is known for being quite sexually active. You're not even the first staff member he's fornicated with. I doubt you'll be the last. I suggest you make the right decision here. Just end things and date someone not associated with the team. Simple."

"Evan had a reputation once, too. And now he and Holly are married with a baby," I argue. "People change, Bud."

Bud shakes his head. "You have two choices, Pam. You can continue to work for the Crush and end your relationship with Georg, or you can continue to see him and lose your job."

There doesn't seem to be anything else to say. At least, nothing that will help. I thank Bud for his time and let him know I'll get back to him later with my decision.

I DON'T KNOW what to do with myself for the remainder of the day.

My mind keeps spinning in an endless cycle of embarrassment, mortification, and pure panic. My first thought is to lay it all out to Georg and let him deal with it, but I know that's the absolute worst thing I could do.

I can't upset him right now with the Crush on the cusp of going to the playoffs. He's just come off IR and is playing so well. I cannot let him jeopardize his focus because of me.

Which is undoubtedly the reason for the Crush organization having their non-fraternization policy in the first place. *Fuuuuck.*

What. The. Fuck. Have. I. Done.

I've created a nightmare.

I caused it.

And now my heart feels like it's being ripped out of my chest.

I'M a complete wreck by the time I pull into Holly's driveway. After enduring a truly torturous day as the remainder of my work hours crawled by painfully slow, every shred of emotional control I'd managed to hold on to disappears the instant I ring her doorbell. She answers the door with the baby in her arms and a smile on her face as if all is right in the world. Because right now, everything *is* right in her world.

Oh, dear friend, have I got a story for you.

Annnnd that's my cue to bust into a seriously ugly cry right there on her doorstep.

"Oh my gosh, Pam, what is going on? Get in here and talk to me."

I follow my friend into the house and to the kitchen, where she gets to work setting a tea kettle to boil. She does all of this efficiently while swaying sweet baby

Danya in her arms. I plop myself into a seat at the kitchen island, drop my head in my hands…and sob.

"Bud says it's my job or my relationship with Georg," I tell her after I've had a good minute of pity-crying.

"Wait, what happened? How did he find out?" She pushes a box of tissues toward me.

"A coworker outed me…I think." I valiantly attempt to wipe away my tears before more of them spring from my eyes. I've never felt more like a ridiculous mess than I do right now. "There was audio of a, um, very graphic make-out session in the therapy room."

Holly's eyes go wide and her mouth puckers into a O.

"Yeah, not my smartest choice. But Bud made it sound like I was just one in a string of women who fall into bed with Georg. He treated it like I was a victim or something."

"Well, Georg does have a reputation," Holly says. "But they all kind of do, honestly. And I'm proof that they can maintain real, healthy, long-term relationships."

"Holly…"

"What are you not telling me, Pamela?"

"Georg and I spent the weekend together after his first game back. He told me he loves me. And I told him the same."

Holly's eyes go even wider. They look like they might pop out of her head. I feel awful for not telling her before now, but there hasn't been time to simply hang with her. I've missed that. "Whoa. I think I already knew that. You wouldn't be sitting here crying if you didn't feel the same."

"I do," I say. "I don't know how or when it happened.

It seemed casual, kind of. A date here and there. Some mix-ups. Some jealousy. A lot of making out. Normally, I'd be done with someone after this long."

"But you don't want to be done with Georg," my friend says softly. "Because you love him."

"Yes, I love him. But if I stay with him, I'll lose my job, not to mention cause a whole blow up between management and staff relations.

"I think you can get around that though. I didn't lose my job. I was worried about it for sure, but once we had Max in our corner, everything was fine. So maybe you just need to go to Max?"

"I don't have that relationship with Max Terry," I say. "I've only met the man in passing."

"Well, maybe Evan and I could—"

"No." I shake my head definitively. "Just—no. I can't ask that of the two of you."

"Well, we'll think of something," Holly says confidently.

The tea kettle sounds and she pulls it off the burner. She preps two cups before taking the sleeping baby and wandering toward the living room. When she comes back empty-handed, she hands me a cup of tea and then brings her own so she can sit down.

"Is she fussy?" My valiant attempt at changing the subject to anything that won't make me burst into tears again.

"Dany? No. She's normal, I think. Overall good. I mean, I think so anyway. I don't have a lot of opportunity to compare."

"You're calling her Dany now. Cute."

"Yeah," she says with a smile. "Evan and I both really like it. Danya seems very formal. She'll need to grow into it, I think."

"I like it too." Grasping at straws to find anything to talk about that's not about me, I ask, "How's Scarlett doing now that she's demoted back to press passes and releases? I haven't hung out with her in a few weeks."

"She's fine," Holly says. "Well, at least from a work perspective. Did you know she grew up in Vegas?"

"I think maybe she told me that. And that she moonlights in one of the casinos to make extra money."

"Yes," Holly answers excitedly. "And her father disappeared under very suspicious circumstances. Gambling debts or some such thing. She knows a lot about the gambling underground. I guess her last boyfriend was a big name in competitive poker? Did you know that?"

"Nope. She talked about owing money and knowing mobsters when she saw them, but nothing about a poker-playing boyfriend."

"Well, he passed away, I guess," Holly says. "Apparently, he committed suicide. And Scarlett's barely like twenty-three. She's been through a lot already. It's a miracle she can function in life, I'd say."

"Was this recent? I don't think she ever mentioned having a boyfriend. She's always been flirtatious and fun when we've gone out. Like nothing was wrong. But you're right. She's a young thing so it can't have been that long ago."

"Not sure," Holly says with a shrug. "She didn't go into detail. I can't remember how it came up—we were talking about celebrity poker for the foundation with the players or something and she ended up telling us."

"Wow, I had no idea about any of that. I'll have to check in with her."

Holly sighs heavily. "So...what are you going to do about Georg?"

"That I do not know."

I can't talk about it anymore with her though. Because if I do, I'll start up with the ugly-crying again and that solves nothing.

In my heart, I know exactly what I have to do. There is no other option for me.

Tomorrow or the next day I'll go into work and tell Bud I've made my decision.

I'll text Georg and make some excuse why I can't FaceTime with him tonight. Because how can I talk to him? How can I look into his loving and insightful eyes knowing our lives are about to change and not lose it completely? He knows me too well. He'll see it in *my* eyes. I'll text him I love him, because he needs to know that. He needs to know how incredible my life has been since I met him. How incredible *he* is.

And then my heart will officially be broken into a million tiny pieces.

That can't be put back together.

25
it's hard being in love

Georg

We won three in a row on the road and are now headed to the playoffs with home-ice advantage. There's a very real chance we might take home the cup a second year in a row—by the skin of our teeth, so to speak. This was a hard year.

In spite of the excitement around another playoff berth and a multi-year, multi-million-dollar contract, courtesy of super-agent Scott, I can't enjoy it. Why? Because my girl has gone silent on me. Nearly the whole time I've been gone. She messaged that she couldn't make our FaceTime date but never explained why. I've called and left messages with no callbacks from her. I've texted and gotten emoji replies only. It's not like her at all, and my senses tell me something's not right.

"Maybe she's sick?" Evan offers as we board the plane back to Vegas.

"I doubt it. If she was sick, she'd tell me." Hell, she'd waste no time telling me if she didn't feel good. I know her.

"Let me text Holly real quick. She'll know if Pam's okay." Evan sends Holly a text while we're boarding. A few minutes later he looks up from his phone and says, "She's dealing with some work stress per Holly."

"Why wouldn't she respond to me, though? If it's just work stress?" I know I sound like a big baby, but I can't help it. My gut is telling me something is wrong. I have a very bad feeling about this.

"It's hard being in love, isn't it, G? Hard worrying about someone other than ourselves."

"I can't tell if you're being sarcastic or not."

"I'm not. And I am. It's both things really. I understand how this feels. Remember how I fell on my face for Holly just last year? It changes things. It changes you." He pauses and narrows his eyes slightly. "You love her."

"With everything I am, yes."

"And you believe in her? In you both?"

"She's my *vozlyublennaya*."

"Your true love. Okay, well in that case, if Holly says it's work stress, then it should be okay, yes?"

"I hope." I'll find out when I see her in a few hours' time. "Ugh," I groan. "Feelings suck."

"Yeah, man, icky feelings very much suck."

Evan says it as a joke, but it's nothing but.

THE FIRST THING I do is make a beeline to Pam's apartment, flowers in hand.

She answers, but she doesn't look particularly happy

to see me. In fact, she looks like she hasn't slept since I last saw her.

"Hey, Georg." She says it quietly in a way that sends alarm bells clanging inside my head. I do not like the way she just spoke my name. Usually the sound of my name on her lips is huge fucking turn-on. Right now? Not so much.

"Hey. I've tried to ring. Text. No talk. I was worried about you."

"Yeah..." Her shoulders slump as she lets out a huge sigh. No kiss. No throwing herself into my arms. No smile. Nothing to reassure me that everything is okay with her and me.

"Can I come in?"

She nods and turns away, leaving the door open. I follow her in, back toward the kitchen. She pours herself a cup of tea. I watch her do all of this silently, admiring her long hair down her back, her toned, tanned legs-for-fucking-days, topped by a pair of white shorts. She's absolutely gorgeous, and all I really want to do is pull her into her bedroom and fuck away this worry that's starting to squeeze around my throat.

After we fuck it out, we can talk about whatever's bothering her.

"You want some?" she asks, her back toward me.

"No," I say firmly. "I want you to tell me what's going on."

She fiddles with her tea bag. Puts sugar in her cup. Stirs. She still won't turn and look at me.

"Pamela." The frustration is enough to make my voice break on that one little word. Her name. The name of the woman I've grown to love. This is some fucked-up bullshit that's going on right now.

She turns and takes a sip of her tea, but her hands are shaking. "We—we c-can't see each other anymore, Georg."

I'm pretty fuckin' sure someone just flipped the world upside down. "What the fuck are you saying?"

"I spoke to Bud while you were gone. Or rather, he spoke to me. One of the computer cameras was on that night we...well, you remember the night in the therapy room. There's no video, but very explicit audio. Bud said very clearly that it's my job or my relationship with you. And I need this job. I have a mortgage to pay, and I can't afford to leave my first employment under these types of circumstances. I'll never be hired again."

"There's audio? How the hell?"

She shrugs. "Does it even matter? And it doesn't matter who told him, or showed him, or whatever, either. What matters is that he has it. That he's listened to it. That my job is forfeit if I keep seeing you. He gave me an ultimatum."

"I'll go talk to him—I'll tell him it was my fault. I'll tell him I coerced you."

"But you didn't. I did it willingly, knowing it could get me fired. I did it because my body feels weird things when you're around. I sort of lose all my self-control. It needs to stop. I have to focus on my career. So, I told Bud yesterday that I was committed to the team, and that I would end things with you as soon as you were back."

"That's ridiculous. We don't have to do this. I can go talk to Bud and Max."

"No," she snaps. "You can't. This isn't about you. You're the superstar. The guy with the hot, new, upgraded deal. You're the playboy, and I'm just the girl who got sucked in. At least, that's what they think. That's the only reason they're even considering letting me keep my job. What I did was so unprofessional. I fucked a client. In the professional workspace. There's little that would be considered a worse infraction than that."

"We didn't fuck that day," I say, cringing at the word. "We fooled around, but we didn't go all the way."

"Irrelevant. My point still stands and you know it, Georg."

"We can go to them together. Tell them we're in love. That it's not a fling—"

"Georg." She levels me with her tone. It actually makes my heart beat faster. "It's over. I can't see you anymore. They're not interested in love stories. They're interested in having a physical therapy team that can be professional with the players. So from now on, you are a client, and I am a therapist. And that is all we can be."

"So you're choosing your job over me? After all we've been through?"

She makes a derisive sound. "What have we been through, Georg? We went on a few dates. We made out. We fucked. Just because we didn't both run away after the third date doesn't mean it's a forever kind of love. We're both in uncharted relationship territory here."

I feel like I've been sucker-punched. I can't breathe. I can't comprehend what she's saying. I know it's all over my face and while I want to pull it all back, act like I don't care...but that's not the truth. I care. A fucking lot.

"Pam, I know you're telling yourself this because you're scared. You love your job, and you're really good at it. But Holly loves her job and she's really good at it, and she married a player. We can get through this. This is real. You know it. I know it. And you're stronger than this."

"You don't get it, do you?" she bites back sharply. "You're celebrated. You can get away with whatever you want, pretty much. I'm a physical therapist. A dime a dozen. There will be fifty people in line behind me for a job like this if I walk away. And for what? I'd walk away from a career I love for something that *might* work out? Might possibly be more than a fly-by-night thing?"

"No, you'd walk away from a career you love for *someone* you love. Because I believe you love me, Pamela. And I love you. And I'm willing to fight for this. For us. Why aren't you?"

"I guess you're stronger than me, then. Because I'm scared. And I'm not willing to risk my livelihood right now. I worked hard, put myself through undergrad and master's programs to get here. I'm still paying student-loan debt. I'm still establishing myself. This is a career ender if they fire me."

"I can take care of you, and we can even get married like Holly and Evan." I sound completely desperate I know, but I don't care. "Do you want to? Get married?"

"No. I don't want you to take care of me, and I don't want to get married—not like this!" She's crying now. The tears are flowing, and I think that alone is making her bravado crack. "I don't need someone to take care of me. I never have. I've always had to take care of myself and I've gotten pretty good at it, too. So, don't come in acting like some golden knight in shining armor because I don't need it. I don't *need* you, Georg Kolochev."

"Pam, you don't know what you're saying—"

"I do." She slashes at the tears on her cheeks with the back of her hand. "I'm saying this is done. Please, you have to go now. I—I can't—do this."

We stand there staring at each other, both of our chests heaving, the air heavy with anger and frustration. I step forward and put my hand on the back of her head, pulling her to me. My lips touch hers for only an instant before she turns her lips away.

"Please...leave," she begs while hot tears continue to make trails down her cheeks. "You h-h-have to go." *How the fuck am I meant to leave her like this?* How am I meant to leave *her*? My everything. *My future...*

A heartbeat passes. Then another. "Fine," I finally say. "But know that I love you. I'm really fuckin' disappointed in you, because I know you're stronger than this. And I also know that you really don't want this."

And I turn. I walk out her front door, dropping the bouquet of flowers on the front step.

I go to the car, start the engine, put it in drive. I'm on autopilot. My ears are buzzing, my head swimming with a million thoughts. When I arrive at my apartment building I park, but I don't go up.

No, I walk to a place that I know I shouldn't go, but I do it anyway.

The nearest bar where I can drown my sorrows in the bottom of a glass.

A few drinks into my pity party I realize that it will

take a lot of glasses to drown my sorrows. But more importantly, that even if I drink all the glasses, it won't make a difference.

I stop drinking before I'm unable to walk myself home. Barely. But I manage to make it inside my apartment and into the shower when I have my come-to-Jesus moment. A lifeline of self-preservation. Strength and determination that rises up from somewhere to reason with my fucked-up, aching, torn-to-shreds heart.

Kind of a miracle actually given the way I feel right now.

Having Pam or not having her—I cannot go back to the partying I did before. Just because I'm hurting. Pamela Jenson is a beautiful, intractable, talented, and brave woman. I *get* what she's fearful about, but she's given up. *What the fuck do I do about that?* I don't know how I'll dull the pain, but I can't go back there to that dark place again.

Because I won't make it out the other side in one piece if I do.

26

this is no fairy tale

Pam

As soon as he leaves, I fall to the floor in a sobbing heap. That is one of the worst things I have ever had to do. Telling him to go. Telling him it's not real love. I hurt him. I hurt my Georg and sent him away.

But I had to do it. Everything I said about my student loans and paying my mortgage—all of that was true and real, and I wasn't lying when I said I don't want someone else to take care of me. I have to establish myself on my own terms. I don't know another way to be.

I'm so angry at myself. For allowing myself to cross a professional boundary. For losing myself in this man. I've never let things go so far before. Why did I do it this time?

Because this time was different.

This time you fell in love.

I tearfully gather up the pink and purple bouquet now scattered on my steps and bring them inside to the sink. I arrange the unbroken stems in a vase, through a veritable river of tears, while reliving the words from Georg that hurt the most: *I can take care of you, and we can even get married if you wanted.* He can't have possibly meant it that way. There's just no way Georg Kolochev wants to marry me or anyone else, even if he did offer it as a solution in a moment of rejection. I saw the hurt in his eyes. I put it there.

Much later, after my tears have stopped, and when I'm utterly exhausted from the emotional roller coaster I've been stuck on, I still can't sleep. Instead I lie awake for what feels like hours.

Staring up at the ceiling in the dark.

Clinging to the idea that pushing away the man I love...was the right thing to do. Clinging to the lie that someday I'll find love again.

THE FOLLOWING day I let Bud know that my relationship with Georg is officially over.

"This really is for the best," Bud says. "Staff and player relationships very rarely end well. There are reasons for our policies."

I bite my tongue to keep from asking why Evan and Holly were allowed to move forward with their relationship. It doesn't matter. I've ended things with Georg, so it just doesn't matter anymore.

Dale and I start planning some conditioning clinics for the players in preparation for our expected trip to the cup series. The coaching staff wants the whole team to be as fit and strong as possible.

I go to lunch with Dale so we can do some planning.

After we order our food, he blows his straw wrapper into my lap from across the table.

"What are you, ten?"

"I'm flirting." He grins widely, his attentions doing absolutely nothing to lighten my mood.

"I'm not dating people at work. Focus on the task at hand."

"I'll wear you down one of these days," he promises.

"Yes, just the way I want to get a date. By wearing me down." I roll my eyes. "You need to mature your methods of wooing women, dude."

He chuckles at this and switches the subject back to our strength and conditioning clinics. He is fun to collaborate with, no doubt. We work really well together, and while he's attractive, he just isn't my type.

The worst strike against Dale is that he isn't Georg.

No other man is Georg.

Later in the week, I watch an away game on television with Scarlett. Holly is back to work, and back to traveling with the team to manage their social media from the ground. She wears the baby in a little carrier the whole time, and it's super cute. The press loves her as much as they love Evan, and every chance they get they put the camera on Evan's little family in the stands. It makes me so happy for my friend. She looks so confident and happy.

But it makes me sad for myself. Because she got her fairy-tale ending and I got told, under no uncertain terms, that I would no longer have a job if I continued a relationship with Georg.

The team is playing well. Georg is being uncharacteristically aggressive on the ice, but it's working, and in the third period, the Crush is winning by two goals.

"He doesn't look very happy out there," Scarlett comments as she picks her way through a bowl of popcorn.

"I wouldn't know," I say sourly.

"Why not?" she asks, concerned. I've forgotten that we haven't talked about any of this. I've only talked about it with Holly. "I thought things were progressing with you two."

"I was told by management that it was Georg or my job."

"Oh no." Her mouth goes wide. "But Holly and Evan—"

"I know," I say, putting my hand up. "They don't view Georg as a settling-down guy. They view me as some dumb woman who fell into the trap of a playboy...blah, blah, blah. It's ridiculous, but there you have it."

"Well that *really* sucks. If it were me, I'd quit. I'd quit and go get a job somewhere else and keep seeing him. I mean, you're a physical therapist. And a damn good one. You can get a job anywhere."

"But I really want to work in sports. And I love hockey. And I love this team."

"And you love Georg." Scarlett gives me a look that dares me to challenge her assessment. "This is Vegas. There are all kinds of performers—dancers and acrobats and gymnasts—and they get hurt. And there's arena football and soccer, too. There is plenty to do if you want to treat athletes. It doesn't have to be here."

"I can't believe you're telling me to quit my job."

"And I can't believe you're letting a great guy go just because of a job. A job is a job, Pam. It pays the bills. And yes, it's good if you enjoy it, but you can enjoy working somewhere else. But there is only one Georg Kolochev." She shakes her head at me slowly. "If you love him and he loves you then it's just stupid that you're not together."

"You make it all sound so simple."

"I know it's not simple," she says sharply. "I'm not naïve. But I lost someone I cared about and while we didn't have a perfect relationship, it still hurt like hell when he died. And I don't know if I'll ever fall in love again. So, all I'm saying is that it's worth it to hold on to it when you find it."

"I pushed him away, though. I hurt him and I told him I didn't need him. He probably hates me."

"He doesn't hate you," Scarlett says. "Look at him. He's hurt. He's angry. But you don't feel that way unless there's love there, too."

"Maybe so, but I can't just be like, *oh, I'll quit my job. Take me back.* And what's more, I don't want to quit my job. I want both. Why is that too much to ask?"

"I don't think it is," Scarlett says with a soft shake of her head. "And if anyone is sassy enough to make that happen, it's you."

I hug her and thank her for the support, but it's really so much more than that. Scarlett has given me a thread of hope. It might be a very thin thread, but it's there.

I think about what Scarlett said for a couple of days.

And then it comes to me when I'm lying in my bed at night wide awake and miserable, missing the man I love because *I* sent him away. *I* sent away a beautiful man who loves *me*.

Dumb.

So very dumb.

I have absolutely no excuse for doing it either, other than the heavy anchor of fear that's trying to drag me to the bottom. I let my fear win the day I told Georg we had to break up. But I'm done with fear ruling my life's decisions.

I am so done with that. Fear ruled my life for two incredibly unspeakable years. It eroded my confidence. It destroyed my innocence. It nearly destroyed me. But I don't have to let fear rule my life now. What was absent in those years was love. Unconditional, patient, unselfish love. *"If you love him and he loves you, then it's just stupid that you're not together."*

I'm done being stupid. It's time to get my fight on.

And I know exactly what I must do.

27
some bunny loves you

Georg

The Cup.

We have home advantage to start out the series, but the DC team is on fire this season. They're having the season we had last year and it's only Vegas luck that has us squaring up against them for this final playoff series.

In games one and two, we played well, winning both games in the desert at the best-of-seven cup series. In the games directly after Pamela threw us away, I played like a rookie. Tight, aggressive, total chip on my shoulder. I didn't play badly, but I definitely wasn't a star. It says a lot that it was hotheaded Tyler and hotheaded Mikhail who pulled me aside and told me I was going to get injured again if I didn't get my head in the right place.

Evan told me not to squander the good deal Scott worked out for me by getting injured again. Another concussion could be a career-ender, and that seemed like a big waste to him.

They're right, of course, but I'm having a hard time

channeling my anger over this fucked-up situation with Pam. I started down the hallway one day, determined to get her back, to make her listen to me—but I stopped myself before I got to the door of the therapy room. Instead, I drove all the way out to visit Ned at his rehab facility. Poor old Ned. He'd lost weight and looked good, wide-eyed. But he said it's been a hard road, finding sobriety and rebuilding his relationship with his family.

The visit helped me focus on my own sobriety, my own career goals…even if that meant I must do it without Pam. Her choice not to be with me is something beyond my control. My career and my life choices are within my control. I feel like fucking shit on the inside, but I can still do my job and do it well, and that's something.

So, when I went back out on that ice, I was a machine. Or, even better, part of a very well-oiled machine. Because Viktor, Tyler, and I have really meshed well on defense, and we just stopped allowing goals. There wasn't one goal scored on our line in the final six games of the regular season.

Now we're in DC for game three, playing against a rowdy, noisy, opposing crowd that wants nothing more than to see our championship restricted to one year.

The crowd is deafening as we head out into the second period, owning a 1–0 score. I take a look around and can't believe how many people they've crammed into the arena here. Looking up into the owner's box, I see Holly and the baby with Max Terry at their side. They all wave and I raise my hand, only to realize they're actually waving at Evan, who skates up beside me. I catch the rear view of a blonde and my hopes soar, but she turns and it's not Pam. I shove my mouth guard in and skate into position, allowing the frustration to fuel me.

We play well, holding off a flurry of shots on goal, but in the last few moments of the period, Viktor gets distracted and the puck slips by our goalie, allowing the red-and-white to score. The next shot they take is deflected by Tyler, who puts a little too much chine on it, resulting in an icing call. It's a stupid mistake, one that results in a faceoff and another score for the home team.

Evan gives us a "get your fuckin' heads in the game" speech during the break, and as we head out into the third period, I can tell our energy is just not in the right place. We fight and fight but they score once more. Despite Evan going full hockey-hulk mode we can only get one more in, and we end it in a loss.

We lose the fourth game as well, mainly because Tyler starts not one, not two, but three fights that put us on the losing end of a power play. Coming out tied in the series, Coach Brown threatens to bench him for the rest of the playoffs if he doesn't get his temper "under fucking control."

After the game, a few guys ask me to head out for drinks. I could use one, but I haven't had a single drink since the series started. I'm determined to never have to check myself into rehab like Ned, so that means self-regulation.

I go, but I get a club soda, and of course, the guys end up at a strip club. I pretend to be delighted by the attention of a very attractive dancer who makes it clear that she'd love to go into a private room with me.

"I'd take her up on whatever she's offering," Tyler says in my ear. "She's super hot."

"She is. I'm just hanging, though."

The fact is—she's not Pam. No one is Pam, and I want Pam. I get out my phone. I type, "I miss you" into a text and then delete it.

I end up going back to the hotel early, spending a restless night watching television.

At noon the next day, there's a knock on my door. When I open it, there's a scantily clad playboy bunny holding a basket. She's wearing the ears and silky butt-shorts and the little cotton tail. There's little left to the imagination, her long, toned, tan body on full display.

"Are you Georg Kolochev?" she asks in a high-pitched, girly voice.

"I am."

She holds out the basket. It's filled with bath items. "Some-bunny loves you," she says as I take the basket, a surprised look surely splattered across my face.

She walks off, leaving me holding this basket full of girly stuff like bubbles and body wash and loofahs. And she said "some-bunny" so, what the fuck does that even mean? Just a play on words because she's a Playboy Bunny? Or is it from a puck bunny?

Weird.

I toss the basket onto the counter and go turn on the shower. The team bus will be departing for game five in a couple hours. Here's hoping this weird start to the day doesn't stick with me as we move onto a pivotal game.

The whack-off session I intend to have in the shower will probably help some with the tension. But the only thing I can picture is Pam as I work my cock over in the palm of my hand beneath the spray of hot water and some soap... The two of us together at the ranch making love. Her first time having sex. How she looked as she came with me buried deep inside her. How generous she was with me. How trusting she was of me. I felt all those things. It was real.

Her name slips off my tongue as I come.

28

god love a feminist

Pam

"You sent him what?" Holly asks over the phone.

"A basket full of all of the soaps and items we used at the B&B that night we said we were in love with each other," I answer.

"That's very—umm, will he even know that's what it is?"

"I don't know. It's meant to be mysterious. I had it delivered by a Playboy Bunny."

"He's not going to get that, Pammy. He's not that smart. Sorry, friend."

I burst out laughing. "Well, he's not dumb, and he put a lot of thought into that night, so I bet you he will get it. But I didn't send a card or anything, so we'll see. And there are other gifts, too, so he'll see the pieces come together, and he'll get it eventually."

"It's weird."

"Shut. Up. Evan planned a big ice-skating outing to get your attention. It's not that weird."

"Pam, he was trying to woo me. And get past the non-fraternization policy by pretending to teach me to skate."

"Well, I'm wooing Georg. So there."

"You're already in love with each other. Just go tell him you were stupid and you want to get back together."

"Nope. I want to do the grand gesture. I need him to know I'm willing to put myself on the line for him. And he needs to feel it coming from me one hundred percent."

"Okay, fair enough. Well, speaking of which, how did your meeting go with Bud?"

"It wasn't just Bud," I say. "I had Devon, Max Terry, and Patrick from HR in there. I explained that Georg and I met prior to my working for the Crush. I told him about the night of the fight with Viktor, and that we tried to ignore each other for the sake of the team's policy. I shared that we were in love, and that I knew I could manage my relationship with him in a more private manner, but I was willing to leave the Crush organization if they were inflexible."

"And what did they say?" I can hear little Dany cooing in the background, and it melts my heart a little at the sweetness.

"Devon said she felt that Georg's focus on career and personal health has been spurred on by his positive relationship with me. Max Terry said he wanted his players to be happy and healthy. He felt Georg was integral to the integrity of the team, so he wanted Georg to be happy off the ice as well."

"Well, it's all good, right?" Holly asks hopefully. "Max was our saving grace, too."

"Yeah, that was all good, but HR said the biggest

problem is we had sexual relations on the property. Patrick felt that alone was a dismissible offense. And he's not wrong. But Devon pushed back and asked him if he would also fire Georg, or if it was a one-sided, sexist policy that would allow players to do whatever they wanted while staff took all the hit for it."

Holly snickers. "God love a feminist."

"Right? Anyway, they ended up agreeing that I was an asset to the therapy team, and made me promise that my relationship with Georg would in no way be played out at work. So I promised that, though I intend on it being very much a part of work if we make it to game seven."

"Oh boy," Holly says. "I guess there's still time to get fired, then?"

"Most definitely." But I'm smiling to myself this time, because I now know what I really want.

Make that *who* I want.

We finish up our conversation so she can get some pre-game work done while the baby naps. Me? I'm planning my next delivery.

I've put a lot of thought into expressing how my feelings for Georg developed. It might seem quick. I mean, we've just been an on-and-off thing for a little less than a year. But each experience with Georg has chipped away at my heart, bit by bit. I've realized that while we've certainly had some seriously hot sexual moments together, our connection is so much deeper than that.

So, I put the finishing touches on my second gift. I've gathered a pack of playing cards, some Texas hold 'em chips, bar snacks, and other fun, Vegas Strip-related items in a basket. The main item, though, is two passes to ride the LINQ.

I wrap up the basket and tie it with a bow, then call to have it delivered to Georg as soon as he gets off the plane when the team returns from game five.

I get a text from Holly as all of the pre-game activity is happening, telling me Georg came on the ice and immediately scanned the crowd and the owner's box. I know he's looking for me, hoping I'll be there.

As it is, I haven't really watched many of our games from the stands. It makes me too nervous, so I prefer to watch from home still. Also, I yell a lot and it's less embarrassing to yell in my own home than in a stadium full of people.

The game is really exciting to watch, meaning I do a whole lot of the aforementioned yelling. Evan and Georg are a machine out there, working hard to keep the puck in range of our goal. But despite a flurry of shots on goal and a big power play early in the first period, we don't manage to score, so we sit at zero-zero heading into the second period.

The second period is fast and furious, too, with both teams playing dynamic offense. There's a short fight between Mikhail and an opposing defenseman after Mikhail gets checked while making a breakaway toward the goal. Both players get sent to the penalty box for the outburst as the DC fans scream for blood.

Two quick shots on goal after the melee result in one goal for our opponents, and we head into the second break with a deficit.

When the team comes out for the third period, I can

see on their faces the resolve, the will to win. The camera focuses on Evan and Georg as Evan puts his gloved hands on the sides of Georg's helmet. Their foreheads press together as Evan says something to his friend, who nods sharply in response.

Suddenly I find myself in tears and shaking with anxiety. I pull out my phone.

> Pam: I 'm such a jerk. I didn't even text him to tell him good luck in the series.

> Holly: Yep, that's pretty jerky.

> Pam: Not helping. You're supposed to be my friend.

> Pam: I'm freaking out, here.

> Holly: As your friend, I'm also here to tell you the truth.

> Pam: He must hate me. I've really screwed this up.

> Holly: You can text him now.

> Pam: What good will that do?

> Holly: He'll see it after the game. He'll know you've been thinking about him.

> Pam: Ugh. I'm an idiot.

> Holly: Hang in there. Stick to your plan. GTG

I pace the room, crying like a baby all through the third period. When the Crush lose, two to nothing, I fall into a heap on the floor. It's not about the loss, though that sucks. It's really this awful realization that a person who loves another person should have at least reached out with well wishes. I'm horrible for not even supporting him with a "good luck tonight" at the very least.

I don't recognize myself anymore and it makes me sad. Hurting Georg makes me sad.

I grab my phone, starting and stopping several texts. *Coward much?*

Finally, I shut the thing off, take two Melatonin, and force myself to get some sleep.

Holly's right. I have my plan, and now I just need to see it through.

29

miss march...so hot

Georg

The team is quiet, sullen, on the flight back to Vegas after our loss in game five. Now we're in a corner. We absolutely have to win game six or we've handed the series to Washington, DC. Evan's sitting at the back with the offensive coaching staff, talking about how to better capitalize on our shots on goal.

When we land, all I want to do is to crawl in a cab, go to my apartment, and sleep for the next fifteen hours. But as I walk down to get my bag, I'm greeted by yet another Playboy Bunny in a skimpy costume. She's holding a dry-erase board with the words: "Some-bunny really, really loves you, Georg Kolochev."

She hands me another basket, and I sigh as I take it. The other guys are looking at me like, "What the fuck?" but I just grab my bag and leave, not even bothering to look inside this new basket.

We have a full day off before game six, and I end up spending it with Dale in the gym. We work on stretching and strength training, and then I alternate from an ice bath to a hot tub. When I get home, there's another stupid basket sitting in front of my door. I bring it in and heft it onto the table, next to the one from the airport, realizing I never even looked inside.

When I dig into the second basket, it has a bunch of card games and snacks. There's a card and if I was hoping it would be signed, I'm disappointed. Inside, there are passes to ride the LINQ.

"Weird," I say out loud.

This third basket has some funny stuff in it:

A new men's dress shirt.

A sexy green dress that looks vaguely familiar.

Boxing gloves.

Mix tape with a random assortment of songs ranging from techno to country, including *Night Fever* by the Bee Gees.

And then it all makes sense. *Holy shit. This woman...*

The baskets are all from Pam. She's the 'bunny' that loves me.

These things represent different times we've hung out. Different moments we've had together.

The first basket was a nod to our time in the bathtub, the moments we spent together making love, expressing our love. The second basket, silly little reminders of the Strip and our fun night on the LINQ. The third basket, a story about clean shirts and dancing and the fight with Viktor. She hasn't used words, but she's shown me how much she loves me. *God, I fucking love her.* It's been miserable without her, especially before our most recent game. But this? Her gifts intended to prove her love to me? Hell, yes, I'm smiling. Like an idiot. But who the fuck cares?

I pick up the phone to call her but my finger hovers over her name and I find myself unable to make the call. Maybe I should text her. I don't know. I mean, she hasn't reached out once since we broke up, or whatever that was when she broke my heart. Nothing. Not even a "good luck" as we headed into the series.

But the thoughtfulness of these baskets, the story they tell...it makes me want to go straight to her apartment, tell her I love and forgive her, and make love to her until my dick stops working. As much as I want that option, I know it's not what I should do. The way we left things was fucked up sure, but we both knew how we felt and what needed to happen in order to move forward. Pam needs to make these gestures for herself. She's the one who must take the first step back to us, and she knows where I am. And I don't mean that in a selfish way at all. Her past has left her with a lot of baggage to unpack and move on from. I get it. Only she can make that happen. This is her way of telling me she's working through it I suppose.

I need to keep my head in the game, though. We need to advance to a game seven, and I need to stay focused. So I don't call. I don't go see her. I don't text. But I do go to sleep with a smile on my face. I'm going to get my Pamela back, because she does love me after all.

I can wait for her as long as it takes.

The next night, we're suiting up and Tyler is babbling about some woman he took home the night before.

"I just need to bury my sorrows in pussy," he's saying.

"She was okay in bed. Hot chick. Great body. Amazing tits. But, you know, kind of boring in the sack. But whatever, I got off. That's what's important."

"Was I like this before I got married?" Evan asks, making a disgusted face.

"Maybe not quite so bad," I answer, side-eying Tyler, "but I probably was though, huh?"

"You were definitely like this," Evan agrees. "Pam got your whoring ass straightened out."

"Yes, and then smashed my fragile heart to pieces."

"I thought you said things were looking up with you two, G?"

"They are. Just trying to focus on the game. One thing at a time, you know? But I am hopeful."

Holly has set up a social media staging area in the previously mirrored tunnel. There are pre-recorded messages for all of us to watch on screens lining the walls, and cameras on each of us to capture our reactions for social media as we watch our personal messages.

I'm far back in the line, so it takes a few minutes. I bounce from skate to skate, trying to stretch out, limber up, preparing myself mentally for my job. Some of the guys have funny messages from fans, some have sweet messages from family.

When I finally get up to the screen, there are two messages with my name on them. I push the prompt for the first and am astounded when my father's face pops up. He's got hair like mine, but his is gray, thinning. His eyes still have the sharp look of a longtime coach.

"*Privet, syn,*" he says before switching to broken

English. "I—hearing good things of your recent… agreement…of the Crush team."

I let out a little laugh and mutter, "Contract. The word is contract."

"Las Vegas is very far from home, but we are to pay attention to your…work…there in the America. I am coach of past and proud of your playing. Also, I am your father and proud of my son."

I feel a little crunch in my chest, the want to cry, which I will absolutely, totally, never, ever do in front of my teammates. But this is really something. I call home sometimes, but my father has never told me he was proud of me.

As the message ends, I push the button for the second message. As soon as it opens up, I let out a loud bark of surprise. Because there's Pam, in one of those satin bunny costumes. She has a pair of ears on her head, a tiny little puff of a tail on her rear end. Her curves are on full display, and she definitely looks better than the real bunnies who delivered those baskets.

"Hey, Georg," she says. "Through this series, you've received several messages from a special bunny who loves you. Hopefully you've figured out that it was me. And hopefully you've figured out that I am fully aware of what a total idiot I was."

Evan pops up at my shoulder and asks, "Is that Pam?"

I nod vigorously.

"Hot," he says.

I just keep nodding.

"I love you, Georg. And I got permission for us to see

each other. And I get to keep my job. I was an idiot for not fighting for this sooner. But these past weeks, I've realized that loving you is really real. It's the most real thing I've ever known in my life. And I want to be yours. Always, if you'll have me. I have a proposal for us, and I can't wait to tell you. I'll see you soon."

The video message ends with her blowing me a kiss, and I'm frantic. That can't be it, right? There's got to be more. I look around, at every angle of the tunnel. The opening music is playing, and the players are about to get announced. I have to skate out onto the ice with the team, but I need to know where she is, if she's really here. *I need to see her* with my own eyes.

After most of the players are announced, the starting offensive line gets announced with a video of their best goals all season. Following that, there's a montage video that plays, showing Viktor, Tyler, and me making a bunch of crazy saves. We all hold up our sticks as they announce our names, and the crowd goes crazy. But then, an even crazier thing happens.

A song starts playing. And it's live. There's a platform being pushed out to the center of the ice, and red carpet rolled out to meet it. A guy with a big pompadour starts singing a song about the Vegas lights.

"Panic at the Disco," Evan yells into my ear. If I thought the crowd was crazy a minute ago, they are breaking the sound barrier right now. "Holly arranged this, because she's a big friggin' music nerd. He's from Las Vegas."

The guy has a great voice and a big-band, Frank Sinatra-like sound that mixes with a pop, dance, alternative feel. It's hard to describe, but the crowd is up and moving as he sings.

When he finishes the first song, he gives a speech about how proud he is to be here to cheer his hometown team toward a second championship. Then he says, "Now, I have a special guest joining me for my next song."

And out comes my Pamela, in full Playboy Bunny getup, high heels like skyscrapers, her blonde hair down her shoulders the way I like it best. She looks amazing, and I literally let out a groan of want and desire.

"Easy there, big guy," Evan says with a chuckle.

The singer hands Pam the mic, and she starts to speak. "I have an important proposal to make, and the answer will determine Brendan's next song. She turns to me and, to my total surprise, she falls to one knee. My heart is going to bust out of my chest I'm sure, but I don't even care, because I only have eyes for my beautiful sexy bunny.

"Georg, I told you earlier that I had something important to share. As you know, I love you. I realize I can be annoyingly stubborn sometimes, and I make the worst decisions because I've lived most of my life avoiding commitment. Before I met you. Then you came along and broke down every one of my walls with your love and your charm, teaching me that what we have together is something very special. I don't want another day to go by without you, so...with team permission, I'd like to fraternize with you every day for the rest of my life. You once told me that your younger self wanted to marry Miss March someday, so, Georg Kolochev, wonderful man that I love with all of my heart, may I be your Miss March?"

I don't know what I expected to happen next when I saw Pam's video message in the tunnel, but a marriage proposal during the pre-game was not it. I love it though. I love *her*. And now the whole world knows that she loves me enough to lay her heart into my hands for all to witness. During a nationally televised game in the Stanley Cup Finals no less. She did that to show me I'll never have to doubt her love for me again. And I don't. I won't, ever.

My face feels like it might break in half from my smile, but it feels so fucking good because she's here and I can see her. I pull off my helmet so she can see me too and nod my head so there's no doubt about my answer. A big, mute, stunned dummy. That's me. Nodding up and down over and over and over. *Yes. Yes. Yes, baby, yes.*

Evan gives me a push at my back and one foot goes in front of the other until I've reached the base of the platform where she's still kneeling. I pull her off the platform and give her a quick spin on the ice before dipping her back and kissing her fiercely. I don't want to stop kissing her, and I couldn't care less that so many people are watching. The crowd absolutely explodes.

The cheering is so loud my heart is literally pounding along with the thumping beat coming from the Crush fans. When I can finally bring myself to release her back up to standing, she gestures to the singer, who breaks into a song about *The Death of a Bachelor.*

It's perfect. I grab her again and skate her to the gate.

Once she's off the ice, I can't resist another kiss, before murmuring against her lips, "I love you, Pamela Jenson."

"I love *you*." She puts her hand to my face and smiles at me with happy tears shining in her dark brown eyes. "Now go out there and win this game, and then afterward I can show you just how much. I'll be here waiting for you."

"The six best words I've ever heard."

30
and he scores!

Pam

Even the high of proposing to Georg, being engaged to Georg, can't override the feeling of total exposure in this skimpy bunny suit. I make a beeline down the tunnel, high-fiving strangers as I head down to slip into something a bit more comfortable. The adrenaline is still pumping through my veins. *I can't believe I just proposed to Georg at a game. In front of so many people.* But I did, and I have the puffy lips to prove that my Georg said yes. *Oh my God, he said yes!*

Still shaking as I remove the bunny costume, I switch it out with a fitted black dress and heels before heading back up to the owner's suite. I'm greeted with hugs and words of congratulations as I enter, and I can't wait to get a drink to calm my nerves. I want to just sit and watch the game and let it all sink in for a while. I think I'm still in shock to be honest. Out of body experience, anyone?

Max Terry approaches me, clinking my glass with his as we look out on the start of the game.

"So, there must be something in the water here, huh?" he muses. "First Evan and Holly, now you and Georg. Who's next to topple our fraternization policy for the sake of true love?"

"I don't know, but I'm really grateful to have this job despite it. Thank you for giving me a second chance. Thank you for giving Georg a second chance, too. This team means the world to him."

"He's really grown into a valuable player," Max says. "And you did amazing work getting him back on his feet after what could have been a season-ending injury."

"Well, thank you, he was worth the effort."

We're quiet for a few moments, watching the action. Max lets out a frustrated groan as we miss a shot on goal. Then, very casually, he asks, "Why the bunny costume?"

I take a deep breath. "So last year, remember when Georg, Evan, and Viktor got in that bar fight?"

"Ugh. Yes, I remember. Stupid boys."

I nod in total agreement. "Indeed. Well, that night, I went back to Georg's hotel room. I was a little post-traumatic I think, from getting knocked down, but Georg was in a rage about it. So it took a really long time for both of us to calm down enough to have any kind of intelligent interaction. I started asking him random questions. Like, if you could be any kind of animal, what would it be? And, when you were a boy, who did you want to marry?"

"What kind of animal did he want to be?" Max asks.

"Oddly, an orangutan," I answer. "And he said that his thirteen-year-old self really thought he would grow up to marry Miss March from the Playboy he stole from under his dad's mattress."

Max lets out a big belly laugh. "So, you're his Miss March."

"In the flesh," I say, grinning.

"That's really clever. And cute."

"And embarrassing to be seen in that ridiculous getup in front of a gazillion people. But…that was how I needed to do it, so *c'est la vie*."

"Indeed," he says. "Well, cheers to you both."

The game is surprisingly normal for the first two periods. Each team scores in each period, so the game is tied at two-two going into the third.

I can see the concentration on the first-string line's faces as they huddle on the ice prior to the start of the period. Evan is talking a lot with his hands. Holly is literally bouncing up and down in one corner of the suite, biting her nails.

The period kicks off with Evan in control of the puck right off the bat, making it close enough to shoot before getting checked at the boards. DC seems to be resorting to a lot more physicality in this period than in the previous two.

Mikhail gets tripped on a breakaway, resulting in him on his face and an opposing player in the penalty box. Ready to fight back, Viktor levels one of their offensive players, sending him to the bench on concussion protocol. Ouch.

The minutes tick down, with no more goals, but several hard hits. The game gets to the last two minutes and it looks like we'll go to overtime, but then I see Georg stop a goal and wing the puck right over to Mikhail. The opposing team would have expected him to send it to Evan, so they're not in position to stop Mikhail as he nears the goal. The goalie looks ready, though, and someone skates fast to get to him, to provide just a little extra support. Just as Mikhail gets sent to the glass, he pushes the puck backward. Doesn't take the shot. No, he sends it to Georg, who is right behind Evan. Evan moves to the left, closer to the net, and just when I think Georg will pass it to Evan, he doesn't. Instead, he takes a shot.

And he scores!

My Georg. My fiancé. A defenseman. He just scored what is likely the game-winning goal in a game the Crush *had* to win to push this series to a seventh game.

The energy in the arena is electric. The sound in the owner's suite is overwhelming, with cheers and crying and all kinds of emotional outbursts, including my own. Weeping. That's me right now, full-on weeping, exposed out in the open where people can see the tears streaming down my face. But I don't care about either. It's not something I'm used to feeling, but then none of this is familiar because I've never been in love before. I didn't know love like this was even possible for someone like me.

But with Georg Kolochev it is. *It so is.*

A MILLION HOURS between his goal and the moment I'll finally get to be with him again are passing at a snail's pace. I realize he had to do the post-game press with some of the other players and shower, but I'm terribly impatient waiting in the hallway for him to finish up. I pull out my phone for what easily could be the tenth time, when I feel familiar strong arms wrap around me from behind. A sigh of pure relief comes out of me as he presses his body flush with mine. His spicy cologne fills my nose as his damp hair falls forward to brush against my cheek. I close my eyes and just take him in. *Finally.*

"I'm looking for my smokin' hot fiancée. Blonde. Legs for days. Rocks a bunny suit like a Playboy model. Wears it better, actually. Seen her?"

All is right in my world again.

I'm in Georg's arms and he's kissing me. I'm pretty sure we're both crying. It's the best feeling in the world. "What do you want to do tonight?" I ask once he lets me come up for air.

"You." He's not even joking. His eyes take on a serious note as they move over me intently.

"Well, that's a given, but were you planning to go out if you guys won? I know I was a surprise for you tonight showing up like I did, and maybe you had plans for after the game with—"

I don't get a chance to say more because Georg shuts off my babbling with his beautiful lips. Beautiful lips I've missed so, so much. Showing me how much he's missed me too. Kissing me senseless, until I don't remember the question I even asked.

Doesn't matter.

Don't care.

Pretty sure Georg doesn't care either.

WE END up doing the most mundane thing ever. Pizza and salads while watching the post-game cuddled on my couch. His physical exhaustion pretty much matches my emotional exhaustion right now, so when he told me he wanted to go home with me, where we could be alone, I offered my very enthusiastic approval to his "plan."

I ordered our dinner from my phone as he drove. To my place. I wonder if he wants our reunion to be back at my condo because that's where we left things, and he needs to cancel that other sad memory out. I sense he's deep in thought from the intense expression on his face. Every few moments he looks over at me and smiles. He holds my left hand in his right until he needs it to drive, but then it comes right back to find mine again. Now that I think about it, his hands have been all over me since we met up in the tunnel. It feels to me as if he's worried. Like if he lets go of me, I'll slip away or leave him. That thought gives my heart a sharp pang for hurting him., but I tell myself he'll never have to worry about me leaving ever again.

"How long until the food gets here?" he asks the minute we're inside.

"Forty-five minutes to an hour," I whisper, barely able to get the words out. I'm nervous, and the predatory gleam in his eyes as he backs me against the wall ratchets up the tension another notch.

"Perfect. Just enough time to take the edge off, because that's all it'll be. I need you over and over again until this ache I've been carrying around for too fucking long is totally obliterated."

His words cause tears to spring to my eyes as I nod up at him. "Whatever you need, I want to give you."

That gets me a smile.

It's not long before his fingers are up my skirt and he's sliding his palm over my thigh, covering as much skin as he possibly can. I return the favor by unbuttoning his shirt and tugging it free of his pants. The defined planes of his pectoral muscles, as always, look good enough to lick. When I do exactly that with a wet kiss over a peaked nipple, he shudders into my neck. "I love you so much, and I hated every day that I couldn't be with you."

"I hate that I caused all of those days apart for us. I'm so sorry."

"You were scared, I get it. But we can get over our pasts. We can move forward together. Right?"

"Together," I say, dipping my hand down into his pants to find his cock. After releasing him from the confines of his boxers, I stroke the silky length to full, erect hardness. It doesn't take long. "I want that very much, Georg. In fact, that's all I want."

He groans, pushing himself hard into my hand. "Feels so good...Pamela, more like that."

His palm grinds between my legs as I stroke him, his lips kissing down my neck to find my mouth periodically, our tongues mingling before retreating again.

"I don't want to come like this," he says pulling me over to the couch. "I want to be inside you when I come."

Happy to oblige, I straddle him after he sits. With zero hesitation, his fingers push my panties aside for quick access. *Thank God, because there isn't time to take them off.* Roughly, he plunges inside me at the same time his mouth claims mine in a blistering kiss. I'm full of him. He's everywhere. So deep, so big, so penetrating. I can't help the sound that comes out of me—a cry of pleasure and pain in equal measures. He swallows that too. The pleasure is because he's inside me once more, but the pain because I was the one who caused us to be apart in the first place. I don't have long to ponder though, because he begins to move. Hands at my back, in my hair, at my neck, working my body to fit his need of me. I'm lost in the sensation of being claimed by my man. Totally and irrefutably claimed. His mouth skims along my jaw, moving down into my cleavage where a nipple peeks out from the low neckline of my dress. He nips at it, shooting heat straight to my core as his cock spears into me.

His palm finds my clit and grinds at it, the pressure intense as we pick up the pace. I can't get close enough, can't move fast enough. The pressure builds and builds, and I can hear myself moaning. Over and over he slams into me, melding our bodies into something fucking wonderful. *Wonderful fucking for sure.* Georg knows what I need, because his free hand pushes at my ass, pushing me forward so his other hand is a constant pressure against my clit.

I see stars when the climax hits. Literally, my vision goes fuzzy. My breathing halts. I'm in outer space, for all I know. All I feel is the pulsating vibration of being thoroughly and truly loved tingling through my whole body.

When I come back to reality, I'm sagged against

Georg, barely coherent, but enough to see that his eyes are closed, his chest is heaving, and his cock is still shuddering inside me as he works out the end of his own orgasm.

"We came together," he finally breathes. "Like it should be."

Georg

GAME SEVEN REMAINS AT HOME, and the streets of the Vegas Strip are lined in Crush colors. People, flags, lights...it's all for us. We are at a pre-game signing party, and I've probably had four women tell me they should be my fiancée instead of Pamela Jenson.

Of course, they're completely wrong. After a long night of reconnecting—in about every position possible— I woke up early to a text from Scott, congratulating me on the engagement and the big bonus he just scored for me based on my goal in game six.

I promptly kissed my sleeping fiancée's head and snuck out to meet a jeweler I know so I could blow that bonus on a ring. I've now had forty-eight hours to soak her in, and think I'm leveled out back to normal again.

When the conversation got around to talking about our wedding, I was the one to bring it up. Would we have a long engagement? Live together for a while first? Pam rushed in saying that we didn't have to get married right away, and if I wanted to wait indefinitely it was okay with her. I put a stop to that noise immediately. I took her face in my hands, looked her right in the eyes and said, "I've just gotten you back and I'm not interested in waiting to make it official. I'm marrying the fuck out of you just as soon as we can arrange it."

That earned me some happy smiles. I think she really had worries that she'd pushed me with the proposal at the game, but I assured her she was wrong. I have ways of convincing my woman that I love her. In the end, we both agreed a Vegas wedding was totally for us, but lying on a beach somewhere was what our honeymoon needed to be about.

I need to get through this game tonight, because while I love hockey, I love my woman, too. And I just got her back, so I have some time to make up in the bedroom.

After our fan experience event, we all head to the arena to suit up. The whole therapy and conditioning team is on hand, offering stretching, massages, and warm-up support. Pam's supervising therapist, Andy, tells me with a wink that if Pam gives me a massage today, we need to keep it PG. I decide to let it go, though part of me wants to clock him since he was obviously the one who shared that audio file with management. Dickhead.

In pre-game, Evan and the offensive coaches decide that our play at the end of game six will be considered a fluke, so we devise a plan to get me to scoring range once more. We can only make it work once, and if we fail, we won't be able to get away with it again.

When we skate out onto the ice, among on the pre-game excitement, the league's executives are on hand with the cup, which is on the display during the National Anthem. Max Terry is there, too, and as he welcomes everyone to game seven, he also says that it is his pleasure to award this year's Norris Defensive Trophy to one of his own.

"This player has demonstrated a resolve this year that I haven't seen in a long time. Personal resolve, physical resolve, and team resolve. We would not be where we are tonight without him. I give you Georg Kolochev."

I'm stunned. The Norris Trophy? Seriously? I swear I've died and gone to heaven.

I go up and hoist the trophy, giving Max a hug and posing for pictures. And then it's time to play. The starting music plays and Coach Brown gives a few last-minute instructions as the ice is cleared.

When the first period starts, there is literally nothing that can bring me down. Nothing that can stop me. I have my team. My career. A new trophy. And Pamela. I have her, and I couldn't be happier.

So, when Evan gives the signal, the stars are aligned and I know I can't be stopped.

Goal!

epilogue

Georg

Two weeks later.
Fripp Island, South Carolina

So Pam found this destination wedding package to Fripp Island that is fucking amazing. We invited my parents and sisters to join us on our honeymoon for a beach holiday, after we'd had a few days to ourselves first. Well, not exactly with us, but nearby in their own cottage. We see them at the restaurants sometimes or when we feel like being social. They all absolutely love Pam, and she's fit right in with my sisters like they've known each other for years. I think with her in my life, Irina and Zoya might finally be able to convince my father to allow them to come to Vegas for university. We'll see how it goes, but the possibility is not as remote as it once was.

Fripp Island is all about privacy and fun activities like kayaking and windsurfing, anything beach related, really. I'm improving at windsurfing every time I go out. I also like that the privacy means I can have time with my woman in a beautiful place and not have to worry about someone spying on us and spreading shit. We are one-hundred percent legal now regardless. Our wedding was a fun Vegas party with all our friends and families joining in the craziness. Pam's mom couldn't take two weeks away to vacation with us, but at least she was able to spend a few days here on the island with her daughter before she had to head back to work. I like her. She's a tough lady, and I can totally see where Pam gets her independent streak.

We're kayaking over to an adjacent smaller island to check it out a little later with couple we met at dinner the other night. James and Winter Blakney, also on their honeymoon, same as us. He's a lawyer and she's a social worker in Boston. I didn't tell them what I did at first, but then again, I didn't need to. Turns out they hold season tickets in Boston and already knew who I was long before we all ended up honeymooning on the same island. James came up to me, stuck out a hand and said, "My wife is a huge fan." Those were the first words out of his mouth. To which Pam replied, "His wife is a huge fan too," while tucked into my side and winking at them. Winter's expression turned immediately to horrified as she scolded, "Yeah right, that wasn't stalkery at all, James!" It was funny, and we all had a good laugh before introducing ourselves properly. They are a really cool couple, and we plan to connect whenever we're in Boston for a game.

This morning while we were eating breakfast on the deck, we saw dolphins body surfing, shredding waves, having a blast. A few minutes later a mother deer and her two babies wandered into the grassy yard below our cottage. This place is a full-on nature nest. Pam has taken so many pictures that it'll take a year to go through them all.

We've chosen to post some on social media. Nothing too invasive of our privacy, or of our families here on the island, but some fun pics of the two of us to appease the fans. After the proposal on the ice in game six, Crush social media followers became super-crazed, desperate for an official update on what happened with us. It was all over sports news around the world. We knew we had to give them something before things went sideways with the stalker-fans. Yeah, unfortunately they're out there, and pretty much every player has dealt with one or two getting far too close for comfort at least once. There's a whole slew of *stans* trolling Crush players daily anyway. Realizing there was a wedding happening somewhere in the world with the hockey couple of the moment? We needed some professional help in dealing with all the attention.

Lucky for us we know the right people—or more accurately, the right *person*. Holly came up with a brilliant plan to solve the issue. We picked out a bunch of pictures of the wedding and included my teammates in some of the shots, which Holly then made into a fun photo series for the official Crush media accounts. We also send her pictures from Fripp Island and answer one fan question each day, (rated PG of course) and she takes care of the rest.

The team is off for the summer until the season starts

up again in the fall. We spent the week after game seven of the finals moving Pam into my place and speed-planning our wedding so we could have a long honeymoon lounging on the beach. So far, so good. I have another ten days to make love to my wife with only the sounds of the wind and the waves around us.

Every. Chance. I. Get.

I still love the fact I am her first. I fucking love that I was the guy who lucked out being the one to deliver her sin-shot. I ask her all the time if the wait was worth it. She just laughs and tells me I need to demonstrate my technique again so she can make an informed decision.

When I'm not doing filthy things to my wife—in every position imaginable, in every room of our beach cottage —I coax her outside to enjoy the great outdoors with me.

In her orange and pink bikini.

Hot. Off-the-fucking-chain-hot is my wife on the beach in a bathing suit. Needless to say, I spend a lot of time drooling over my spectacular view. I also make sure she has plenty of sunblock on all that skin, so she doesn't get sunburned. I love taking care of her, but mostly I just love her and count my lucky fuckin' stars. There are a lot of them to count.

Because loving Pamela Kolochev is my most important job of all.

She needed me as much as I needed her.

This is our truth. *Eto nasha pravda.*

my thoughts about...

afterword

Extensive creative license was applied in portraying some elements of NHL games, fan events and awards, that would ***not happen in real life***. I did this intentionally to create a more enjoyable reading experience within the storyline. These stories have been carefully crafted for your reading pleasure and in no way meant to be a true and accurate representation of NHL best practices and/or official rules currently or in the past.

Hockey Romance F-I-C-T-I-O-N all the way!!!

vegas crush by trope

All books in the **VEGAS CRUSH** series are *STANDALONES* existing in a connected world centering around a Las Vegas ice-hockey team. You can read them out of order if you wish and everything will still make sense with only minor spoilers. I've made a list of tropes for you here.

CRUSHED

BOOK 1

Forbidden, Reformed "Player", Ukrainian/American Hero, Good Girl Heroine, Office Romance, Love in the Workplace, He Falls First, Sports Romance, Team Captain, Social Media Manager, Risking it All for Love, Band of Brothers

BOOK 2

Bad Boy Russian Hero, Virgin Heroine, Damaged Heroine, Forbidden, Office Romance, Hockey Defenseman, Team Physical Therapist, Love in the Workplace, Band of Brothers, Overcoming Self-Doubt and Addiction, Trust

BOOK 3

Grumpy/Sunshine, Russian Hero, Feisty Red-Haired Heroine, Forbidden, Office Romance, Hockey Defenseman, Public Relations Manager, Love in the Workplace, He Falls First, Brooding Alpha, Opposites Attract, Band of Brothers

BOOK 4

Opposites Attract, Forbidden Romance, Financial Advisor/Client Relationship, Russian/Romanian Hero, Nerdy Young Heroine, Fresh Start in Vegas, Dyslexic Hero, Gentleman Alpha, Good Guy Hero, He Falls First, Age Gap, Vegas Mafia Suspense, Savior Hero, Band of Brothers, Superstar Hockey Centerman

BOOK 5

Friends to Lovers, Teammates Little Sister, Young Virgin Heroine, Russian Heroine, Boston Native, Bad Boy Hero, Forbidden Romance, First Love, Age Gap, Single "Dad" Vibes, Hardscrabble Upbringing, Band of Brothers, Hockey Defenseman, New Adulting, Found Family

BOOK 6

Enemies to Lovers, Forced Proximity, Love in the Workplace, Neuro-Diverse Hero, French-Canadian Hero, Rock Chick Heroine, Socially Awkward w/ No Filter, Opposites Attract, Instant Attraction, Fish Out of Water, Band of Brothers, Superstar Hockey Goalie, Rockstar Heroine, Brooding Alpha, Guitar Lessons w/ Cute Kids, Personal Growth, Sacrificing for Love

BOOK 7

Surprise Pregnancy, One Night Stand, Forbidden Romance, Love in the Workplace, Boss/Employee, Office Romance, Sneaky Dates, Instant Attraction, Age Gap, Mature Hero, Gentleman Alpha, Love After Divorce, Can't Keep Their Hands off Each Other, Career Milestones, Team General Manager, Team Nutritionist

BOOK 8

Friends With Benefits, Instant Attraction, He Falls First, Brooding Alpha, Superhero Complex, Gentleman Alpha, Damsel in Distress, Knight in Shining Armor, Living up to Father's Legacy, Vegas Mafia Suspense, Comic Book Nerd, Wedding Planner Heroine, Band of Brothers, Finding Your Voice, Parent/Child Relationships

BOOK 9

Age Gap, Secret Crush, Surprise Pregnancy, Shotgun Wedding, Opposites Attract, The Owner's Granddaughter, The Brooding Hockey Player, Forced Proximity, Only 1 Bed, Career Milestones, Forbidden, Old Family Friends, *Neanderthal* Hero, *Heiress* Heroine, Parenthood, Beliefs, Growing Up, Manning Up, Facing Your Demons, Family Legacy

BOOK 10

Christmas Marriage Proposal, No Third-Act Breakup, Proposal Problems, Brooding Hockey Player Hero, Buying a Home, Festive Holidays, Dear Santa Letter, Gentleman Alpha, Building a Legacy, Comic Book Nerd, Wedding Planner Heroine, Team Captain, Band of Brothers, Family Relationships, OTT Romantic Gifts

about the author

BRIT DEMILLE is the alter ego of *NYT* Bestselling author, Raine Miller, having an absolute blast writing books quite different from what she writes as Raine.

Stories about sexy billionaires [millionaires make the cut too] who fall in instalove with young women who may or may not be virgins, and then go on to make adorable babies together are her favorite themes. In addition to the billionaires, hot hockey players are at the top of her list of favorite heroes, along with royals and ex-military bodyguards.

Most important when she writes a story is a happily ever after. But during the actual *writing* of the story, the most important thing is a cup of hot tea with a splash of milk (and don't forget the stash of cherry Jolly Ranchers). A dog or two will likely be in between her and the chair at any given moment, which is very handy, because they are the ones who approve everything she writes.

RAINE MILLER is a #2 *New York Times, USA Today,* and *Wall Street Journal* bestselling author since 2012. Before that, she spent two decades teaching kiddos to read—something she's most proud of. These days, writing steamy romance books pretty much fills up the hours... for which she keeps pinching herself to make absolutely sure she's not dreaming.

#Truth

She has a handsome husband, two amazing sons, and two very bouncy Italian greyhounds to keep her busy the rest of the time. Her boys know she writes romance books but gratefully they have zero interest in reading even a single one. *Thank. God.*

When she's not writing she's likely deep into a hockey game cheering on her beloved *VEGAS GOLDEN KNIGHTS* and dreaming up a new book. The greyhounds are likely to be in her lap while she writes the books or watches hockey—both dogs at the same time of course!

She loves to hear from readers and chat about the characters she's created.

You can connect with Raine on Facebook in her reader group, **Raine Miller Romance Readers**. She pops in to visit most days because it's a super happy place where romance awesomeness abounds day in and day out with the most amazing readers on earth.

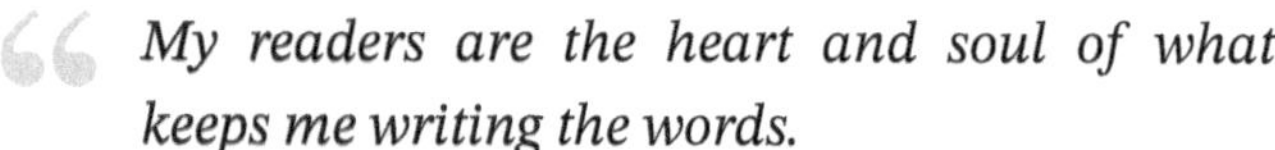

My readers are the heart and soul of what keeps me writing the words.

#Truth2

also by raine miller

The BLACKSTONE AFFAIR

NAKED, Part 1

ALL IN, Part 2

EYES WIDE OPEN, Part 3

RARE and PRECIOUS THINGS, Part 4

The ROTHVALE LEGACY

PRICELESS, I

MY LORD, II

BLACKSTONE DYNASTY

FILTHY RICH, I

FILTHY LIES, II

HOCKEY ROMANCE *as Brit DeMille*

CRUSHED, Vegas Crush #1

SIN SHOT, Vegas Crush #2

RED ROCKET, Vegas Crush #3

PUCK MONEY, Vegas Crush #4

SMOKESHOW, Vegas Crush #5

The KEEPER, Vegas Crush #6

LUCKY PUCK, Vegas Crush #7

Mr. HOCKEY, Vegas Crush #8

CLUSTERPUCK, Vegas Crush #9

Mr. HOCKEY's MARRY CHRISTMAS, Vegas Crush #10

CONTEMPORARY ROMANCE

CHERRY GIRL

HUSBAND MATERIAL

LOVELY PINK

HISTORICAL ROMANCE

The MUSE

The PASSION of DARIUS

The UNDOING of a LIBERTINE

Wedding Night Diaries

LORD BLACKWOOD'S VIRGIN

join raine mail

FOR MY NEWSLETTER and information on upcoming books and events, you should definitely sign up for Raine Mail. Use the QR code below.

whispers *There's so many freebies in that thing.*

subscribe to Raine Mail